Pharaon

Ty Cobb

Pharaoh
An Addictive Political Thriller

Ty Cobb

Copyright © 2020
By Tyrus Cobb & Tyco Publishing
U.S. Copyright Office Registration # TXu002135547

ISBN # 978-0-578-68972-2

Dedication

Dedicated to those in the recovery rooms who are earning their sobriety and helping me to stay sober.

And for me, it wouldn't have happened without Jesus C.

Acknowledgements

Thank you to my family and friends who stuck by me through my lows. Thank you to my God who redeemed me and raised me to my heights. Thank you to the people in recovery who reflected His grace. Thank you to Jason who contacted me every single day during my first shaky months of sobriety. For their help in making this book possible, thank you to Jason, Melanie, Tony, Shannon, Becca Q., Tom M., and Rick Allen- the best design guy in the business.

Prologue

It's been three months since I almost caused my own death, Mark realized as he paused his rhythmic sidewalk pacing. The startling revelation crept into his brain as a grounding reminder in his surreal circumstances. *I'm a screw up, I shouldn't be here.*

He wiped the sweat from his forehead and mouthed reassurances to himself as he restarted on his circular path. The heat and humidity were normal for a place built on a swamp, but the effect it was having on him wasn't helping in his attempt to project a composed demeanor. The anxiety was self-created, after all he was the one who had asked for this meeting, a request that he was beginning to regret. He loosened the tie around his neck, which was so foreign to him that it felt like he was being choked. He fought the urge to check his watch again, but he was out of alternatives to fight back the angst. He had been so worried about being late that he had arrived an hour early, with a bladder full of coffee to boot.

As he resumed his oscillating march in front of the ornate wrought iron fence, he began to panic over the attention that he was generating from the guards monitoring him from the gate. His mind panicked, *I've got to calm down or they're going to lock me up before I can even get inside.* He started rifling through his pockets to find his phone, or anything else that might distract him, when his hand touched something that had been a constant companion since his near-death experience; a photo of him and a little girl.

He stared at it as his heartbeat slowed. He thought about how much he had endured in the time since the picture was taken, a depiction of him when his entire life had consisted of occupying a bar stool in a one-room dive bar outside of Richmond, Virginia.

His eyes moved up from the photo to the imposing building to which he was awaiting entrance, the iconic façade which signified the highest seat of power in the world- the White House. He wanted to keep his mind occupied, so he returned his attention to the photo and allowed it to wander back to a time when he was known to the world as "Doc" ...

- 1 -

He stared down at the empty glass in his hand and exhaled the remnants of his well drink. Doc tried to calculate if he could afford another, but was frustrated in his attempt by the alcohol haze swirling in his mind. He hated to admit to himself that he would once again have to dump out the change in his pockets to see whether or not he'd soon be heading back to the basement he called home.

He pushed quarters across the ash-stained bar top until he reached the magic number, $3.25, just enough for a rot-gut bourbon. He ordered and gave the bartender an apologetic shrug in lieu of a tip. That was how he spent most of his nights, drinking away the modest wages he sporadically earned through his various odd jobs. The bar was a steadier shelter to him than his constantly changing residence, he felt an odd comfort in the stale beer smell and ended up passing out in a secluded corner nearly as often.

"Last one, Caroline," he said sheepishly to the tall, stout bartender as she placed the drink in front of him.

"Yeah sure, I've heard that before, Governor," she said with a smirk in her deep, raspy voice.

Governor. They started referring to Doc by that obnoxious nickname ever since learning that he used to be a "big-shot" Legislator. He hated that they knew about his past, but he had only himself to blame for rambling during a blackout one night. He had come to this place seeking a refuge from that hurtful time and had cherished his anonymity. He cursed himself again for this mistake.

He refocused on the booze and wasted no time in raising it to his lips. As he lowered it back down, he caught his image in the wall-length mirror behind the bar. He was startled at how his mop of black locks obscured his sunken blue eyes. Just four years earlier, he had worn designer suits to match his neatly cropped hair.

He thought about the "Governor" moniker and winced again. If anything, he had coveted his father's title, Mark James Rutherford, United States Senator. It eventually could have been a perfect match to him, save for the middle name. He had instead been saddled with the bizarre family name of "Pharaoh" and because of it, had endured years of jokes and questions from his schoolyard peers. He never forgave his parents for it, one of a lifelong list of grievances he had tallied against them.

He had particularly despised it when his collection of nannies had called him "Junior." To him, "Junior" suggested he was secondary and that he shared a name with another, and sharing was not one of his strong suits. His younger brother, George, could attest to this. He had been a child who needed to be special, to try to bring sense to his painful early existence when sadness and shame had enveloped the life of a previously joyful soul. So when he had watched a movie about a gunslinger named "Doc" who would mete out his wrath upon his opponents, he adopted this name for himself.

Those early years had been spent in the tony West End of Richmond, only a few miles from his current location, which was close in terms of proximity, but certainly not in status. He had been raised as the son of a hard-drinking southern politician, although "son" more described his place in a lineage, not really in a *family*, and despite his current humble circumstances, he was defiantly convinced that he preferred it over the past.

"Cheers Governor," he mumbled to himself as he eased the memory from his brain with another swig.

Although no longer quite anonymous, Doc was still nonetheless successfully in hiding following his public downfall. His now sober father would attempt to contact him periodically, but with no formal job and no fixed address, he remained secluded. The only phone calls he consistently received were unsolicited from people selling car warranties. *So much for the Do Not Call List*, he thought. He had already added that to his list of resentments.

Doc essentially couldn't be found unless he wanted to be, and there weren't too many people who qualified for such a distinction, but his brother was one of them. George still contacted Doc periodically and would even invite him over for dinner or to church. *Imagine that*, he scoffed, *my brother still believes in a loving God even after being condemned to life in a wheelchair*. After all of the pain that Doc had experienced, all he knew was that if God did exist, He didn't embody love.

Doc had declined every invitation from George, but he did eventually divulge the location of his watering hole. That was how George's wife, Linda, found him.

"That useless lump over there on the bar stool, see him? That's your uncle Doc."

His heart stopped as he tried to simultaneously sober up and turn toward the distinctive voice. When he did, he was confronted by Linda's brooding glare, staring out from behind her perfectly coiffed, dyed-blond hair and heavily painted face. Her chubby profile emerged from the doorway holding the shoulders of a four-year-old girl out in front of her. His attention moved down to see a tall, slender child with jet-black hair and big blue eyes. As Linda walked the girl over to him, he couldn't avert his gaze.

"Doc, this is Annabelle. Annabelle, say hi to your uncle Doc."

The girl waved hello to Doc as he struggled to wave in return. He just kept staring at the familiar eyes.

"You look like hell, Doc. Do you live here or something?"

The comment shook him with embarrassment. He sat up straight and brushed the strands of hair out of his face. "Hello Linda, good to see you," he said formally. He leaned forward toward the child and with the gentleness of a light breeze said, "And hello to you sweet girl." He lingered close to her and studied a face that he had never seen before.

Linda rolled her eyes, creasing her racoon-like mascara. "Look, I'm here to tell you that you need to start paying the money that you promised us to help out with George's medical costs. You do remember your commitment, don't you *uncle* Doc?"

Her ripe emphasis hung in the air as Doc chose his words carefully. "Of course I remember, Linda, and I want to help, but I obviously don't have a lot to offer these days."

"Really, aren't you still a lawyer? Seems like you should have plenty to offer." She stared daggers at him with her harsh black eyes. "Would be a shame to have to handle this legally, bringing the courts into it."

Doc froze. His thoughts were muddled with cheap liquor, but looking at her, he knew he hadn't misread her threat. At

6

that moment though, all he could think about was another drink. "Uh, do you want something?" he asked pointing at the bar.

"You think I want to spend another minute in this dump?" she said, prompting an upset look from Caroline. "Or catch up with you over a beer? You're a mess, Doc, look at you."

Doc looked down at his clothes and put his empty glass on the bar. "Linda, I can't just wake up tomorrow and start charging people for legal work. I don't have an office, or access to research, or clients even."

"Then borrow the money, I don't care, but start sending something soon." She looked down at Annabelle. "Honey, give me your camera."

The child pulled an instant camera from her backpack and handed it to her mom. "Go sit with Doc and I'll take your picture."

Before he could protest, the little girl ran over and jumped backward onto his lap. She wiggled around a little to sit on his right leg facing square toward the camera as Doc's body seized from her warmth. Linda snapped the picture and walked over to him shaking the photo it produced.

"Here's a little reminder of what you're paying for, you know, *George's* little girl." She turned and waddled toward the door without her.

Doc sat there motionless, not knowing what to say, when Annabelle looked up at him. "Bye uncle Doc. Love you." She hugged him and jumped down to run after her mother.

Turning back to the bar, Doc dropped his head. Caroline silently placed another drink in front of him.

◆ ◆ ◆

Later that night, Doc stumbled his way home and sat on the edge of his bed, transfixed on the photo which he held gently between his fingers. The girl bore a resemblance to her mother, especially the button nose, but Doc stared at the blue eyes. He forced himself to confront a memory from five years earlier, before she was born.

George and Linda had returned from his first post overseas with the Army and began hosting Doc on Sundays for dinner. They would cook large meals, serve Doc his customary scotch, and spend time cleaning the wine stains from the carpets before Doc would finally call it a night and stagger to his car. After a few close calls driving home, Linda had suggested that Doc just stay the night on Sundays. George, being more concerned about the potential damage to Doc's career than he was, had agreed.

It hadn't taken too many dinner conversations for Doc to recognize Linda's abnormal interest in even the most mundane of legislation as more an interest in him, and after a month of dinners-turned-sleepovers, the two had finally begun their affair upon waking from a leisurely late sleep. Doc had felt pangs of guilt, but his internal excuse was that it was validation that he was just the better man.

This arrangement had become easier to juggle with George away periodically on training assignments, but even still, Doc had already turned his woefully short attention span elsewhere when news of his brother's accident had reached him. George had been in the California mountains for his cold weather training when his Humvee skidded off of a mountain road, badly injuring him. He had been the

8

lone survivor of the accident, and in all likelihood, George would be a paraplegic for the remainder of his life. As always, the news had come as a personal affront to Doc. *Why did this have to happen to me?* he had lamented. However, this setback had felt different to Doc and his unfamiliar selfless demeanor had chafed him like a tight collar.

Linda had publicly assumed the brave face of the loyal wife, but Doc could tell that deep down, she resented her new lot in life. She had been the wife of an Army Officer, reduced to the role of a caretaker, trapped for life. Upon George's return to Richmond, Doc had immediately been at his side, until Linda had cornered him in the kitchen...

"I'm pregnant."

All Doc could do was stare in response, the words searing into his stomach. He had never had much use for the feeling of guilt, but with this piling of news, his world suddenly seemed overwhelmed by it. He attempted a feeble, "Maybe it's not mine," before Linda dismissed any such hope.

"I'm four weeks. I haven't been with George in over a month. The kid has to be yours."

Doc desperately grasped at the kitchen counter while fighting to prevent the ceiling from collapsing in on him. "I can't believe this is happening. George is going to hate me."

"The kid is going to look like a Rutherford, you idiot. I'm going to have the baby with George and our family will be whole, well, almost all of us will be whole." She smirked as she glanced toward George's empty wheelchair. She had obviously had more time to think it through and had settled on her course of action.

9

"I'll give you money every month like I was sending it to support George. I already told him that I would do that."

"Two thousand a month ought to cover it. Just mail it to us on the first and George will never need to know about the real reason you're sending it."

"Two thousand, of course."

The throbbing in his head broke the memory and brought him back to his present predicament as he looked down at the photo again. He thought about Linda's motives and realized that she had nothing to lose. If she told George the truth, she could play the victim of a narcissistic, drunken seducer. If George still blamed her and threw her out, that was her ticket out of her life tied to a cripple. She'd still have her daughter--no court would award custody to a non-biological "parent" like George--and Doc was in no shape to petition for it.

He wedged the photo into the corner of his bedroom mirror and laid back on his bed. He couldn't let his brother discover the truth that the child he deeply loved was not his. Doc had terribly betrayed George, but that was one thing that Doc was not willing to let happen to him. *I've got to find a way to satisfy Linda's demands.*

- 2 -

The morning sunlight pierced Doc's bloodshot eyes as he fumbled for something to shield them. He cracked an eyelid and scanned the room, just now realizing that his windows had been bare since moving in a month earlier. He retreated back under his pillows in a heap of drunken agony.

Hangovers were second nature to him at this point, just the price to pay for the escape that he needed. Without the booze, he would ruminate on his past, conjuring up images of his hubris, failure, and misdeeds, all wrapped in his embarrassing former façade of arrogance. This would lead to a distraught hopelessness and agony that never left him. He awoke most mornings wishing he hadn't.

Since he did, he needed something to numb the emotions while preventing him from detoxing from the perpetual stream of alcohol in his system. He pulled his hand from under the pillow and grasped his tight chest to fight the familiar anxiety that enveloped him in these episodes, wondering when his heart would eventually give out. He had endured the painful process innumerable times- the tremors, chest pain, vomiting, and of course blinding headaches. And detoxing wasn't just an uncomfortable condition, as he had discovered from experience a month earlier.

Unbeknownst to him at the time, alcohol is one of the few recreational drugs that can kill a person due to acute withdrawal. That particular night, after having attempted for the first time in years to sober up, he had awoken in the middle of the night with his heart racing and his chest constricted. Tremors had shaken his body for several hours as he had debated whether to drag himself to the emergency room. He had consulted the internet where he had learned how serious his situation was but had finally decided against the trip, partly due to cost, but mostly due to his indifference toward continuing his life. For hours he had struggled to breathe to keep his heart pumping. Out of desperation, he had crept back inside of a bottle and simply hoped that he would survive the night.

Even this brush with death couldn't break his taste for booze. In the years long past, he had occasionally sobered himself up and resolved to start anew, but nothing had changed, because *he* never changed. He was still the same person, sober or drunk, and one drink couldn't solve that, so he now hoped that maybe ten drinks would. *Maybe this time*.

Eventually, Doc had failed to see the point in not being drunk, because to him, being sober was just staring at the clock until he could justify a drink. He would count down the hours, then the minutes, then the seconds until the bittersweet release, the false promise of relief that never came. He would pour his first drink with a sense of impending doom of what was to come. His life had become a repetitive nightmare with no hope of reprieve.

He slowly dragged the pillow from his eyes and stared at the ceiling. That morning wouldn't be spent in bed seeking solace, his unpracticed conscience wouldn't allow it. He slumped over to the side of the bed and held his head until the room stopped spinning, then he dropped his hands and forced himself to his feet to shuffle back to his makeshift closet. He was shaking badly, so he grabbed the bottle that he kept by his bed to help calm the jitters.

He looked at his suits, the ones he hadn't tossed or sold, and picked a blue one to try to secure a job. He took a swig from the bottle- he had to look presentable, but not necessarily be sober in the process. He knew that he couldn't just walk into a random job interview in his condition and have a prayer of being hired, but he thought there might be a chance that he could convince his old colleagues at the McDaniel Haslet Law Firm that he could be of value to their lobbying group. Although he didn't use it, Doc had kept his law license, *That's one accomplishment that life can't take away*, he defiantly believed.

Doc sat in his idling truck and listened vaguely as the dangling muffler rattled against the frame. He stared from the parking lot at the massive exterior of his former firm. He hadn't returned to this place since the partners had insisted that he resign his position following his humiliating public spectacle and now he was hoping that those same people would look beyond his sordid past and reinstate his employment. He had to admit to himself that such a proposition was a long shot at best.

He had commenced his legal career at this place, where his father had risen to prominence before him, fresh out of law school and with his typical exaggerated sense of self-worth. He had completed his studies by relying on intelligence rather than effort, another dubious confirmation to him of his unique exceptionalism, and he had carried himself with an air that he owned the place, even if the partners had not yet been aware. Firm life had been dull and Doc hadn't understood why he was required to bill hours like a lowly associate, after all, he had been simply biding his time until he could shine in the political arena. *Don't they know that this is an honorary position?* had been his internal query, the honor of course being that they once again had a Rutherford among their ranks.

His daily routine had consisted of billing a minimum number of hours and then escaping to the corner bar promptly in time for the 5:00 PM happy hour. The happy "hour" soon became "hours" and Doc had shown up for work later and later each day. After several years of lackluster performance, he had declared that he was running for a State Delegate seat which had opened up that year. The announcement had been met with great relief by the partners who had assumed that he would at least cost them less by being in the Legislature.

He lowered his gaze from the tower and examined his eyes in the rear-view mirror. It would likely remain unmentioned in a meeting that day, but his time in the Legislature would be front and center on the minds of his former colleagues. His first campaign had been a heady time for him, full of flattery and adulation, until he had realized that the groundswell of support from the Richmond elites had essentially been an homage to his famous father. With only tacit opposition, he had easily won the election for his seat and Doc had embraced his own positive press.

So it came as quite a shock to him that his fellow caucus members hadn't shared the high regard for which he had held himself and he had stewed as veteran members had assumed all of the leadership and chairman positions. He had settled himself into the janitor's closet to which he had been assigned and had begun to plot his way out of his inauspicious trappings. Seeking the advice of one of his father's old legislative colleagues, he had been told that "hard work and silence" would indeed get him far in the building. This hadn't sat too well with Doc, but faking had become a practiced art to him.

His two terms had been fairly uneventful, most notable for his failures of proper protocol when addressing the body, and on one occasion after a particularly late night, for having argued the points of the wrong bill on the House Floor. He had heard constant whisperings of how his rage seemed to guide his actions, anger that Doc knew emanated from his childhood darkness which could never be explained to others. However, astute observers who had penetrated this exterior had recognized that Doc had been capable of cogent statements in committee built on knowledge that he had gained from the study of each bill.

Doc had begun preparations for his third run at the House when he had heard the news- Senator Jenkins, the State Senator in *his* district, would not be seeking a sixth term. Without consulting the party leadership or even his own family, Doc had announced his intention to run for the seat. He hadn't known it at the time, but by the end of that ill-fated campaign, he would be out of politics, unemployed, and headed precipitously toward his current woeful existence.

He exhaled as the sorrow of that past dissipated. He slowly exited the truck, stood outside his old office building, and stole a quick drink from his flask before entering. He walked cautiously toward the unfamiliar receptionist and asked to speak with Kent Jaworski. Kent was the head of the lobbying group and had counted on Doc's support in the House, not exactly an ethical arrangement. Doc was shown to a chair in a small conference room where he shifted awkwardly and attempted to straighten his wrinkled suit.

The door burst open, "Hey Doc, how are you??" Kent's greetings, like those of most lobbyists, were always enthusiastic and over the top, typical of people who peddled legislation like used car salesmen.

"I'm good Kent, thanks for taking the time to see me." Doc took note of Kent's new hair plugs and impeccably tailored suit, designed no doubt to subtly hide the extra ten pounds that the powerful lobbyist now carried.

"Yeahhhh. Sureeee. Of course!" Kent's words were slow and elongated as he obviously needed time to assess the situation to figure out what posture he was to take. "How's your dad?"

Doc coughed a little to stall and said with as straight a face as he could muster, "He's good, thanks for asking," as if he had seen him that morning.

"Oh good, good..." Kent paused while he examined him. Doc was never one for small talk, and now that he had intentionally isolated himself from other people, it felt downright excruciating. Finally, Kent mercifully broke the silence. "Well, what can I do for you?"

"I, uh, was wondering if you needed some help this next Legislative Session in your group?"

Kent nodded his head, but Doc recognized it as a popular maneuver employed by lobbyists to appear to be agreeing with a person while figuring out how to tell them "no." He had experienced it quite often while unsuccessfully seeking support during his final campaign.

"Oh wow, you know we've got a pretty good crew on staff already, and you know Jamal Phillips from Norfolk? He just retired from the House and joined the group as well."

"Right, well, I just thought that you might be able to use an attorney as well as a former Legislator..."

Kent interrupted, "Are you still an attorney?" His astonishment pierced his fake demeanor.

"Yes, I have my license."

He reviewed Doc's rough appearance and asked, "And where are you practicing now?"

"Uh, well, I'm not really with a firm right now. That's why I came to see you. I was of course a lawyer here for several years."

"Yeah, that didn't end well." Kent was blunt. Clearly, he had determined that Doc had nothing to offer him, so the pleasant disposition was jettisoned.

"Not exactly as I had hoped, no, but I still have contacts..."

"Doc, I can smell the liquor from over here. You're in no shape to shine shoes at the Legislature, let alone lobby there. I couldn't possibly employ you at McDaniel Haslet."

The blood drained from Doc's face as he confronted the reality of how far he had fallen. He was embarrassed and just wanted to get out of there, so he thanked Kent for his time and quickly made his way to the door unescorted. As soon as he emerged from the building, he walked directly to his truck to dip into his emergency gas money. He found the nearest liquor store and used it to buy himself another pint of cheap whiskey. Defeated, his only thought was of returning to his isolation where it was safe.

- 3 -

Hidden in his basement, Doc swallowed whiskey straight from the bottle. He was essentially out of options, at least ones that were palatable to his ego, and he stared at his dust-covered briefcase cringing at the idea of having to resume the charade of a legal career. It really didn't matter, though, there wasn't a firm in the state that would hire him.

This was of little consolation to him. He had made a peace of sorts with his drinking lifestyle, but that was before he had felt any type of calling in his post-political life. He had never contemplated a world where he would be needed by others. Sorrow descended on him as he reflected on his own past unmet needs, the family that wasn't, the remainder of which was a father of means. Doc debated calling the Senator as his last resort.

His father had been in the United States Congress for twenty years, with his first eight years in the House followed by two terms in the Senate. Throughout his career, the Senator had been well respected by his peers as a talented deal-broker and orator. His name adorned several pieces of legislation as well as a post office in Powhatan County.

His reputation for hard work and compromise had been only slightly tarnished by his fondness for morning scotch and nightly liaisons. This lifestyle had been permissible in Washington until over time the formerly collegiate atmosphere had become a partisan battlefield. Behavior which for years had gone unmentioned in political campaigns had become moral failings on full display at election time. As the Senator had geared up for his final campaign, the onslaught of women accusers had convinced him that it was time for a "dignified" retirement instead. He decided to move down the Hill to a nicer office on K Street where he could continue his self-indulgent ways in a more luxurious setting.

The move from Congress to the lobbying corps had also afforded the Senator the ability to fully disengage from the family that he had all but discarded years earlier. He reveled for years in his freedom until his drinking had begun to consume his life. While Doc was in college, his father had secretly placed a gun in his mouth and had contemplated a less dignified exit. His nerves failed him and instead, he had sought treatment for his alcoholism in a program in Richmond. The Senator had thrived in the work of the recovery program and emerged from the process as a very different person. Gone was the selfish and narcissistic demeanor Doc had grown to admire and emulate, weaker was what his father had appeared to him.

In sobriety, their father had approached both George and Doc to attempt to rebuild his relationships with them. George had been moved to tears; Doc had been disgusted. To him, the Senator had been a politician of the highest order, a drunk in a successful man's clothing. Doc had revered him and copied his ways, right down to the type of scotch that he had drank. The idea of his idol apologizing for his actions had been a direct rebuke of the man Doc had wanted to be, and deep down, the hurt that Doc felt over his abandonment was something that Doc knew he could never forgive. He still felt this way, but Doc needed his father's help.

He squeezed his eyes shut in an attempt to gather his thoughts; however, every time that he did, he pictured the last time he had seen his father- to seek his support in the race for State Senate.

At the time, his father's embrace of the moral code in his sobriety program had left him with few remaining lobbying clients, but they were loyal and his name had still carried weight in Virginia politics. Although he had remained in Washington for the most part, the Senator had returned periodically to Doc's boyhood home in the West End. One such trip had occurred two weeks after Doc's Senatorial announcement, so Doc had donned his best suit and gone to see him. Doc had been sure that his father could eliminate his competition, *Certainly he owed me this much,* had been Doc's expectation.

Doc thought about the conversation, which had taken place in a study full of moving boxes...

"Are you redecorating?" Doc asked, swiveling his head.

"No, I'm selling the house." His father was curt and typically gruff.

"Oh, I guess it's time to get rid of this old place." This information surprised Doc but his response was designed to keep the conversation focused on the important business at hand. His father looked at him as if Doc hadn't comprehended the significance of what was just said.

Doc pressed on. "So I announced for the open Senate seat here, going to be a tough race if I can't clear the opposition."

Doc said this and then shifted uncomfortably as his father's demeanor went unchanged. The Senator sat straight in his chair displaying his broad shoulders and grim manner. He finally responded, "Yes, a friend of yours named Julia reached out to tell me."

The seconds ticked by on the old grandfather clock in the corner of the room as Doc's hopes of his father's encouragement faded. "Aren't you going to help me in my race?" he finally asked.

"Mark..."

"Doc, my name is *Doc*." His mind seethed, *I may not have this man's support but I damn sure better have his respect. I deserve that.*

His father looked down and exhaled, "Doc, you've barely served two terms and without any real accomplishments and you're trying to tell your leadership that they need to make room for you now? You haven't even suggested to me why you want to run for this seat."

Doc was incredulous, *Imagine me having to explain my ambitions to the Senator. Besides, he has no right to question my decision, he's just supposed to support it.* "It's *my* rightful seat, why would I let some guy who happened to have served more time in the Legislature take that from me?"

The Senator cringed at Doc's impertinence. He stared at Doc for a few seconds with his cold blue eyes and then leaned forward in his chair. "You're unnecessarily making enemies. There's no need for you to run right now."

His father's words fell hard on him as the realization set in that the Senator had already determined that he was not going to help in this move. Doc's disappointment quickly tapped into his reservoir of anger. "I don't believe this!" he said, boiling over. "You've never done anything for me! You went to D.C. and lived it up, and now you're denying me my right to run for this seat?"

His father stiffened a little but remained calm. "Mark, I'm trying to save you from the path that I took. You're right, I wasn't always there for my family and I've tried to make amends for this."

"Keep trying!" Doc screamed. "Start by supporting me!"

Doc jumped to his feet and wandered aimlessly through the boxes in the room. He seethed as he counted the ways in which he believed his father had failed him over the years. The accumulated enmity poured out of him. "Seriously, you've never been there for me and now you stab me in the back?"

His father winced at the accusation. "I made countless mistakes. I should have been there for you and your brother. I should have cared less about ambition and more about my family. I can't change that, but supporting you for this seat isn't the answer."

Doc processed this as his brain told him that if he were to have meaning in his life, it would come in the form of titles and accolades, not from any inherent self-worth; that had been stripped from him in his childhood. His father's refusal to support him challenged this notion. Doc cleared this doubt from his mind and tried to think of a way to guilt his father into supporting him. "Well, I guess I'll have to do this without you," he said as resolutely as he could.

"If that's what you think is best," his father replied as he softened his gaze and leaned back, "but I think that would be a mistake. I'm worried about you. I hear that you're barely in the office at the firm, that you're on the verge of being asked to leave, you're spending late nights at the bars." He left the implication to hang in the air.

Doc's eyes widened as he recognized the comparison. "I'm not you. I'm not some useless drunk," he said wagging a dismissive finger at him. "I'm *much* stronger than you."

He watched as his father shrank into his seat. *I can't believe the nerve of this man trying to lecture me.* "The firm doesn't want me? There will be a dozen begging to add my name as a partner after I'm a Senator." Doc spoke the words confidently even though he himself doubted them. "I don't need a broken-down has-been to get what is rightfully mine." He said this as he stared into his father's now pained eyes.

Doc had enjoyed leaving this dagger in him as he had turned and left. When his campaign had eventually failed, this image became an ever-present humiliation in Doc's mind.

But that memory was all irrelevant now as his father was his only remaining option for the money that he needed for Linda. He stared at his cellphone and tried to compose himself to be able to communicate clearly and avoid slurring his words. He dialed the number and the phone rang.

"Hello?" Doc didn't respond to the greeting. "Mark is that you?"

His father sounded genuinely happy to hear from him, not harsh like in his previous life. In spite of the anger that he had for the man, the sentiment felt comforting. "Hi… Dad." He spoke haltingly and without much of an idea of where to start.

"Mark, how are you son? Can I come get you?"

His voice expressed a sincere desire to save Doc, to deliver him from the misery about which his father had obviously heard and had experienced himself. Doc felt his chest shake with the desire to run to his home and have his pain taken away. "Uh, I'm okay." He looked at the floor. "How are you?"

"I can leave Washington and come get you right now. Where are you staying?" His father obviously knew that Doc wasn't calling to chat.

"I live in the Broderick Row Houses in Midlothian. Just renting a basement from someone I know." *Why am I telling him this?* He shook it off. "I was hoping that I could borrow some money… till I get on my feet."

He father said, almost pleading, "Mark, I know you're in a lot of pain. I can help if you'll let me."

The thought permeated Doc's thick skin. He had often wondered if there was a way to not feel like this all of the time. He forced himself to brush the thought aside to return to the pressing issue. "I just need some money, Dad, I'm sure that I can pay you back when I get a job again."

"Mark, I used to be in pain too, there are people who care about you and will help."

People? Just not you, right Dad? is how Doc's anger interpreted. He took a breath, "Sure, I'd like to read a self-help book about drinking in moderation or something, that sounds like a good idea, but I need money right now."

Sternly, his father replied, "I can give you money for treatment. What you need is to come to grips with your drinking."

Doc interpreted this to be an order and his blood began to simmer. "What I *need* is a father." The rage welled and the contrite tone was gone. "I can't believe this! I need you to act like a father and help and all you can say is 'go get someone to fix you'?"

"That's not what I'm saying, I'll be with you to..."

"You'll be with me?? When have you ever been *with* me?"

"I agree that I should have been a better father to you..."

"You were NEVER a father to me! And you obviously aren't going to start now. This was a waste of time, thanks for nothing."

He hung up the phone. He may not have secured the money that he needed, but Doc received the satisfaction that his anger craved. He breathed in the resentment and scanned the room for a drink, that would soothe the pain.

- 4 -

The sun traced across his room, slowly marking the hours as he sipped the dregs from the bottle he had purchased that morning. He heard voices and movement outside of the basement, a perpetual reminder of the life from which he was now disconnected, like being trapped in a cell.

What logic he could manage strained to justify his words to his father. *The man has no right to tell me what to do, certainly not by pushing me off to some facility. It was just him trying to blame me for his lack of parenting.* However, even in the midst of his exaggerated denial, he couldn't shake the realization of how much he had followed in his father's footsteps. Regardless, what his father had inadvertently accomplished was to conjure in Doc the memory of Julia Sawyer.

Doc had first met Julia in the Legislature as he had stalked its corridors for female companionship. She had been a tall, curvy, middle-aged lobbyist who had taken an immediate liking to Doc as she had mistaken his brash demeanor for sincerity. "Jules" (as Doc called her) had mothered him the way he had never experienced as a child and she had hoped that love would blossom. Love hadn't been in the cards for Doc, but lust had, after all he had a thing for red-heads. He had used Julia like all the others but had kept her around for her nurturing qualities as well.

She had stuck by her infatuation even as Doc's world had slowly unraveled at the beginning of his final campaign. He had always been light on substance, but with his humbling lack of donor support and his misdeeds weighing on him, his confidence had also been shattered by then. He'd had no squad of loyal volunteers, just Julia and her friends passing out leaflets on the weekends, and watching her rally those people to his cause, he had begun to realize that he had no true "friends" to speak of, just "acquaintances" and "colleagues." He hadn't really placed any importance on developing personal relationships since college, that would have required giving of himself and diverted focus from his ambitions. Regret had begun to amass inside of him.

Over time, Julia had come to the realization that there was no future in their "relationship" so this had left Doc to troll for ladies nightly at the bars and events around Richmond, anything to forget that he had been losing his grip on his formerly solid future. One such evening, Doc had struck out at a bar in the Shockoe Bottom neighborhood and had decided that he might dip once more from Julia's well. He had called her feigning over-intoxication and had implored her to drive him home. She had warned him countless times that a D.U.I. would end his career instantly and he had played on this sentiment to have her deliver him home. Doc couldn't help but smile as he remembered his practiced skill that night...

"Take an Uber home, Doc," Julia said dismissively with her country twang.

"But what if I pass out on the street waiting for it?" Doc said, slurring his words just right.

"I have my kids and you know I don't like 'em to see you when you get sloppy like this." Indeed, Doc knew that the kids were not fond of him. He was often inebriated when he was around them and they didn't appreciate how grabby he got with their mother.

"Leave the oldest in charge, he can handle things for a few minutes," Doc pleaded. "Come on Jules."

She exhaled while she contemplated this request and finally said, "Okay, be outside in ten minutes."

As instructed, Doc was outside when Julia arrived. He hopped in her sedan and gave her the best toothy grin he had. "Thanks for picking me up," he said as seductively as he could muster.

"You need to start actin' like a Senator if you want to be one, Doc. Nights like this don't go unnoticed."

He responded to the rebuke with fake humility. "I know you're right, but I'm not that drunk, I just wanted to be able to spend some time with you," he said, still smiling.

"You know that you can 'spend time' with me when you decide that you're done drinkin' like a sailor and chasin' other women. Are you gonna do that?"

"I'm just a southern gentleman who enjoys his whiskey and companionship," Doc said, trying to sound dignified. "You know that's how my father raised me."

"Yeah, and where did that lifestyle get him?"

Doc deflated at the implication of her comment. Julia sighed with regret as soon as she said it. "I'm sorry Doc, I shouldn't've..."

"No, you're right. Who could love a jerk like me?" He might have been tipsy, but he still knew which buttons to push. "You can just drop me at the curb. I'll find my way in."

"Stop, I'll help you into your house."

Once inside, Doc poured himself another drink and deposited it by his bedside. Julia helped him with his shirt and he began to kiss her.

"Okay, that's enough. You know we're not doin' this anymore. I feel guilty that I did it in the first place."

Doc heard her but persisted. She squirmed and maneuvered but Doc countered at every move. "Don't you love me Jules?"

"That's just it, you don't love *me*, Doc. I can't keep doin' this, it's breakin' me up inside."

"You know I only care about *you* Jules." As always, Doc got what he wanted.

The next day at the Legislature, Doc smiled as he approached Julia. "Thanks for the lift, *darlin'*," he said, mimicking her down-home charm.

"You're welcome. You've got two events this week, so be sure to prepare remarks for each."

Doc noted the distinct absence of any detectable accent. "Well, I'm sure that you can help me come up with something," he said as he slipped his arm around her back and leaned in.

Julia pushed him back with a repulsed look. "You smell like a distillery, chew some gum before your next committee."

Doc was stunned. He could tell that this wasn't just a friendly rebuke, but a renunciation of their former relationship. He began to feel hollow inside like he did the night that Linda had told him about her unfortunate condition. He feebly attempted to convince Julia to reverse her course. "Jules, if this is about last night, I liked that you stayed."

"Love," she said, jerking her head up to stare into his eyes. "You're supposed to *love* me, not *like* me. You told me you loved me, but really you just wanted someone there."

Doc averted his eyes from hers, but could still feel them.

She was unphased. "I'm not goin' to be there so that you don't have to be alone in your miserable life. I have a God in my life who wants more for me and He wants more for you too if you could just see that. You could have so much goin' for you Doc, if only you cared."

She paused as she struggled for the right words. She finally just shook her head. "I let Him down, but no more. I hope that you figure it out, too," she said, finally averting her gaze, "but until then, I'm just a political supporter."

She walked away as the misery she had described washed over Doc's body, leaving him empty. Anger rushed in to fill the void, it whispered, *God doesn't love, He takes.*

The smile left Doc's face as the image of that hurtful ending pushed long-suppressed feelings flooding into his brain. He rubbed his face and threaded his hands through his matted hair. The alcohol he was consuming was an emotional suppressant, but it was also a depressant, and engendered self-loathing. He attempted to fight the remainder of his history, but eventually embraced it in a self-destructive crescendo.

He thought back to the end of the campaign. At that point, there had been only a couple of months left until the election and Doc had seemed poised to win against the odds as the Rutherford name had still stood for something in the West End. All Doc had to do was to keep himself clean and handle the one debate he had scheduled with his opponent, but with the looming birth of his love child and the loss of his one true friend, Doc had begun to spiral. He had lost any regard for himself and therefore couldn't fabricate any care for his campaign.

His behavior had grown erratic as he had missed more committee meetings and had stopped billing even his reduced number of required hours for the firm. The rumors of his excessive drinking and partying, which had previously been confined to the Capitol building, had started making appearances in the back pages of the Richmond Post, not that Doc had still read the paper.

It was on the night before his noon debate that he had finished off a bottle of Dewar's, picked up a lady at a bar, and had decided to drive them both back to his house, twelve miles away. He never made it home. The accident report had recorded his blood alcohol content at over three times the legal limit. He had turned too late at an empty intersection and had ended up running off the road and into a tree with the airbags in his S.U.V. having saved his life and that of his passenger. He awoke the next day at the Richmond City Jail, and it was there that Julia had found him seated on a bunk, staring at the ground...

She approached his cell. "Are you hurt?"

"No." He exhaled in fatigue. He couldn't look at her. "I missed the debate, didn't I?"

"The race is over, Doc."

The words piled like boulders on top of him, suffocating his spirit. He couldn't possibly think of what to do next so he just sat there. He had nothing left to say and no will to say it.

Julia drove him home in silence. When they reached his house, Doc felt a wave of self-pity. "My life is over. I can't believe this."

"Stop feelin' sorry for yourself and pull your life back together, Doc. I'll help you."

"This happened because you abandoned me," he lashed out at her. "You're not my friend."

"I was there for you throughout this campaign, what I couldn't be was your fling on the side. I never abandoned you."

"Everyone has abandoned me. What good am I? Nobody would care if I just died."

Julia frowned and looked on him compassionately. "That's not true, Doc. You have so much to offer. You're a good guy, you're just goin' through a rough patch."

"A good guy?? I just destroyed my political career, Julia. I'm sure the firm doesn't want me around anymore. Now I've got a kid on the way..."

Julia's body went limp and her mouth hung open. "You've got what?? You're about to have a kid, Doc?? With who?"

Doc purposefully mentioned the baby, *Why not get all of my misery out in the open?* but immediately began to have second thoughts when he did. He looked out the window to make it easier for him. "I'm the father of George's baby. I slept with Linda."

Julia's face contorted as tears welled in her eyes. "How could you do that??" She screamed. "You're an animal!" Her hands went to her face seemingly more to block the sight of him than to clear her eyes. "I can't believe you, Doc!"

33

He reached over to comfort her.

"Get your hands off of me!" she yelled, swatting him away. "And get out of my car!"

Doc hadn't expected her to react well to the news, but this startled him. He had hoped for her to console him for his troubles and perhaps even escort him inside to "commiserate"; at that point, he was desperate for validation. He was ashamed and scared at the same time and as he opened the car door, Julia shoved him in the back.

"Get out! Don't ever call me again!" She sped away with the passenger door still ajar as Doc dragged himself into his house for a drink. That was the last time that he had spoken to the only person Doc could describe as a friend.

He jumped up from his bed, almost toppling over as the room spun around him. He chugged the remains of the whiskey and smashed the bottle against the far wall, despondent over the recollection of his past. The alcohol made his conscience sag as he pictured his last days in Richmond.

He had finished out his Delegate term in solitude and had been officially removed from the firm's employment roll on the same day. The D.U.I. case had been referred to the court of the Honorable Sanford Quilici, where his father had quietly urged his old friend to show leniency toward his son. The charge had been reduced to reckless driving with probation, not jail time, and since he had avoided a felony conviction, Doc had been spared a disbarment hearing by the State Bar. Soon after, his brother's family had celebrated the birth of a baby girl, but Doc hadn't had the guts to reach out to them.

With the reenactment of his failure completed in his mind, Doc collapsed onto his bed as he succumbed to the booze and faded out of consciousness.

- 5 -

Doc awoke on his stained sheets, which had long since been pulled off of the mattress in a heap. The clock read "6:22," but looking out the window into the darkness, he couldn't tell if it was morning or night. Since his brain was still thick and his body wasn't yet shaking, he surmised that it was night time. He sat up on the side of the bed and rubbed his face, where he caught a glimpse in the mirror and almost didn't recognize himself. He couldn't bear to look for long and his eyes wandered to the photo wedged in the corner.

There she was, smiling so innocently. Her face beamed in contrast to the dark figure next to her, as if a cherub had floated down and sat next to a ghoul. He shook his head and stared at himself again.

The back gate screeched as someone approached his door. Doc stood and held onto the wall to steady himself. Ever since the phone call with his father, he had been anticipating a visit. His anger resurfaced, *If "Daddy" is here to tell me what to do, then I'm going to give him what he deserves.*

As he forcefully opened the door, his heart stopped. Standing where he had expected his father to be was Julia.

"Hi Doc," she said gently, her eyes brimming with concern.

"Julia. What… how did you find me?"

"Your dad called me from D.C., told me you were stayin'
around here. Apparently your neighbors know who you
are."

He scowled, "I guess it's funny to them, a lawyer and
politician who fell from grace." He shifted his feet
uncomfortably. "Um, sorry do you want to come in?"

"Sure thanks."

He regretted it as soon as it was said as he realized that
she would discover what his life had become. His clothes
were scattered everywhere, garbage piled by the door, he
couldn't possibly hide the abundance of empty liquor
bottles; this is where he hid, not entertained. She gracefully
maneuvered her way to a folding table with a single chair
and took a seat.

"I heard that your sister-in-law had a girl."

Doc looked down. "Yeah."

"Have you gone to see… her?"

"Annabelle. I met her a few days ago." He walked over
and gently removed the photo. "Here she is," he said,
showing her the picture.

She smiled. "She's a darlin'."

Doc admired what a sincere nature Julia had about her,
but not knowing how to respond, he managed a barely
audible "Thanks" as he placed the photo back on the mirror.

Julia watched as he lingered on the photo. "Your dad
says that you're in trouble."

Doc's pulse raced as he thought about the money that he
needed. He pictured the massive amount of cash that Julia
must make with her lobbying business. *Of course, I could
work behind the scenes for her*! Excited by the idea, he

37

turned and said, "Well, I just need to start making some money again, so I could help you..."

"I'm talkin' about your drinkin', Doc."

His excitement evaporated as he averted his eyes. *She's not here to make me rich, she's here to save my soul.* He would've been angry with her and thrown her out, but he knew he had no right to ever mistreat her again. "I like to drink, always have, you know that."

"Did you always want to live in a filthy basement with no life to speak of?"

Doc was so exhausted from his existence that he had no genuine response. *Best to let her say her piece and leave.*

"Aren't you sick of this, Doc? I mean, what do you do for money now?"

"I do work here and there. It pays the bills."

"Pays what, the bar tab? Don't you think that you were meant to be more than a drunk?"

Doc's temper flared as he thought about where life had dumped him. "*Meant* to be? I've learned the hard way that life doesn't work that way. My life has been one disappointment after another and now I just drink and watch it go by. It's easier that way."

"*Life* did this to you? What, the universe conspired against you? How is any of this someone else's fault?"

"Then how do you explain it? My life mattered when I was *somebody*. I may have had no childhood to speak of, but it meant that I would have a special life as an adult. That's how I justified it in my mind. Now I'm grown and my life is reduced to this," he said as he spread his arms apart.

He dropped his arms and breathed heavily. The emotions that he had suppressed for years seeped again into his thoughts. "There was supposed to be a reward, I survive the bad and get the good. My life would have meaning, that was the pay off. So I drank to survive, but the pain never leaves, so I drink more. I drink even though I know I'm making it worse because," he shook his head slowly, "because I don't know what else to do. Now I don't know how not to drink."

"Doc, I'm sorry." Her eyes narrowed. "What... what happened to you?"

His mind called out to him, *Tell her*. He turned his head to speak, but his body froze. A wave of shame and guilt coursed through him, he couldn't stand the idea of her knowing. He dropped down and sat on his bed. "You wouldn't understand."

She watched him as silent empathy crossed her face. She sat next to him and gently placed her hand on his leg. "It's okay. Life can be tough, *so* tough. My daddy died when I was twelve and we lived on food stamps to survive. But life can also be so wonderful. I worked my way through Virginia Tech, interned at a consulting firm, and now I lobby at the Virginia State Capitol, me, a country girl from nowhere. But you know what got me through all of that? Having a God who loves me."

Doc winced. His brain flooded with his early understanding of God- confusing secrets that required hiding from others. Anything but love. He shook his head, "I don't get it, if God let your dad die and left your family destitute, how could you continue to believe in Him?"

She was undeterred. "How could I continue on without Him? Everyone goes through difficult times, I just don't have to do it alone." She smiled. "And of course, now I have my kids, too. When I'm at home, sittin' in front of the TV with a mound of popcorn and those three layin' on top of me, everythin' is right with the world."

"That's great and all but I don't have anything, Jules."

"Nonsense. You're a lawyer, you're smart, you're a terrific speaker. When have you ever given the real you a chance?"

He stopped trying to contradict her. *Is she right? What if I was able to just leave all of the pain behind.* His gaze returned to the photo.

Julia followed the focus of his eyes. "Have you thought about the possibility of bein' a part of her life?"

He looked back at her as he shook his head. "I can't tell George the truth, and I don't deserve her in my life." He closed his eyes. "It would be best for everyone if I just stayed away."

"Doc, I'm not sayin' that you stumble into your brother's house and blurt out what you did, but you could at least be a good uncle to her," she paused gauging his response, "if you were sober that is."

His eyes opened. Julia stared at him with a zeal that almost frightened him. Her confidence was infectious. "You really think that I could get clean?"

"Of course I do, Doc. I believe in you and I know that you can." She walked over to the mirror. "I want you to do this for you, but if that's not enough," she said as she snatched the photo and held it up to his face, "then this little girl will always deserve whatever you can give."

It was too much for Doc to handle. He hid his face in his hands as Julia sat next to him and held him. She whispered,

"I will be there for you every step of the way, Doc. Your dad's already called the place that he went to for treatment. Will you let me take you there tonight?"

Without looking at her, he whispered, "All the things I've done, I don't deserve another chance... and I don't deserve you." He leaned sideways and buried himself against her.

"Of course you do. It's what you do with that chance that matters."

At 9:00 PM, Julia dropped him off at the Faraday Center in Richmond with a duffel bag of clothes and a carton of cigarettes. His truck was already on its last legs, so he had simply deposited his keys in the front seat on his way out of Midlothian.

As he exited her car, Julia called after him. "I know that you're afraid, Doc, but remember, *God has not given us a spirit of fear, but of power, love, and sober thought.*" She giggled, "Love that last part, but it's true, God didn't set us out as weaklings."

Doc scoffed but nodded. He checked in with the on-call staff and blew a 0.22 blood alcohol content. He was placed in the temporary medical facility room where he could be monitored and treated for his detox. In there, he had nothing except the clothes he wore in and a picture of a little girl sitting next to a man she didn't know was her father.

- 6 -

Doc spent the next two days in the "Med Room" as it was known and although he was confined to his bed for most of that time, the detox process was still painful and physically draining. At the beginning, the staff attempted to prepare him for the agonizing trial, but they were astonished when he announced to them that he had detoxed on his own innumerable times. They confirmed to him that he was lucky that he had survived past detoxes without a seizure which could easily have killed him. To avoid this, he was given drugs to lower his blood pressure and calm his nerves. Doc couldn't sleep for more than an hour at a time, so he laid in bed and shook in pain.

The solitude of the Med Room also afforded him the ability to contemplate his future. He hadn't fled to this place for a momentary reprieve from his drinking, he had sought refuge to find the answer to his misery. He was skeptical, but he knew that the program it espoused had turned former helpless addicts into functioning men and women again, among them, his formerly drunken father. *They have to know something*, he was sure of that much at least.

After three days, Doc emerged shaky and scared. He hadn't realized it, but this was the first time that his body had been completely free of alcohol in over six years. It was breakfast time as he wandered into the cafeteria/meeting room where a sparse group remained slurping coffee and talking about the day's schedule. He was met by one of the staffers who handed him the recovery guide titled

"Alcoholics Anonymous," known as the "Big Book" to those in the program it described. He wandered over to the cereal selection which was all that was still available. He carried his corn flakes and coffee over to an empty table and stared at the meal in silence.

"You need to hurry up," an annoyed woman spat at him from behind. "I have to clear this table before the morning meeting starts in twenty minutes." Doc turned and looked at her, but the remaining pharmaceuticals in his system fogged his brain.

"I'll get him set up," a rotund man with a patchy beard said in response. He sat down across from Doc who stared at the bear of a man in bewilderment.

"Names Aaron, Aaron A. I know, A.A., it's been a source of amusement here at the 'Farm'." Doc didn't laugh. "You just get out of the Med Room?"

Doc registered the question and eventually replied, "Yeah."

"Well it'll take a bit to get used to this place. I chugged about a dozen airplane bottles of vodka before I came in, so I had to shake it out in there for a couple of days myself."

Doc silently stared.

Aaron pressed him, "You from the area?"

Doc's brain was beating against his skull, hampering any desire for the meet and greet, so his anger took the wheel. "Look, I'm not really in the mood for polite conversation, tubs."

"Oh I get it," Aaron laughed. "I'm overweight so you called me 'tubs'." He kept laughing until his insincerity was obvious. He mimicked a tear-wipe for good measure. "You better eat something if you want to feel better there, Jeff Foxworthy."

Doc realized that it might help the pounding in his head to get some food in his stomach, so he slowly pulled a spoonful of cereal to his mouth. He was still shaky, so it slopped about and fell mostly on his lap.

"Whoa there, Jazz Hands." Aaron's smile revealed the good nature of his ribbing.

The scowl on Doc's face was intended to show that he was not in a receptive mood for the man's humor, but he also didn't want to be known as "Jazz Hands" for the entirety of his 30-day stay. "Call me Doc."

"Right on, Doc. Eat up and I'll meet you outside. I've got to grab a smoke before the morning meeting."

After eating a breakfast that he ended up mostly wearing, Doc wandered outside to try out smoking. Doc had never been a fan, *But this is rehab after all,* he thought. He saw a large group of about twenty people puffing away and made his way over.

"Hey," he managed with a slight wave.

They all stared at him with looks anticipating his self-introduction. Instead, after a few seconds of awkward silence, Doc started fumbling with his pack.

"So how do you like the place, Mark?"

Doc was startled by the mention of his name and looked at the speaker with astonishment. The group snickered.

"It's on your nametag there chief," the guy said pointing a cigarette-clenched finger at Doc's chest.

Doc's eyes moved down to the sticker on his t-shirt which had been affixed unbeknownst to him. Apparently, his name was now "Mark R.," in conformity with the anonymous program.

"His name is 'Doc', *Reginald*," Aaron interjected. Reginald, a gangly guy with a large loop earring, scowled at him. Apparently he wasn't fond of his given name either.

The group returned to their earlier banality as Aaron ripped the sticker from Doc's shirt. He was still too jittery to spark his lighter, so Aaron lit his cigarette for him as well. He choked and hacked out a puff of smoke as Aaron took a step back.

"Easy there, cowboy," he said laughing.

The one-minute warning bell rang and the mob extinguished their cigarettes to file into the building. Doc took a few more drags and coughed some more. *Well, I won't be picking up any more habits here at least*, he surmised.

The room was filling with haggard-looking souls as Doc found himself a seat in the front row next to Aaron. A staffer walked to the front podium and recited an "uplifting thought for the day"- this one apparently written decades before by a former drunk. At the end of the schedule review, assignment of chores, and recitation of the rules, the staffer pointed to Doc and asked him to stand.

"Everyone please welcome our newest victim, Mark R."

Doc stood as the group golf-clapped its greeting. "Doc… is what I… go by," he managed to stammer out. *All those years of delivering speeches to supporters and fellow Legislators and that's all I can come up with?* He was not impressing himself.

The group then adjourned to the "smoking section," as the outside tables were called, to inhale a five-minute cigarette before the first session.

After about a week at the Farm, Doc's wits were back about him and he was able to mingle with the larger group. The more separation he had from the misery of his recent existence, the more confidence he perceived in his ability to deal with alcohol on his own. He hid in the safety of the self-assured persona that he had crafted over the years and became less interested in the spiritual program that was being taught. The sessions began to bore him and he defiantly vowed early on that he wasn't going to identify as an alcoholic at the evening 12-Step meetings. He convinced himself that he just needed some alcohol-management skills, not membership in some cult as he saw it to be.

Before long, Doc began to separate himself from Aaron who had consistently held a seat for him up front. He and Reggie (formerly Reginald) began hanging out in the back of the sessions, poking fun at the people they considered to be nerds for paying attention, chief among them, his former chum. The staffers would ask them politely to quiet down, but they weren't there to babysit, and as far as they were concerned, Doc could quietly goof-off all he liked.

At the conclusion of Doc's first week was the start of his counseling sessions. His counselor would be Cedric, who also doubled as the Head of Staff for the Farm. Doc waited outside Cedric's office and sauntered in with a little sober cockiness when he was called. He willfully stood across the room from Cedric and read the diploma hanging on the wall from Hampton University, a traditional African-American college located near Virginia Beach.

"Doc, how are you enjoying your stay here at Faraday?" Cedric's muscular physique, tattoos, and facial scar clashed with his professional clothes and reading glasses.

Doc slumped down into his seat. "It's fine. The food sucks but I appreciate all of the second-hand smoking that I get to experience on breaks." Doc's smirk was full of his nascent confidence.

"Sorry to hear about the food," Cedric replied as he opened a file with Doc's photo on it. Doc didn't remember such a photo being taken, and judging by his disheveled state, it must've been on the day of his arrival.

Cedric said, "I've been noticing that you don't care much for the lectures and classes either."

"You've been watching me? That's kind of creepy," Doc said with a chuckle.

"I watch everyone, that's my job here as a servant of my fellow man. My Higher Power saved me from my addictions, *plural*, and I continue to stay sober and give thanks to Him by working with fellow addicts."

Doc rolled his eyes slightly at the allusion to God. Undeterred, Cedric continued. "I've been watching you in particular because I specifically selected you to be one of my counselees. I take notes and have an initial evaluation of each of you."

Doc sat up a little to try to see the writing in Cedric's file. "And what did you write about me after the first week?"

"Self-absorbed ass."

Doc began to laugh and then his ego kicked in. "Well, that's not very fair. This is the first time we've even spoken."

"And yet your true self was still so apparent."

Doc wanted to argue with him over his characterization, but he knew that he didn't really have a leg to stand on. "Well, you can think what you want about me, but my dad was an accomplished drunk and if a weak s.o.b. like him can quit, then I know I can... if I choose to."

"If your dad is sober, then he is *recovering*, but he is still an alcoholic."

"He doesn't drink, he can't be an alcoholic."

"It's a process of growth and progress, not an attainment of some goal of perfection. Just refraining from alcohol doesn't mean that you're cured of alcoholism, and I'm sure he didn't manage to achieve all that he has by being weak... or combative and recalcitrant for that matter."

Doc deflected the criticism with a sigh and a disinterested looked out the window.

"Look Doc, if you're here to appease your family or just get sober for a while and then return to your drunk fest of a life, that's your business. But I hope that you'll give this program a chance before you pass judgment and tune it out." Cedric leaned forward. "I will tell you this though, you will NOT continue to be a disruptive force for others who need this program or I *will* kick you the hell out of here."

Doc's eyebrows furrowed as he thought, *That's a little harsh for a "Godly man."* Nevertheless, watching Cedric's aggressive posture in defense of the addicts seeking help at his facility, he believed what the man was telling him.

"Do you have a Higher Power, Doc?"

"Uh, well if you mean God, then no, He's been no friend of mine."

"He got you here didn't He?"

Doc sneered, he wasn't buying that idea.

Cedric continued, "Regardless, a Higher Power is an entity greater than you- any force or being that you understand to be what people have traditionally called 'God'. It doesn't have to be the God that your family taught you, it can be the power of your ancestors, the nurturing force of nature, the vastness of the universe, whatever is your true understanding of God."

"So if I have a problem with the old God, then just pick a new one."

"In essence, through your action of coming here, you're admitting that you already had picked one."

Doc just gave him a puzzled look.

Cedric explained, "If you have reached the point in your drinking where you can't control it, then alcohol has become your Higher Power. You have relinquished your free will to it."

Doc self-consciously averted his eyes.

"For now, just work on the idea that there could be a power greater than yourself out there and that It wants what is best for you. If you need help with this, just have faith in the idea that I and countless others have placed our faith in a Higher Power and found refuge from our addictions in It."

This sounded crazy to Doc, but he nodded his head to get the session over with.

Cedric leaned back in his chair and observed his hostility. "Okay, Doc, we can leave it there for today." As Doc got up and started for the door, Cedric added, "Oh, and here is your phone back. I'm sure that you'll want to check in with your loved ones and tell them that you're," he looked Doc up and down, "well, alive at least."

Doc snatched the phone as he strolled out of the room, looking expectantly toward the numerous well-wishes from friends that he could respond to sober. When he opened the phone, his ego sank- after a week without access, the phone still only had one friendly message, which was from Julia. There were several missed calls from unknown numbers (the regular unwanted solicitations), and a text from some religious group, but no other friends had contacted him. He was forced to acknowledge that he had essentially shunned having a group of meaningful people in his life.

As the familiar self-pity enveloped him, he opened the religious text. It read "Verse of the Day," and he thought, *Julia must have signed me up for some brainwashing.* The previous day's verse was the first one on there, *Now faith is confidence in what we hope for and assurance about what we do not see.*

The next day, Doc was back sitting in the rear with Reggie, joking about the class and the people he disliked, people like Aaron who seemed to buy into the idea that God would actually care about some helpless drunk. Secretly he envied him, *How has this guy come to believe that the alcohol he needed every day was somehow now unnecessary?* He pondered Cedric's instruction, "Have faith in the idea that he has faith."

Doc was listening to the speaker describe the process of a Higher Power lifting the "alcohol obsession" when Reggie became perturbed. "What're you, joining the Moonies up there?" he said pointing to the front.

"Ha, I was just trying to figure out what this guy was rambling about. Do you feel this 'obsession' to drink that he's describing?"

"Hey man, I just like to party. Ain't no God gonna ruin my good time by taking the fun away."

"Yeah, it's not a big deal, I should just drink less I guess." *Right, if only I had tried that concept before*, he said sarcastically to himself.

"Sure, do that. Me, I have to be here. Got my third D.U.I. and I'll do jail time if I don't sit through this crap."

Doc was astonished by this information. He looked at him and thought, *Three D.U.I.'s and this guy still thinks he's just partying and having fun?* He hoped he didn't sound that ridiculous when he defended his own drinking.

At the conclusion of the class, Doc walked out past the smoking section, ignoring Reggie's calls to join the crowd there, and took a seat by the pond out back. He knew that he felt this obsession, he had felt it for years but couldn't quantify it, all he could do was abide by its demands. When he had dared to question the need to drink, the craving overpowered him and made him do it, even in the face of the inevitable negative consequences. From then on, fear had dictated Doc Rutherford's life- the familiar fear that had made him hide behind a false front in his personal and professional life and then finally just hide from the world. Thinking about all of this made him ache for the escape of a drink.

Absent this option, he grabbed a shower and headed to his next counseling session with Cedric. Doc's head still hurt from his weighty considerations, and combined with his unabated compulsion to drink, it was not a good recipe for thoughtful conversation. Before he entered, he checked his phone and found a new verse waiting for him. *But he said to me, 'My grace is sufficient for you, for My power is made perfect in weakness.'* He shrugged it off and took a seat.

"So Doc, did you think at all about what we discussed yesterday?"

"Yeah, some."

"And?"

"I mean, my life sucks, but lots of people have tough lives, so that's why I drink."

"You think that you drink because your life sucks or your life sucks because you drink?"

"Well, drinking doesn't help."

"No it doesn't, does it? And yet you can't stop."

Doc was a little surprised to hear that Cedric intuitively knew this about him. "Yeah but I'm working on that."

"Oh, got it. How's that been going?"

Doc rubbed his head as the line of questioning compounded his pain. "I'm not an idiot, I'm a smart guy. I'm assuming that I'll be able to figure this out on my own."

"Okay. Your mind took you down this road which has essentially turned your life into a dumpster fire, so you're going to count on your best thinking to bail you out?"

"I mean, my life isn't great, but..." Even Doc couldn't justify a completion to that sentence. Cedric waited patiently to allow Doc to attempt to do so. After a few seconds, Doc began to feel persecuted. "Isn't this a disease that you claim that I have? Shouldn't you be a little more understanding?"

"We don't diagnose you, you must decide for yourself if you're an alcoholic."

"Okay, well, let's say I'm an alcoholic, that means that I was born this way, right? I mean, you wouldn't give a hard time to a person born with diabetes."

Cedric laughed at the notion. "Doc, I don't go out and hunt down alcoholics to chastise them about their drinking. You came here seeking answers and it's my responsibility to give it to you straight."

"Is that what you call this? If alcoholism is a disease, then I'm to be pitied, not berated."

"Narcotics Anonymous has a saying, 'although we are not responsible for our disease, we are responsible for our recovery.' It means that people who suffer from addiction are sick with an illness, but not terminally so. We can recover if we accept the treatment, but it is up to us to embrace the path to an addiction-free life."

Doc was frustrated. He couldn't argue with the logic of what he was hearing, but he was still angry over the idea of being born with an infirmity with which he was forced to deal. His life was already dark before adding addiction to it.

After silently watching Doc digest the discussion, Cedric asked, "Did you try to talk with your Higher Power about relieving your obsession for alcohol?"

Doc's anger spoke through the darkness. "Yeah, sure. I said, 'If there's a God, then help me to not drink as much.' Still feel like drinking, though. Guess it doesn't work for everyone."

Cedric smiled. "And this didn't work?" he said with mock surprise.

Doc, unphased by the ridicule, pressed on. "Nope, your God apparently doesn't want to cure me."

Cedric's smile became a smirk as he stared at him. The office went silent except for the distant sound of voices in the other rooms. Doc grew self-conscious about what he knew to be his childish attitude and he finally averted his eyes.

Cedric broke the silence. "You're a lawyer, correct?"

"Yeah, and I was a Legislator."

"Oh, well excuse the hell out of me. I didn't realize what an important person I had in my care."

Doc shifted uncomfortably.

Cedric was done with the sarcasm. "Do you think I'm asking you for your life story or do you think maybe I'm asking questions to get to a point? As a lawyer, approach this logically. If you were to argue before a judge and say, 'Your Honor, I deny your power and authority, but on the off chance that you can, then grant my client everything that he wants,' would you expect the judge to respond favorably?"

"No."

"Right, and you would never approach in that fashion. You would be humble, respectful, acknowledging the court's authority, etc." He leaned forward. "And you would certainly have to *believe* in what you were requesting."

"But even if there is a God, why do you assume that He loves us?"

Cedric sat back. "Why do you assume that He doesn't?"

Doc's mind flashed to his childhood and the pain that his mind attributed to God. He thought of the place with the large cross as shame and self-disgust enveloped him. "Because of all of the evil in the world."

"Don't you think that the evil could be because of us and that the good comes from Him?"

The idea that there could be perfect love soothed Doc's head. Cedric seemed to acknowledge it on his face. "We are His creation, His children. Why would He hate us?"

Doc grew receptive, but the memories of his past actions now derailed him. "But how do I know that He would respond to me? I don't exactly deserve any kind treatment. You wouldn't believe the things that I've done in my..."

"Yes I would, I've heard it all before. I've probably done them myself. If you would like to discuss those things so that I can confirm to you that there is no depth to which you can sink that your Higher Power can't find you, then I'm happy to do so. But don't wallow in your past as an excuse to avoid God's help now. As the Big Book says, *We will not regret the past, nor wish to shut the door on it.* It means that it is important that we always remember how addiction caused us to destroy our lives, but we will not allow the wreckage of the past to define us moving forward."

Doc leaned forward in his seat to listen more intently.

Cedric concluded, "It's not what we *deserve*, it's what God has offered to us out of His grace and love for us, even in our weakness, but we've got to be truly willing to accept His outstretched hand to experience it. *Willingness* is the key."

Doc thought about the idea of grace and the willingness to accept it, such foreign concepts that he had never felt and certainly had never practiced in his own affairs. Cedric ended the session to allow him to consider it further.

He shuffled back to his room and checked his phone. There was an encouraging note from Julia waiting, to which he thought about responding, but his guilt prevented him as he knew that he was not approaching treatment in the right spirit and couldn't lie to her about it. He noticed a new "Verse of the Day" and opened it. *For if the willingness is there, the gift is acceptable according to what one has, not according to what one does not have.* Doc began to feel as if some ridiculous prank was being played on him, *It certainly couldn't be divine intervention.*

He shook his head and closed his phone as he contemplated the last counseling session. He couldn't help but respond to Cedric's reasoning, he was a drunk, no argument there. He had tried to quit or at least cut back innumerable times and failed miserably. His life was a mess, even if he didn't want to admit to it, one look at his intake photo would confirm that. Now what? These alcoholics had obviously discovered something with God, because they were *willing*. He felt distaste grow in his heart over the thought of "God" being his only hope. *What I wouldn't give for a drink.*

As if on cue, Reggie found him sitting on his bed. "Hey man, I've got a surprise for you."

"Oh hey, I'm not really in the mood to hang out."

"Really, how about now?" With that, Reggie produced a thin cigarette. Looking closer, Doc knew that it wasn't tobacco.

"Yeah right, we'd get kicked out of here."

"Dude, we've got like an hour of free time. The counselors are busy getting ready for the nightly meeting, so there's no one going to see us in the woods on the other side of the pond."

Doc stared at the joint as his alcoholic mind took over. *Just a little weed to take the edge off. This God nonsense isn't going to work anyway, might as well.* He dropped his head, "Let's go."

They made their way past the main building and walked straight toward the pond. The crew in the smoking section called to them, but they just waved and kept walking. Their path took them directly past the counseling offices as Doc felt a shiver. His mind shifted and started warning him about the risk involved. It was no use, he had decided, he didn't want to have to deal with any of this anymore. He just wanted to go back to hiding from everything, even if he had to admit that it was just the illusion of safety.

They reached the far side of the pond and found that the trees provided much less cover than expected. Doc began to waiver but Reggie assured him that it would be fine. He pulled the joint out of the inside pocket of his jacket and quickly attempted to light it. Doc sensed that Reggie was trying to get the process going before Doc could bail. Reggie took a long drag from the joint and held it out to him.

"It's not the best stuff but it's all I could get my friend to toss me over the fence," he said straining through the exhale.

Doc held it in his hand. His head was screaming for relief, the obsession to alter his mind and to escape from the world, but his thoughts were dark. *What if this is it? What if*

I never get this opportunity again? He felt defeated. His hand was shaking as he raised it to his mouth and drew in a short toke. He could barely hold the hot smoke before coughing it back out.

Reggie's initial reaction was to laugh and mock him for his amateurish behavior, but looking at Doc's face left him silent. It was obvious that Doc was despondent. He just gripped the joint until Reggie felt the urge to break his trance.

"Ha ha, okay Doc, you need to learn to share," he said, taking back the joint. He was half way through his massive inhale when they heard the voice.

"Put that out now."

Doc whirled around as Reggie choked and expelled the smoke. Cedric was standing at the entrance to the woods, staring at Doc. Without averting his eyes, he said "Reggie, you're out of here. You've got thirty minutes to pack your things then come see me for your car keys and other items we have up front. Doc, you come with me, I'll out-process you first."

Doc was in a daze when he reached Cedric's office and took a seat across from his desk.

"Okay Doc, you get to go back to drinking yourself to death, enjoy," Cedric said as he intently filled out the required discharge documentation.

Doc's mind grasped for excuses to try to salvage the situation. "I don't even like weed, it was just to let off some steam, you know..."

Without looking up, Cedric replied, "You knew the rules. You purposefully violated them. You're gone."

"Because of one slip?"

Cedric seethed at the lie. "That was not a slip, Doc, that was a conscious decision on your part to announce to the world that you don't want help. You are a self-pitying drunk who thinks the world owes him something because he was born with an illness. But this is not an incurable cancer, this is a disease with a treatment, hand-delivered to you if you'd only be willing to embrace it. You want me to feel for you, but how many of your fellow men would you pity if they, like you, refused to help themselves?"

Doc understood the rhetorical nature of the question and his mind ran dry of excuses. His eyes went blank as his head wilted toward the ground. For the first time since he had arrived at the Farm, he did not wish that he were free of the place. His heart sank as his throat tightened- not in his familiar self-pitying fashion, but instead, in recognition of a deep loss. He could only manage a whisper. "What if it didn't work for me?"

Cedric froze. His eyes widened with delayed comprehension as the seasoned counselor said astonished, "You're afraid."

Doc couldn't raise his head. "I've seen people try to stop drinking and fail. Good men, better than me. I'm nothing, I'm a fraud. I talk big and act confident, but I know that if I try and can't do it," his throat closed and a tear trailed down his face, "I'll have no hope left."

"Doc, *Rarely have we seen a person fail who has thoroughly followed our path.* As those of us in recovery can attest, all things are possible through your Higher Power. *God could and would if He were sought.*"

Doc looked up at him. His entire body cried out in desperation. "I want to believe that God is real, I just can't

59

believe that He would want anything to do with me. That He loves me."

"I know exactly how you feel. I couldn't imagine it either until I came to believe it in my heart. I had pushed Him away, cursed Him, and refused His every offer of relationship, and yet there He was with His hand extended, just waiting for me."

The words were pure comfort to Doc's pain. He imagined a life without the obsession to drink, without the feeling of hopelessness, without constant regret. He wanted that so bad. His voice cracked, "Please don't let me ruin this. Please tell me that this was meant for me."

Cedric's eyes narrowed as he pledged to him, "If you are desperate, if you are at your end, if you are willing to go to *any* lengths, then you simply cannot fail."

"I'm so scared. Oh God Cedric, I'm so scared."

Cedric's eyes welled as he smiled. "Doc, it is written, *If God is for us, then who can stand against?* It's not a question of will God help you, it is a question of will you let Him."

Doc heard the words and believed them for the first time. The God of the Universe, *his* Higher Power, could do anything. God had never abandoned him, had never wanted him to fail, had never delighted in his despair. He had been there all along, waiting for Doc to reach out and accept His hand.

Doc collapsed to his knees and wept into his hands. "Please God… please help me."

Cedric quickly moved close and wrapped his arm around him. "You are free, Doc. You are a free man for the first time in your life."

- 7 -

Doc stumbled out of Cedric's office, back to his bunk, and collapsed. He slept through dinner that night, through the evening meeting, through morning prep, and through breakfast. His body was exhausted from carrying the weight of a world that he himself had created.

When the other guests grew irritated at his absence from the morning meeting and began organizing to rouse him, Cedric intervened sternly. They were puzzled, asking each other, "Why would a no-nonsense guy like Cedric provide cover for a goof-off like Doc?" They assumed that Doc had been a part of Reggie's pot rebellion and would have been expelled already.

Thirty minutes into the meeting, Doc came running in wearing the same clothes in which he had slept. He took an immediate seat and focused on the printed agenda. Cedric nodded in his direction and returned to the rules of the day without even a word of admonishment. The group was stunned.

After the meeting, Doc quickly grabbed a cup of coffee and found Aaron. "Hey man, how are you this morning?"

Aaron stared with a jaundiced look at his capricious friend. "Uh, I'm good. You feeling okay, Doc?"

"Yeah, thanks for asking. I needed to hibernate." He laughed lightheartedly.

Aaron relaxed a little and smiled. "Yeah, you should be caught up for a good month."

"The session is about to start, let's grab a chair." Doc gestured as he started toward the front of the room.

Aaron still appeared a bit confused, but followed him to an adjacent seat nonetheless. He watched Doc open his Big Book and prepare for the class. The book creaked as if it were being opened for the first time.

Over the next two weeks, Doc consumed the program as he was consumed by it. His doubts about the program were gone- if a God that he had shunned, disavowed, and even cursed still accepted him and cared enough to relieve him of his unceasing obsession to drink, then He could help Doc accomplish anything that was prescribed for his recovery. That was his belief.

He learned about the basic recovery tenets of rigorous honesty, selflessness, and most important for the ego-driven alcoholic, the substitution of God's will for that of his own. As was his new practice, he checked the latest Verse before entering his next session, *Trust in the Lord with all your heart and lean not on your understanding; in all ways submit to Him, and He will make your paths straight.* He contemplated the words and had to admit to himself his reservations. Doc was a new man, but even a spiritual awakening as he had experienced when asking God to free him from the stranglehold of alcohol did not immediately relieve his bondage of self. He was still in charge, that was, until Cedric discovered his holdout.

"Your best thinking left your life in a shambles, right Doc?"

"Yeah, but I'm thinking clearly now."

"Good, then you should just tell God that you don't need His will to govern your obsession anymore and let your will take back over. I'm sure that He'd appreciate your candor."

Doc was horrified. He couldn't go back to the way he was before. He felt almost stupid for thinking it. "So what, I'm just a mindless drone now?"

Cedric laughed. "Do I look like a mindless drone? Do the sober people that you know look like they're worse off because of their submission to a Higher Power? We still make our daily decisions, but we consult with God to be sure that we're in line with His perfect direction."

"So, I'm supposed to find a burning bush and have a chat? This seems so humiliating to me."

"You're supposed to maintain conscious contact with God. If you're humbly praying to Him, He will guide you. Humility is not humiliation, nor is it thinking less of yourself, just thinking about yourself less."

"Sounds crazy."

"Two weeks ago you were a fall-down drunk whose life was unmanageable. Now you no longer have a debilitating craving for alcohol because you surrendered and asked God for help, but asking Him for guidance in your daily affairs is crazy?"

Doc stared indignantly. "Okay, fine, you're right."

"See, God told you to say that."

They both chuckled. Cedric tilted his head in contemplation. "Remember that this is a relationship. All relationships require communication and this is accomplished through prayer and meditation. Just make sure that you're not the one doing all of the talking."

"What do you mean by 'surrender', though? All I did was ask God to use His will to help me quit drinking."

"And in so doing, you surrendered your will to His. Both of you can't be steering the ship." Cedric observed the concern on Doc's face. "What comes to mind when you think of the word 'surrender'?"

"I think of being beaten into submission, weakness, etc."

"Okay, your drinking did beat you down pretty good, but God didn't, did He?"

"No, I guess not."

"What He did was offer you relief from that misery through following Him. Surrender means to simply stop fighting your Higher Power, to stop fighting His perfect, benevolent will for you."

Doc nodded as the light came on in his head.

Cedric closed his folder to signify the end of the session. "That is the essence of acceptance. We stop fighting and accept His will in our lives. We restore ourselves through the process outlined in the Twelve Steps and grow in our understanding of our Higher Power through study and communication, which is the key to our long-term sobriety."

Doc internalized these ideas and explored the work of the program. Rigorous honesty was a prerequisite for any true assessment and understanding of one's life and standing therein. Humility prepared the individual to seek God's direction and to improve one's self. Gratitude provided contentment and cheerful disposition. Willingness is what made it all possible.

With a firm start on his relationship with his Higher Power, Cedric began in their next session to walk him through an inventory of his character defects and resentments and how they had caused pain for himself and others around him. He admitted his flaws- even things that hurt his ego, especially things that did. This bred life-saving humility.

They reviewed Doc's initial Fourth Step list of resentments and defects, which he had prepared during his down time. Cedric considered the list to be understandably spotty, as it was with most newly-sober people on their first attempt, but still, he tread lightly in his criticism.

"This is the process that separates the men from the boys, Doc, and you either decide to stay the man you were or become the man you want to be. I'm glad to see that you're willing to be so honest with yourself in reviewing your shortcomings."

"Thanks, but I'm not really sure why people are so scared of this Step."

"It can be difficult for people to confront their deep-seated defects and the harmful actions that these flaws have led them to take. But it's important to remember that you're simply *admitting* these things, so they're already known to you and weighing on your conscience, you just hadn't yet consciously acknowledged them."

"Well, I find it freeing to understand why I do the things that I do. Changing them, that's another issue."

Cedric chuckled. "Yeah but that's really the key. Not much point in identifying all of the traits that drag you down and then calling it a day."

Doc shrugged, "I've cataloged them and now I'd like to get rid of them."

"Then you're ready to ask God to remove them from your life. You meditate on your faults, understand how they've misguided your thoughts and actions, how they've negatively affected your life, and when you're ready, you prepare yourself to have them removed and humbly ask God to do so. You've done a great job here. It is crucial to remember that this is a list of defects for you to continuously work to overcome while adding to the list itself through your spiritual journey."

There was an awkward pause. Doc could tell that the wheels were turning in Cedric's mind, but he was feeling fearless at this point. "Okay what is it?" he asked.

"At the end of the day, this is your list, and you've got to complete it in your own time and in your own way." Cedric paused again. "But I think this would be a good time to discuss some flaws in particular."

"Oh, sure, which ones."

"Well, really one. Your anger."

"Okay, I admit that I acted angrily toward people and wronged them. I'm absolutely willing to own that."

"Good, but dealing with these character defects isn't just about preventing harm to others or avoiding mistreating yourself. The true curse of the defect isn't in how it manifests in your actions, but in how it governs your mind."

Completely aware that he was walking into a trap, Doc still asked, "So how is anger governing my mind?"

"You need to tell me that. I can help with what I've seen, for starters, you harbor resentment over your alcoholism."

"Yeah, I'm not exactly happy about it."

"Understandable, but you need to come to grips with it or it will monopolize your thoughts." Cedric hesitated again. "You are also very angry with your father."

Doc sat up. His temperature grew for the first time since he had embraced the serenity found in the program. "You mean the guy who abandoned his family, abandoned *me*, and pursued his selfish desires instead?? Uh, yeah, I'm still pissed."

Cedric replied gently, "He was a sick man with a disease that caused him to indulge his defects."

Doc's thoughts jumbled in his head. He was certainly open to the idea that his old conceptions were flawed, but his assumptions about hating his father *had* to be correct. "Well, sick or not, he treated me like dirt and doesn't deserve anything from me."

"Are you any better? Did you *deserve* your Higher Power's grace when you received it? You treated people poorly your whole life, but somehow you now *deserve* their forgiveness? I'm not going to make you forgive anyone, Doc, but don't fool yourself into believing that any of what we have been freely given through this program is something that we earned. It has been given through grace, not merit."

Doc folded his arms and seethed at the ground. Cedric reacted to his posture. "You feel that?"

"What? Hatred? Yeah, I feel it."

"Feels familiar doesn't it?"

"Yeah. It feels..." Doc trailed off.

"Feels like when you'd escape into a bottle?"

Doc's stomach churned. He hadn't felt this urge to drink since he had asked his Higher Power to lift his obsession.

Cedric nodded, "That's what our defects do to us, Doc. If we hold onto them and let them rule over us, they force us back to our old coping mechanisms. Drinking, isolating, the path of death and destruction."

"I'm just not ready to forgive him for the pain that he caused me."

Cedric slowly shook his head, "That's okay, I'm not expecting miracles, but the same man will drink again. If you hold onto the anger, and refuse to forgive those who have contributed to its cause, you will eventually suffocate from it and find yourself a drunk once again."

Doc lowered his head and exhaled loudly. "I want to stay sober, but the idea of forgiving him is so painful."

"All growth is painful." Cedric cocked his head reflectively. "What did you do when you had difficulty in taking any of the other Steps so far?"

"I asked God to make me willing."

"Then let's leave it there. As we've discussed, willingness is the key to the entire program. If you sincerely ask your Higher Power to make you willing to take any Step, then you *will* become willing to do so. Notice how many of the Steps simply involve becoming willing or asking God for help. Willingness and prayer are actions, not concepts."

Doc nodded his head. At that moment, that's all that he could give.

After a short break to clear his head, Doc moved straight into Step Five. He admitted out loud, with Cedric as his guide and witness, the things that he had done to others. He felt a great weight lifted off of his shoulders as he was no longer resigned to a life of regret and self-punishment for the past through hiding and isolation. Drunkenness ceased to be his coping mechanism.

When he reached the moment to admit to betraying his brother, he cringed but asked God to help him be willing. He felt the words escape his mouth and waited for Cedric to gasp and rain down a fury of condemnation on him, but there was none. When Doc gathered the courage to look up at him, Cedric was just sitting there looking expectantly.

"Okay, so is that all of it?" was his only reaction.

Doc was astonished, even a bit indignant. "That's it? You're not disgusted, or even angry?"

"Uh, do you want me to yell at you or something?"

"Well, I guess I expected you to be upset, yeah."

"Do you think that I'm any less of a sinner? Or that any person in this program is pure? Doc, this is about freeing yourself of the wreckage of your life, not languishing in it."

Doc breathed a little easier and sank back into his chair.

Cedric said, "Now..."

Doc thought, *Of course there's more.*

"The final Steps to clearing the wrongs that you have done is to admit them to the people affected by them and to humbly seek their forgiveness. When you're ready, you'll pray and meditate on them, list them, and then take them to God to ask Him to make you willing to make amends. Only then do you approach those people."

"I can't tell my brother about this, it would kill him to learn that he is not the father."

"That's up to you and your Higher Power. Making amends is about setting things right for your own conscience. It's not even about the other person's reaction, if they refuse to forgive you, that's their prerogative. You've still completed your work by sincerely admitting the wrong and asking if there's a way for you to make it right. However, if approaching a person with the truth would cause further harm to them, then you wouldn't be making things right, you'd be making them worse."

Over the final week of his stay at the Farm, Doc approached each day as an opportunity to practice, in a safe environment, the principles that he had learned. He showed greater understanding toward his fellow man, was slow to anger, and was less selfish (he was in fact on the brink of becoming *selfless* for the first time in his adult life).

As his departure became imminent, he contemplated the many people he had wronged, regardless of whether alcohol had been involved. The list grew sizable as he cataloged their names and his infractions against them, both in vague and specific terms, and prepared himself to apologize and make amends to them all. He was downright pleased with himself as he checked the Daily Verse and entered his final session with Cedric.

"How are things working for you, Doc?"

"Great. It seems pretty simple, just abide by all of the directions in the Big Book."

"Yeah, that's the gist of it. It has been read, reviewed, and re-issued repeatedly since the 1930's, so you can pretty much count on the fact that it won't lead you wrong. But keep in mind, it is a *simple* program, but not an *easy* one. It is a lifelong pursuit of spiritual progress, not a one-time attainment of perfection. You'll stumble, you'll rebel, you'll fall away, just as long as you maintain your spiritual connection to God."

"Spiritual life is not a theory, *we have to live it*," Doc said smiling proudly.

"Oh perfect, you've been studying 'The Promises' on page eighty-three. That is in essence what you can expect from humble adherence to this program, even before you've completed the Steps. In fact, that's a good place for us to end. Why don't you read them out loud for us."

Doc was a bit surprised by the request, but he opened his book to do as instructed. "If we are painstaking about this phase of our development, we will be amazed before we are halfway through. We are going to know a new freedom and a new happiness. We will not regret the past nor wish to shut the door on it. We will comprehend the word serenity and we will know peace. No matter how far down the scale we have gone, we will see how our experience can benefit others. That feeling of uselessness and self-pity will disappear. We will lose interest in selfish things and gain interest in our fellows. Self-seeking will slip away. Our whole attitude and outlook upon life will change. Fear of people and of economic insecurity will leave us. We will intuitively know how to handle situations which used to baffle us. We will suddenly realize that God is doing for us what we could not do for ourselves."

Cedric smiled and interrupted, "Doc, 'are these extravagant promises?'"

Doc smiled and continued, "We think not. They are being fulfilled among us- sometimes quickly, sometimes slowly..."

Cedric concluded the passage, "'They will always materialize if we work for them.' Those Promises are in essence the culmination of the program. They are the answer to the proposition posed right before the listing of the Twelve Steps, which states 'if you want what we have'. Note the phrasing: if you want all that we *have*. It doesn't say 'if you want to get sober', it's saying that we, as new creations, now have endless opportunities in our lives, as outlined in The Promises in particular."

Doc nodded his head, to him, it felt like the perfect summation to a logical thesis.

Cedric looked up and recited, *"These are the promises that enable you to share God's divine nature and escape the world's corruption caused by human desires."*

Doc looked puzzled. "Where is that found?"

"In the New Testament of the Bible. The words of the Big Book are based on the Christian text so it is often insightful for me to go directly to the original inspiration. Jesus led a life that reflected the ideals of this program and He is the reason why we have it today. Only you can determine what your Higher Power is to you, but regardless of your conception of God, the Bible is a useful resource for understanding our principles."

After a pause, Cedric said, "You've heard me quote the various principles and you will hear people in the sobriety meetings quote from their religious texts as well because the Big Book instructs us to consult those resources. Your Godly inspiration will come from prayer and readings, both the Big Book and the teachings of your Higher Power. This is how God provides direction in black and white, so that you can ponder His words and incorporate the concepts into your life."

Doc nodded his head in understanding. "The Big Book, religious verses, and prayer are my new guides. Got it." He closed the book and sat back feeling content. "I don't know how to thank you, Cedric."

"Well, don't thank me yet. There is one final thing I want you to do. I want you to help a fellow alcoholic."

Doc was perplexed. He had been taught that alcoholics helping other alcoholics, as outlined in the Twelfth Step, was how the program thrived and it was this service that helped those in recovery to maintain their sobriety for the remainder of their lives, but such work was reserved for those who had managed months if not years of temperance and program work. He thought, *Twelfth Step work already? But I'm just a newcomer. Oh well, anything for Cedric.*

"Your father is here, I want you to meet with him and receptively listen to him make his amends to you."

Anything except that. "What the Hell, Cedric??"

"Wow, that didn't last long."

Doc stood and crossed the room. He felt intense resentment, a sickening reminder of his old self. He extended his arms to the wall and breathed as he stewed in the request. "I don't know if I can stomach listening to him, let alone forgive him."

"You're telling me that if he humbly approaches you to honestly admit his wrongdoing, you're just going to turn him away? Is that the response you're hoping for when you attempt to make amends with the people who you've harmed?"

"No, I want to unburden myself and I hope that they'll understand how genuine my regret is."

"That's the same opportunity that you'll be affording him. Nothing more, nothing less."

Doc's impulse was to bolt, but he had learned that his first thought was often wrong, so instead, he practiced using prayer. He was learning that God asked little of him and all of it was designed to help him stay sober and create a new life. This can't be beyond His power, after all, *God could and would if He were sought.* He inhaled a deep breath and asked God to help him be willing. "Okay, I'll sincerely listen to his amends."

"That's all that your Higher Power asks of you."

Doc remained in his chair with arms crossed staring at the door. It opened slowly and his father walked in. Seeing Doc's posture, he did not attempt to approach him.

"Hey Doc, you look great."

"Yeah, I'm doing well now. The people here explained about alcoholism and how to deal with it effectively. Really nice to have some people in your life who care enough about you to show such concern."

Doc suddenly felt like a little kid again, hiding his feelings from his daddy. The anger was still there, but the embarrassment and shame of his addiction flooded his brain as well. He hid behind his familiar confident façade.

His dad nodded in agreement, "This is a great facility. I owe my life to the staffers here and to this program."

Doc looked around the room to convey his disinterest, "Yeah, I do too."

"I appreciate your willingness to listen to me. You don't owe me anything, so I'm very grateful for the opportunity."

Doc relaxed a bit when he looked at him. He appeared so old and frail, not gruff and imposing like Doc remembered. Yet even with the physical infirmity, his father looked strong in his demeanor.

His father breathed deeply. "I ruined my life, son, and I irreparably damaged our family in the process."

Doc nodded his head and thought, *Amen to that.*

The Senator continued, "I don't need to tell you all the ways in which I failed you as a father. But even as I was still indulging my drinking, I couldn't shake the feeling of inadequacy and shame, so I hid from you."

Doc perked up when he heard this as he empathized with every emotion.

His father said, "I couldn't believe that there was a way out, that I could stop my destructive lifestyle and attempt to correct what I had done. The misery, the sorrow, the shame… it just suffocated me to the point where I attempted to take my own life."

Doc's arms unfolded and dropped to his sides. He leaned forward as if he didn't know the end of the story.

"I thank God that He found me there, a completely broken and helpless man. He guided me to this place and to His salvation. He never abandoned me in spite of all of the horrible things that I had done."

The words mimicked Doc's own story. His obstinacy crumbled as he became willing to acknowledge the similarities instead of focusing on the differences.

His father sighed, "I told you that this place saved my life, well the people here did more than that, they gave me a life worth living. Doc, I can't tell you in any simpler way how sorry I am and that I want to do anything I can to make amends."

As Cedric had suggested, Doc made the connection of his own laundry list of wrongs and his desire to be forgiven, to the request now laid before him. No other words were needed.

After a further thirty minutes of discussion, Cedric knocked on the door and peeked his head in. "Sorry to disturb you guys, but Doc, you have your final meeting tonight. I was hoping that you would say a few words to the group before you leave tomorrow."

Doc smiled, "You think I wouldn't?"

The father and son chuckled. The Senator said, "I better get out of here to let you prepare. I don't know your plans, but you're welcome to come stay with me when your stint here ends."

Doc nodded and said, "I might just take you up on that."

With that, the two hugged.

Exhausted, Doc returned to his room and laid down on his bunk. The day's events replayed in his head as he closed his eyes.

When he awoke, the sun had faded and the building was silent. He sat up on the corner of his bed in the dark. He thought about his dad and how good it felt to release the anger he had toward him. Cedric was right, he couldn't harbor resentment against his father, they were both sick and their actions had derived from a common depth of addiction. But his unease lingered, he still felt like he was sullied and broken. He thought about the Lord's Prayer that the group recited at the end of each meeting, "Our Father..." but where had his Heavenly "Father" been when Doc needed Him? When he was just a child? His brain began to spin and he held his head to keep from spiraling.

"You look like you're a bit overwhelmed."

Doc jolted out of his thoughts to see Cedric's outline in the doorway. He sat straight and tried to compose himself. "Uh, yeah. Just some bad memories."

"I think at this point you understand that this program isn't just about sobriety, Doc, it's about healing your past and living free of it. Call them 'memories' or 'traumas' whatever they may be, they will fester into resentment and eventually lead you back to drinking as the solution. Whatever it is that is weighing on you, have you taken it to God for resolution?"

Doc exhaled and crumpled forward. "What if God *is* the resentment?"

Cedric nodded his head knowingly. "Sure, that's valid. It's quite natural to blame God for our condition."

He shook his head lightly. "I don't resent Him for that anymore. It, it's not that."

Cedric was silent. Like most of the counselors that Doc had encountered in the meetings, his tendency was to tread lightly with a fragile newcomer and he left it up to Doc to share further.

After a moment, Doc continued. "I agree with you that man is capable of evil, not God, but surely God is capable of preventing evil. I just don't understand why He would allow evil to happen to me."

Cedric began to answer, "We don't know God's will for us. It could be that…" but he trailed off as he watched Doc and seemed to recognize that this was not an ontological discussion about good and evil in the world. Even in the dark, it was clear that Doc was distraught over something tangible, not theoretical. "What is it, Doc?"

He sat motionless on the bed and continued to stare toward the abyss, searching for divine presence. Cedric spoke soothingly, barely above a whisper. "Son, it's just the two of us. I'm here for you, tell me what happened."

Doc breathed deep and looked down at his lap. "My parents weren't there when I was growing up. They weren't there physically or emotionally. Eventually they just completely abandoned me. That was my resentment against my father. I forgave him for that, but when he left my brother and me with my mom, she made it clear that she wasn't going to be bothered with having to raise children. She wasn't just distant, she was… cold. Even with nannies there to watch us, it must've still been too much of an inconvenience for her to have two of us there, so she placed me into a daycare at a local church. I remember the large cross at the front of the building as I entered, a place where the name 'God' was repeated over and over." He looked up as if admiring that cross.

He smiled slightly. "I loved it from the start. Unlike home life, it was full of children and activities and love, love in the form of hugs and kisses. The hugs were more plentiful when the parents left. Alone with the loving adults. Teachers really. Teaching the children how to love. How to love one another. *Physically.*"

Cedric winced as Doc's lips pursed to continue. "You know, kids want to learn, they want to please their elders, they want intimacy. It was so easy to take part. It felt so right that I took this home with me. We weren't supposed to tell anyone, but my best friend Timmy could be trusted." He shrugged, "I mean, he deserved love too."

He dropped his eyes. "We would hide in the basement guest room under the grand antique bed and love each other. Hiding, where it was safe. Away from the parents, just like at daycare. One day, my mother stumbled into the room with a glass of wine in hand, and just like that, she ended the play dates then and there; no explanation given to me and none sought by her. But somehow, *I* was to blame."

Doc breathed deeply to maintain his composure. "I was a little boy, so vulnerable, so innocent. The people there, *God's* people, they violated me, they robbed me of that innocence. They took away my ability to love, to be in relationship with others. They took all of the joy and the love from my life and I hated God for this. How could that be His will for me, Cedric? You tell me that to stay sober, I must follow His will now, but how can I trust Him?"

Cedric closed his eyes and shook his head. "The program is full of people who struggle to gain sobriety only to give up or take their own lives over their inability to reconcile the pain of their past, either the pain that they have created in other's lives or the pain that they themselves have experienced. Oftentimes, substance abuse is a coping mechanism for the pain to which the addict eventually succumbs. It must have been so confusing to you, Doc, a place of safety that became your source of anguish. You are absolutely right to be angry, but you know God now, *personally*, would He have done this to you?"

"He did do this to me."

"People did this to you Doc, not God. I know how hard it is right now for you to accept the difference, but God never wanted this to happen to you. He never wants any of us to do anything unkind to one another, but that is the essence of man's free will, and that is the result of sick people hurting others."

Cedric moved over and sat next to him. He placed his hand on his shoulder. "Doc, we can't know God's plan for us, that is the immensity of His being, but you and I have both experienced His love for us. When we were stumbling through the darkness, He never left our side, He was there all along. He wouldn't rescue you from the torment of your addiction to then force you to live in the nightmares of your past. It is written that God has a plan for you, *Plans to prosper you and not to harm you, plans to give you hope and a future*. That is His will for us."

Doc breathed deep and uttered a simple prayer, "God please help me to heal." He felt an immediate relief. The cloak of misery which had smothered him all of his adult life felt loose as if it no longer had power over him. As he breathed freely, he felt light filling the dark corners of his soul.

As the evening meeting began with familiar ritual, Doc and Cedric stood together in the back. Cedric looked at him. "Doc, you're not perfect, but you're perfectly placed where

80

God wants you." He winked and walked forward. The edge of Doc's mouth crept upward as he nodded his understanding. As Cedric completed his introduction, Doc walked to the front and stood behind the podium. He reviewed the crowd and found his friend Aaron looking back. They exchanged hopeful smiles.

He looked down at the podium. "I appreciate the opportunity to humbly share my strength, hope, and experience, both before and after my Higher Power lifted my obsession to drink." He looked up and knew what he wanted to say.

"My name is Mark, and I'm an alcoholic."

Doc was dead. Mark was alive in his place.

- 8 -

The next morning, Mark hugged his goodbyes to the staff and fellow addicts before he emerged from the main building of the Farm. Their appreciation for him grew more animated when he began to pass out his remaining packs of cigarettes to the smokers.

"Well Cedric, any final words of advice?"

"It's a long path ahead for you, but it's designed that way to be a constant pursuit of progress. I would just remember the farewell words of our co-founder, Dr. Bob. He said 'our Twelve Steps, when simmered down to the last, resolve themselves into the words *love* and *service*.' Abandon yourself to God, abide this direction, and you cannot go wrong."

Cedric smiled as they hugged. Mark absorbed the words and repeated the concepts in his mind: *Trust God's will, maintain my spiritual condition with Him, love, and serve.* He looked down at the only items he had left to his name, a duffel bag of clothes and a photo of him and a little girl. He began to walk toward the main road to hitch a ride when Cedric called after him.

"Oh by the way, Mark, your dad left you these," as Cedric tossed a set of keys to him. He stared at the unfamiliar metal and looked up at Cedric puzzled.

"It's the Chevy Nova in the side lot over there." Following the direction of Cedric's finger, Mark recognized an old mustard-yellow two-door, his deceased great-aunt

Ruth's car, which was older than him. He smiled as he filled with gratitude.

He slid behind the wheel and started it up. He had no money, no home, and no career, but he had something much more important than those, he had hope. He guided the old heap out of the parking lot, narrowly missing the front gate. He hadn't driven a car in over a month and trying to maneuver one that lacked power-steering proved difficult. He made it out to the freeway and aimed it toward his first destination as a sober alcoholic, the home of Julia Sawyer.

It was a Saturday morning, so Mark was confident that he'd find her there. He pulled up to the house just outside of Richmond and turned off the engine. As instructed by the program, he had mentally prepared himself for this moment. He had meditated on his wrongs, considered what defects had caused his damaging behavior, asked God to remove those defects from him, and was completely willing to accept responsibility for the harm that he had caused her. In spite of all of this, fear gripped his body. All he could do was sit there and pray as he had been instructed, "God, please help me have a humble and accepting attitude no matter what may come."

He took a deep breath and slid out of the worn leather seat. His hand was shaking when he reached for the bell and after a few seconds, the door was opened by a nine-year-old girl. Mark hadn't counted on this. "Oh… hi, is your mom home?"

The girl stared at him and finally turned and yelled, "Mom! It's the turd!"

Mark's eyes widened with surprise.

A voice from inside of the house called back, "What? Hold on." He heard footsteps as Julia approached the door. "Honey, what have I told you about usin' language like..." she reached the door and saw Mark. "Oh, it is the turd. Thank you, sweetie, go clean up your room."

Mark grinned at his new nickname. Julia hid part of her body behind the door while she held onto it. "Hello Doc, you look well."

"Hi Julia, you look great too."

They stood in the doorway observing one another. Mark read the concern on her face and realized that she must be unsure of why he was there. He gleefully blurted out, "I just completed the thirty-day program at Faraday and was hoping that we could talk."

Her eyes narrowed. "Uh huh, and did the program do you any good?"

He smiled. "Yeah, I came to believe that my Higher Power could lift me from addiction. He gave me what's called the 'gift of desperation' which allowed me to break down my barriers and be receptive to His help."

Julia examined him further. She looked guarded, but she nodded as she considered his appearance and demeanor. She managed a smile, "Okay, Doc, come on in."

For the next few minutes, Mark discussed the transformation that he had experienced through the program and admitted how he had wronged her. He intuitively knew when to stop speaking and to just listen to Julia's feelings.

She had a lot to unload on him, but she eventually told him that she was happy to forgive him.

He took a deep breath and said, "There's more I want to tell you about. It's not an excuse for my behavior, but I know that it will help you to understand."

He avoided her eyes to prevent the shame he felt from enveloping him. He then proceeded to tell her about the darkness in which he had lived his early life and how it had corrupted his understanding of love and relationship. She was sobbing but reached out to hold his hand, and after an emotional hour together, she walked him to the door.

"So now what?" she asked.

"Well, I've got a law license, but no firm in its right mind would hire me to handle cases for them."

She nodded her head in agreement.

"But I've got a desire to do something more meaningful than billing hours anyway."

"Oh yeah, what's that?"

He smiled, "I'll tell you when *I* know."

She looked him in the eyes, "Well, I know you'll find somethin' you love. Whatever it is, just remember, *I will honor him who honors Me.*"

Mark shook his head, "Who said that?"

"God silly." She laughed. "I'm proud of you, Doc."

"Uh, Jules. I'd prefer it if you call me Mark," he said haltingly. "If you would."

"Okay… Mark," she smirked, "but I've only ever known Doc."

He no longer had a home in Richmond--a voicemail from his landlord had made this clear--so Mark confirmed with his father that he could stay with him. However, not wanting to lose the momentum that he had in his sobriety work, he hurriedly tracked down a few more surprised people with whom he wanted to make amends before heading north. He knew that getting on his feet after being down for so long would take time and there was probably no safer place for him to be than with a fellow alcoholic who was actively progressing in his own recovery.

It was dark when Mark reached his father's townhouse in the Old Town section of Alexandria, a few miles from Washington. He was exhausted, but his body was still amped from the cleansing work he had been performing, so he convinced his father to brew a pot of decaf coffee and sit on the back porch with him where he shared all that he had accomplished that day.

His father seemed impressed. "So, the guy was so surprised that he dropped his coffee mug and it shattered?"

Mark laughed, "Yep, couldn't believe what I was telling him. I think at first he thought that I was there to ask for money, and by the time I had told him about all of the changes I've begun to make in my life, I think that he thought I was trying to convert him or something. He seemed pretty relieved when I suggested that I leave."

His father was smiling and nodding, "Yes, I had similar reactions from some, however, I generally called ahead of time to prepare people for our meetings."

"Yeah, that's probably a good idea. I just wanted to keep it going, this is the best that I've felt in my life."

"Good, this program isn't about being morose or somber in our sobriety, it's about alcoholics truly experiencing the joys of life for the first time."

Mark sipped from his cup and breathed in the crisp night air.

His father thought for a moment and added, "This part of the program is also about clearing away the debris that used to weigh us down and changing our lives to avoid adding it back again. I'm proud of you for engaging in this like a man."

Mark smiled at the encouragement. He watched the stars and thought about next steps. He looked over at his father and his conscience called to him. "You know, Dad, I owe you an apology as well."

His father cut him short. "Mark, you could sit here all night and apologize to me and it wouldn't mean a fraction of what your actions have meant. Of course I forgive you. That's not to say that your actions didn't merit an amends, but the importance to your sobriety in the process of seeking amends is in your acceptance of responsibility and your desire to rid yourself of those traits."

The Senator placed his cup on the ground while leaning in. "You're seeing now the danger that character defects such as anger can pose to your very survival. As the Big Book says, anger is the 'dubious luxury' of the non-alcoholic. All human beings need to appropriately manage their emotions, but to the alcoholic, it is an even graver proposition because carrying those feelings will eventually drive you back to the drink."

"Yeah, well I'm never going back to that," Mark said as he yawned and started for the door. "I'm beat, goodnight."

His father cast a wary eye toward him as he disappeared inside. He whispered, "I hope so, Doc."

The next morning, Mark was energized. He attempted a four-mile run but was forced to break it off at two. Unlike the work of the program, he'd have to ease back into the exercise. Later, he and his father attended a recovery meeting at King Street Baptist Church and grabbed a burger at the Hard Times Cafe. The conversation inevitably turned to Mark's future career and his father was keen to share his thoughts on the subject.

"I could certainly talk to some of my friends in the legal community in Richmond. There are several people in recovery who would be understanding of your past."

Mark was reading one of the Washington papers and nodded his head. "That's definitely an idea." He wasn't trying to be inattentive, but Mark was enraptured by an article recapping the first few years in office of the new President. The New York businessman was an abrasive, vulgar, and egotistical anti-establishmentarian who had been elected by a disaffected populace because of, not in spite of, his complete lack of political experience.

His father attempted to peer around the paper. "Or maybe you would want to stay up here for a while and get your sea legs beneath you in your first year of sobriety? Our estate lawyer is in Arlington and I could see if she could use some help."

"Yeah, I'll take a look at that."

The Senator looked a bit perturbed by his son's disinterest. "Or you could dig ditches for a living, maybe be a longshoreman."

Mark folded the paper down and shot his father a dismissive look. "Sorry, I'm reading about President Davenport. On paper it seems like he should be doing much better in the polls than he is. The economy is booming, he's making demands on countries that used to eat our lunch on foreign policy and trade, he's not afraid to get out there and mix it up for what he believes is best for the country."

"True, but he's kind of a blowhard with all of his inflammatory rhetoric if you ask me. Not the way you did things in my day."

"Yeah, but I think that's the point. You and I have seen the political world from the inside, and I don't know about you, but it made me sick, even as I have to admit my role in it."

His father put his arms up, "I'm not going to defend that part of my life, but you can't be an effective leader if you're constantly dividing the people you claim to serve."

Mark nodded in reluctant acknowledgement.

The elder Rutherford fished for his wallet. "Now, do you want to spend the next several years sleeping in my basement and reading newspapers or do you want to start working on a legal career again?"

Mark rolled his eyes and laid down the paper to fully engage with his father. He promised he would go meet with the estate attorney in the next week, but in reality, his thoughts lingered on the new President.

As Mark had assumed, the meeting with the estate attorney had been cordial but fruitless. He didn't blame the attorney however, as Mark couldn't manufacture any enthusiasm for a job which consisted of billing hours again, especially given his new-found penchant for speaking openly and honestly in his dealings in accordance with the tenets of his program. As he sat at his father's kitchen table, he ran his fingers through his freshly clipped hair. He consoled himself, *At least I look like a professional again.*

He opened his father's laptop to begin scrolling online for jobs and decided instead to take a detour to research further into Davenport's first term. As he scanned various news sites, the President was portrayed as either a savior or a devil, depending upon which source one believed. Objectively though, Mark was able to glean that the President had successfully negotiated trade policies which promoted U.S manufacturing, agriculture, and jobs. His foreign policy was designed to force allies to fully participate in, and share the financial burden of, their own security. He pushed tax cuts and more reasonable government regulations that, combined with these more favorable trade deals, resulted in record-low unemployment, higher wages, and nationwide prosperity. It seemed to Mark like he was laser-focused on pushing American interests, except he had a severe problem maintaining a coherent, thoughtful message. Much of his bombast came across as the rantings of a belligerent and imperious C.E.O. who's not used to answering to people. Not to mention his veracity issues.

He closed out the browser on the President and returned his attention to his fledgling job search. Up until then, he had been considering legal career options, as limited as they were, but he started to contemplate possibilities across the Potomac River in Washington. He could be a low-level drone in a public policy institute, he could sell his soul (and probably his body) and join the lobbying corps, maybe be a bureaucratic paper-pusher for the rest of his life. None of these vocations appealed to his new sense of calling in life. The prospects were disheartening.

Feeling defeated, his eyes wandered over to the Washington paper laying on the table. He picked it up and began reading an article about the White House which contained a photo of the President's Chief of Staff, Retired Gen. Stephen Hastings. Mark's father walked into the room, stopped, and looked.

"Oh General Hastings, I remember when *Major* Hastings was a military aide in my Senate office decades ago."

Mark stared indignantly at his father. "You know the Chief of Staff?"

"Know him? He used to report to me. Sharp guy. Not sure how he's managed to stay with Davenport this long, this President seems like he would burn through staffers pretty quickly."

Mark looked down at the photo and then turned back to his father. "Do you think that he would be interested in hiring me to work in the West Wing?"

The Senator gave him a pitying look. "Uh, you might have some issues with that given your past."

"Understood, but you could get me a meeting with him, right? The rest would be up to me."

"I'm guessing that I could. There's little chance of you working in the White House, but he might point you to something in an Executive Branch Department."

"The job title doesn't matter to me."

His father saw Mark's mind working. "You may have other obstacles. Generally, an Executive Branch appointment is dependent upon a person working to help the President during the election, of course with the unorthodox route that this President took, that's perhaps not an issue. The other problem might be a background check for a security clearance. I can make a few calls to my old contacts to see if your history precludes you. These days, I doubt it will."

"Okay, so you'll give him a call?"

Mark's father began feeding off of his son's excitement. "I'll call and see if he would be willing to meet with you. When dealing with a meeting like that though, where you don't have any particular skills that set you apart from other interested parties, I would recommend that you go in merely seeking his advice. That's the old adage in fundraising, 'If you want advice, ask for money, if you want money, ask for advice.' He might have a useful referral, but you had better read everything that you can to get up to speed on current policy initiatives in preparation."

Mark nodded his understanding and smiled as a potential meeting scenario played out in his mind. A recovering alcoholic lawyer with nothing to lose.

- 9 -

Mark was standing directly in front of the Southwest Gate to the White House when he turned his attention away from the photo of him and his daughter. The memories it had conjured of the last two months of his life were intense, but after spending the better part of an hour reliving them, they had been helpful in re-focusing him on his task. He looked back up at the commanding building and said a quick prayer of thanks as he wiped more sweat from his brow. The time for his appointment finally arrived and he was met by an assistant and escorted inside to the Chief of Staff's office, by way of a bathroom so that he could relieve himself of the multiple cups of coffee he had consumed.

As Mark walked, he ran through the information that he had learned on General Stephen Hastings. He was a retired former Army Chief of Staff who was close to some of President Davenport's most trusted supporters. It had leaked that Davenport was originally eyeing the president of one of his companies for the position of Chief of Staff, but he was convinced otherwise by these men and women. He was told that he needed either a Hill-savvy influencer or a soldier with Washington experience and a knowledge of managing large bureaucracies. Given how much he ironically despised politicians, Davenport had chosen the latter.

Hastings had accepted the position mostly out of a sense of duty and, according to Mark's father, had immediately regretted it. Since it was widely known that he had been a consolation selection by Davenport, the General was treated with less deference by other Advisors and Washington insiders than past men and women in his position. This made getting things done much harder and it gave him a persistent complex about his standing with the President. That aside, the General was a strong leader and organizing force within the chaotic environs of the Davenport White House. He spent an inordinate amount of his time hunting down leaks and putting out fires, many of which were created by his own boss.

Although Mark technically arrived on time for his appointment, he found himself sitting outside the General's office for almost twenty minutes. It was illuminating to say the least. He heard Hastings scream at the Press Secretary for five minutes and then turn on a dime and speak soothingly to some staffer who apparently wanted out of the harsh working environment. When all of the fires were out, the General appeared in his doorway and summoned Mark in with a wave.

"Come in, Mark. Sit down." The invitation was delivered more like an order from the short, barrel-chested man.

"Thank you, General, I really appreciate you taking the time to meet with me," Mark said as he hurried to an open seat.

"Certainly, your father was very kind to me when I was a young Officer on the Hill. He asked if I could give you some advice about a job in Washington." He sat behind his desk and opened his hands invitingly. "I'm happy to help."

Mark opened his portfolio. "Yes, that would be great if you have any ideas. I brought a copy of my resumé with me and of course I can email a copy to your office as well."

He handed the General his resumé and allowed him a few moments to review it. Mark's eyes were drawn to a corner of the General's office where a life-size cutout of Davenport stood. He chuckled. "He's quite a character," Mark said, relaxing a bit.

Hastings looked up from the resumé and over at the cutout. "You think he's a little crazy, right?"

"Well, I'm impressed that he won. And for a billionaire, he has a surprising understanding of the priorities of blue-collar Americans." Mark grinned, "But man does he say some goofy things."

The General looked at Mark and smiled. "Yeah, he keeps us on our toes. For all of his success to date, he has a tough time staying out of his own way."

Mark nodded his head.

Hastings continued, "But he's certainly accomplished some remarkable things already," the General's face went blank and his sharp, hazel eyes narrowed, "and I guess we all do stupid things in life, don't we?"

Mark's eyes widened and he instinctively sat back up straight. His father, in the interest of full disclosure, had obviously informed the General about Mark's downfall and recovery. He sheepishly directed his gaze toward the ground.

Hastings returned to Mark's resumé. "Your father mentioned that you were a lawyer and a Legislator, that combined with his contacts would probably suggest a position with a Hill Office or Committee. Have you thought about applying there?"

Mark pretended to write this down on the legal pad he had in his portfolio. "Yes, those are great ideas." He looked up from the pad. "Though, I was really hoping to explore opportunities in the Executive Branch."

"Oh, well I'm sure that I could refer you to a few folks in the Departments and Agencies to see what they might have available."

Mark smiled and nodded outwardly but he knew that his sordid history would preclude him from any competitive opening. He needed to be selected for a position by someone who was inclined to help him out or he would be going home empty-handed. "Those are all great ideas and I would certainly appreciate any referrals." Mark took a deep breath. "Do you perhaps have any openings here on your staff?"

The General reclined in his chair as the realization of what Mark was after crossed his face. "Oh, sorry Mark, those slots have been filled for quite some time and require years of D.C. experience. I should have explained to you that White House positions are reserved for seasoned policy experts and Washington insiders."

"Oh of course," Mark said shaking his head, "but I meant working directly for you. I would imagine that it is extremely difficult to keep track of all of your areas of responsibility and I'd love to help."

"I'm sure that you'd be a great addition, but I have my staff in place already," he said dismissively.

"Right, but what about your intern positions?"

It took Hastings a second to comprehend what Mark was suggesting, but even after he had, he shook his head in disagreement. "The intern positions are filled by college kids who help fetch coffee and staple press packets. They're paid a little over minimum wage. You wouldn't want to be doing that work."

"No, you're correct that I wouldn't want to be stapling press packets, but I would be happy to provide you with legal and research work for nominal pay. I'm not interested in making a fortune, I'd just like to work for you and help out the Administration while gaining White House experience."

Hastings looked at Mark, contemplating his proposal. "You'd want to work for nothing just to be in the West Wing?"

"No sir, not just to be in the West Wing, but I would do it to work directly for you." Mark knew that the idea was a long-shot to begin with, but if he could make it more enticing to Hastings, he might have a chance. Every White House Chief of Staff was overwhelmed, as Hastings certainly was, so Mark was offering a virtually free legal and political mind to help.

Hastings remained silent, so Mark continued. "It would be an honor to work for you and on behalf of the Administration," it couldn't hurt to play on the man's ego as well, "and of course, in theory, anything discussed in my presence would be protected by legal privilege."

The General's bushy eyebrows raised at the mention of confidentiality. It was well known that Congressional Committees were always seeking to question White House staffers in an attempt to dig up dirt. Hastings thought for a moment about the idea, but appeared to allow caution to take over. "Well Mark, it's an interesting idea you have. I'll think about it and let you know."

Mark knew that this was Washington talk for "not bloody likely." The General began to collate his papers to signify the end of the meeting. Mark could tell that Hastings was intrigued by the idea that he had brought him, just not the person. He leaned forward, "I also have some ideas about policy initiatives, ideas that I would want to pursue if I were advising a Federal official."

The General stopped shuffling and looked up at him. Mark's father had let slip that the President was a fickle man who always wanted to hear the next idea and the General was running out of them. If he couldn't present new ones, his days would be numbered no matter how competent he was at managing the West Wing.

"What ideas would you suggest?" Hastings was willing to entertain Mark's suggestions, but he presented a skeptical front obviously meant to keep Mark moving quickly to the point.

"Well, sir," Mark said, surprised by the General's quick interest, "I think that the President would be wise to push hard on better trade deals with the Europeans like he did with the Chinese. He's right that they take advantage of the U.S. in foreign policy and exemptions for certain protected industries. He should hit them hard on tariffs and not blink until they lower theirs across the board. And of course, he should pursue the second round of trade talks with the Chinese. Their ruling regime is essentially a house of cards with the populace in check only as long as the economy is growing. The leverage is there."

Hastings responded unimpressed. "That would be the President's stated intention already."

"Right, but I think that he's perhaps being pressured by his own Party to back off of this position, which he shouldn't do."

Hastings stared at him. Even though Mark was somewhat unprepared for this discussion, he needed to dig deeper. "Uh, and if the President is intent on building a wall on the southern border and he wants it paid for by those nations whose citizens attempt to enter the country illegally, as he has suggested, I would recommend that he implement fees on international money transfers, specifically to Mexico and Central and South American countries if such a fee structure is otherwise legal. For example, monetary remittances, mainly from the U.S., is Mexico's largest source of foreign income."

"Right, it's not a bad idea. We've discussed the concept and it is being examined from a legal perspective."

Mark could tell that he was close, but the General wasn't swayed. *What else would matter to the President?*

Hastings stood and resumed the preparations for his next meeting. "Well, I've got to meet the Director of National Intelligence here in about five minutes, so I'll let you know what I decide."

Then it hit him. Mark remembered the old adage that "All politics is local," even for the President. The saying referred to the need for elected officials to keep their fingers on the pulse of their constituents and to always be looking for ways to stay connected to the people who elected them. For Mark, the idea here was to connect Davenport to the households of everyday Americans.

"What about the Do Not Call List?"

Hastings barely looked up. "Huh? What about it?"

"Well sir, it essentially doesn't exist anymore."

Hastings was confused and out of patience. "Yes it does, there's a website for people to sign up. You enter your phone number..."

"No, I don't mean there isn't a concept called the 'Do Not Call List', I mean that the List essentially isn't effective anymore."

"Oh, well I guess you would call the Federal Trade Commission and..."

"Yeah sure if you were a Congressman or a White House official," Mark said, gesturing to the one standing before him, "but if you're the average person working full time, raising a family, trying to get through your busy day, and you were constantly being harassed by solicitors and scammers about car warranties and such, would you really want to sit on the phone for hours to try to reach a bureaucrat in Washington who probably doesn't care?"

The General stopped and pondered this concept. Mark continued. "The whole reason people signed up for the List in the first place was so that they wouldn't have to constantly lodge complaints about harassment. That was the beauty of the program."

"Okay it's annoying, but it doesn't rise to the level of a Presidential initiative," Hastings argued.

"For *you* maybe." Mark could tell that he had surprised Hastings with his pointed comment. "I mean, I'm sure there are people who are so well connected that they can call someone in the government to do something about the calls, but the average person can't."

The General crossed his arms and ran his fingers down the sides of his square jaw. "What are you proposing?"

"The power of the Federal government to regulate communication lines is extensive and almost absolute. Shift the enforcement of the regulations to the service providers. If someone attempts to make robo-calls or uses a clone or fake-ID generator, make the communications companies responsible for identifying this abuse of their infrastructure. If a phone line is misused, require that the service provider cut off all of the lines owned by the offending company, its principals, its investors, etc., until the matter is resolved. And update it to include unsolicited text messages as well. You think that any legitimate business or investor is going to knowingly allow a company to *ever* misuse a communications device again?"

Hastings laughed, "Do you really think that would survive a challenge in the courts?"

"A challenge from whom? Do you think that an enormous telecom company is going to stand with the hated telemarketers? The government delivers the names of the offending companies and then the providers shut down the offenders and blackball any and all of the participants from future service. To avoid a potential court challenge, you co-opt the telecoms to your effort ahead of time. Look at how Obamacare was passed, they brought in the insurance carriers. And even if the initiative were to be challenged and overturned, in whole or in part, the President is still the man who stood steadfastly with the American people."

"Okay, but it's still just an issue of inconvenience."

"It's a national security issue. It's a health, safety, and welfare issue." Mark tried to remember all of the legal catch phrases from law school, whether they applied here or not. "International scammers are calling our citizens and stealing their money. I'm sure that terrorists somewhere are profiting from this like all untraceable illicit activity." Seemed legit to Mark. "The President calls AARP, low-income advocates, immigrant groups, etc., to rally on behalf of an initiative that would fight the scourge of exploitation. While of course preventing the pain-in-the-neck telemarketer calls that were supposed to be prohibited in the first place."

Hastings nodded his head and cracked a slight smile. He paused and looked back down at Mark. "You think you can pass a background check?"

"Yes sir, my father has already used his contacts to look into that. Should be fine."

"Okay, be at the Southwest Gate at 0700 Monday. My assistant, Tina, will give you the details."

Mark celebrated internally as the General gathered his things. "And Mark," he said with the smile gone, "if I even imagine that you're drinking again, I will eighty-six your ass immediately."

With that, the General walked briskly past Mark and toward his next appointment. Tina copied down Mark's information and escorted him out to the gate. As he stood outside by the fence, Mark turned and looked at the White House. *We will intuitively know how to handle situations which used to baffle us.* He hoped to God that was true.

His father couldn't believe the news. "He hired you? On the spot?? I thought he would maybe give you a recommendation to some remote Department in Maryland or something, but to work on his own staff? I guess I still have some pull."

"Yeah, he said that he owed you big time and that he would do anything for you, even hire your ne'er-do-well son."

The Senator looked at him with a brief moment of surprise before Mark shot him a wink. His father shook his head and grinned, "Well, whatever the reason, this is quite an honor for you."

"I'm pretty excited. It doesn't pay much, but I'll be able to do the work that I think I'm called to do in this new life."

"Yeah, well focus more on the 'work' and less on the 'life-calling' aspect of the position," his father said with a knowing glance. "And don't worry about the money, I'll float you while you work toward a permanent position in the future."

Mark smiled. Even while he was celebrating, he was still secretly praying that God wouldn't let him screw it up. It grew quiet in the house as the two men sat at the kitchen table. Mark looked over at his father and realized that his recent sobriety was the first time as an adult that he had just casually spent time with him. An age-old question percolated to the front of his mind. "Let me ask you something, what is the deal with the name 'Pharaoh'?"

His father cocked his head back and laughed. "I wondered at what point in your life you'd ask me about that. It's an old family name. Back centuries ago, when our Scotch-Irish ancestors settled in the Appalachian Mountains, there was a tradition started by your great-great-great, however many, grandparents to name the first son 'Pharaoh'. This continued for several generations until the family fought for the Union in the Civil War. After this success, they were able to move to Richmond and finally join proper society, which apparently killed-off the tradition. I wasn't going to name you Pharaoh, but thought it would be an interesting middle name for you."

"I didn't think so. I hated it growing up."

"Yeah, I can imagine that it caused some joking and kidding."

Mark nodded his agreement in exaggerated fashion, then turned serious. "But do we know why the name 'Pharaoh'?"

"Well, when I was growing up, the kids in our family were forced to read through the old journals and records of our ancestors. The name appeared to be a way for the family to set a new course when it had arrived in America. It makes sense I guess- to the ancient Egyptians, the Pharaoh was more than the leader of the people, he was the conduit to a new life that all those people sought. His death was viewed as a necessary bridge for the people to access a better world. There was allusion to that concept in the writings."

Through all of his years of college and postgraduate studies, Mark had never bothered to examine the significance of the name Pharaoh in the context of his pioneer family. Hearing this explanation, it began to grow on him.

- 10 -

The next morning, Mark's alarm clock sounded and he opened his eyes to the unusual feeling of waking up as opposed to coming-to. He had spent so many years passing out, oftentimes in strange places, that being alert and productive first thing in the morning was foreign to him. As he had been instructed, he offered a "thank you" to show gratitude to his Higher Power for this simple miracle. He intended to take full advantage of it, and after completing a four-mile run, he ate some breakfast and headed to a meeting.

Sobriety meetings varied based on the location and intended audience, but they all had in common a basic formula: the Serenity Prayer, introductions (first name only), a reading from an A.A. approved text, and then individual "shares" lasting a few minutes, which hopefully were at least tangentially related to the reading. Given his lingering embarrassment over his disease, Mark avoided sharing most days, but this enabled him to listen fully to the wisdom (or lack thereof) from more seasoned adherents. As one old-timer had once whispered to him, "Listen carefully for examples of both what you should and *should not* do."

As with any other meeting that he had attended, he passively gleaned bits of wisdom from the day's shares. He heard one man talk about relapsing, repeatedly using the term "slip" to minimize the conscious decision that he had made to abandon his sobriety. Mark shook his head while quietly judging him, *The guy's just fooling himself.* Next, an impeccably dressed man admitted, "I liked drunk me, problem was, drunk me liked cocaine." Mark smiled at the morbid humor.

The final speaker was a middle-aged woman with runny mascara who was asked if she'd like to share given the obvious pain that she was experiencing. "My name is Denisha and I'm an alcoholic. I'm really struggling today and so grateful to be in a meeting with fellow alcoholics. You all are my support... I don't know what I would do without you."

She paused and dabbed her eyes with a tissue. "As I've mentioned before, I had my kids taken away a couple of years ago and I've been working this program, really, to get them back. I worked the Steps, I have a sponsor, I've been sober for over two years now..." She trailed off as she lifted her eyes straight up, seemingly in search of a lifeline from above.

"I got visitation with my kids now from the state, but they don't seem to want anything to do with me. My youngest hid behind his foster parent, just kept crying like I would hurt him again."

She leaned forward and breathed deeply. "I had to leave early and come to this meeting." She moved her hand onto her knee to support her faltering body. "That's tough, that's tough. But you know what? It taught me that I'm either in this for my sobriety, and not just to get my kids back, or I'm not really in this at all."

The group nodded and added a chorus of muted approvals.

"And now I know that I'm in this for me, so I can be there for *them*." She raised her clenched fists to shoulder height in a show of triumph as the other members clapped and smiled. Mark clapped along but his mind was miles away, Richmond to be exact.

As he exited the church basement to return to his father's house, Denisha's story focused his mind on his daughter. For the first few years of her life, Mark had been absent, and for good reason, but now that he was sober, he entertained the idea that things could be different between them. *Could I be involved in her life? Is it wrong for me to want that?* His feelings were intense and frightening.

When he arrived home, he laid down on his bed and ran through the knowledge of his program. *Practice these principles in our daily affairs*; *The next right thing*; *Acceptance.* He knew that he had to be prepared to accept life on life's terms, but he also knew that he had the ability to change things that were within his control, as long as it was the right thing to do.

Mark embraced the peace and solitude of his room as he meditated on his quandary. He thought about how to reach out to his Higher Power for inspiration and then realized that he hadn't really "put a name to the face" yet. Cedric had connected the tenets of the program to the principles of Jesus and his followers, which seemed like a useful starting point.

He pulled out his phone and checked for the Daily Verse: *For it is God who works in you to will and to act in order to fulfill His good purpose.* He nodded his head at the obvious similarity to his service-based program, but he was still unsatisfied. He pondered where to start. After a moment of contemplation, he realized that he was over-complicating things.

It took him only a few seconds to pull up a webpage with the search "Christian Principles." It described Jesus's life purpose, as best as Mark could discern, that all people fall short of God's prescribed hope for us and that to rectify our broken relationship to Him, He had sent his Son out of His grace to teach us the proper way to live. He scanned for the concepts that Jesus not only taught, but lived: love and serve all (including your enemies); practice kindness, honesty, patience, and gratitude; support the poor and defend the weak; be humble and forgiving; avoid self-centeredness and pride; confess transgressions and reform character; commune with God and substitute His will for yours; witness to others. The further he read, the greater the origin of his new principles became solidified.

The passage was concluded with a verse for those seeking guidance, *Do not be anxious, but in all things, by prayer and petition, with thanksgiving, present your requests to God.* He reached into the drawer of the nightstand and pulled out the picture of him and Annabelle. He smiled and then furrowed his brow as he whispered to his Higher Power, "What is the right thing?" His answer, as best as he could tell, was simply to call George.

As the phone rang, Mark panicked with the realization that he hadn't yet prepared to address George on his list of amends. The program encouraged easing one's way into such a difficult restitution, oftentimes after less trying exchanges had provided needed confidence, and of course only after much preparatory thought and prayer. The weight of the matter still burdened him.

"Hey Doc!"

Mark snapped out of his apprehension. "Hi! Uh, George." He paused. "How are you, bro?" He registered alarming guilt in his voice.

"I'm doing okay. Just surviving." George's demeanor seemed low, causing Mark further pain. George rebounded, "How are you, though? I can't believe that you're sober now. That's great, so proud of you."

Mark smiled. "Thanks man, that means a lot." As his thoughts jumbled in his head the line went silent. He took a deep breath and considered his first move. "Uh, so I was wondering if I could come visit you sometime?"

"Yeah, that would be great, Doc! I'm obviously free all of the time, but this weekend Linda will be gone with her girlfriends again. She does that quite a bit, I guess she needs that time off."

Mark's eyes widened as a smile crept up his face. "Great! How about this weekend?"

The Nova cut a wide berth into George's driveway as Mark stared at the front door. He was shaking slightly trying to predict how the encounter would play out, but at least the fact that Linda would be absent was a huge relief to him. He closed his eyes and prayed for strength as he forced himself out of the car.

As he ascended the ramp to the front door, it was swung open by George. "Doc, you made it!"

Mark bent down and hugged his brother. "Great to see you George. Sorry it's been..." He froze as he looked up and saw, in the flesh, the face that had been hidden deep in his subconscious since he first met her in a dingy bar. "Hello Annabelle."

She crossed her arms and replied, "I'm Bella."

George led Mark into the house, "She recently decided that she wanted to be called Bella, so that's what we call her now. Kind of like you, Doc." He cast a smile over his shoulder at him.

Mark chuckled. "Yeah, like me." Then he remembered himself. "Uh, by the way, I go by Mark again."

The three snacked on some chips and drinks while catching-up until Bella made an announcement. "I'm bored, Daddy."

George's eyes widened in mock panic, "Well we can't have that! What would you like to do?"

She led the two brothers over to her play area. "We can play dolls, or Candy Land, or jacks."

Mark's mouth dropped as he recalled his own love for the children's game. "You like jacks?"

"It's her favorite," George said with a roll of his eyes. "She'll play it by herself for hours."

Mark looked back at her and smiled. "Let's see what you've got."

The two brothers watched as Bella got lost in her game. Mark looked over at George and could sense the unease in his eyes even while outwardly smiling. "So, how's things with the Army?"

"Well, they cover most things here and I'll continue to receive a check for disability, but I'll be discharged soon and I'm not sure what the future holds." He sighed, "Linda doesn't want to work, but I keep telling her that we won't be able to afford things like braces and college for Bella if she doesn't. And then she spends so much, like these weekends away. She told me that I should just stop spending money on myself if we're so hard up."

Feelings of anger and guilt battled for supremacy in Mark's mind. "That's tough," he managed to say through gritted teeth. He breathed purposefully to calm himself, and as he was now instructed, he thought about his part in the matter. "I'm sorry that I don't have anything to contribute."

George looked over at his dejected brother. "Oh no, Mark, I didn't mean to make you feel responsible."

Mark nodded his head, feeling every ounce of responsibility.

- 11 -

On Monday morning, Mark was at the gate at 6:30 AM with three forms of identification. After clearing security, he was escorted by an aide to Hastings's office, who was of course already there.

"Morning Mark. Are you ready to get to work?"

"Yes sir I am." Mark smiled as he was legitimately excited.

"Good, I'll have a workstation installed for you by Tina's desk, but you'll still be managed through the Intern Program."

"Sounds good, sir."

"I'll walk you down to Jamie Thurman's office and get you set up with him."

Mark followed the General through the hallways past the National Security Advisor's office and toward the Press Secretary's suite. Behind the main offices was a room that was subdivided into at least a dozen cubicles- "The Rat's Nest" or just "The Nest" as it was known. At any given time, this was home to the dozen or so interns who actually worked inside of the West Wing. Many more were scattered throughout the Executive Branch at the various Departments and in the Eisenhower Executive Office Building (E.E.O.B.), which was the only other structure inside the Pennsylvania Avenue campus.

At 7:30 AM, the Nest was empty save for a slight-statured man in a loud suit. The General walked Mark up to the man's desk. "Jamie, this is Mark Rutherford. I believe Tina submitted his information to you last week."

"And good morning to you too, sir!" He smiled with all of his teeth showing. He was outwardly very pleasant, but Mark could tell that he wasn't pleased with the new intern. "I'll be happy to take care of this young..." he hesitated and looked Mark up and down as he held his chin delicately in his hand, "well, this *man*, and help him get situated."

Hastings turned to Mark. "Get all of your credentials handled and then report back to me. Every morning, you will check in with Jamie, who is the head of the Intern Program, before assuming your post outside my office."

Mark noticed Jamie cringe slightly when Hastings said his name.

"Thank you, Jamie." Hastings said gruffly.

"Yes sir," he said, continuing to smile. As Hastings turned and marched toward his office, Jamie said softly, "And it's pronounced *Ja'mae*," well out of Hastings's earshot. As his hand moved to his forehead, he shook his head. "I swear that man intentionally mispronounces my name." He stopped shaking and turned his attention to Mark. "So, you're the, *intern*?"

Mark became self-conscious. "Well, I'm a lawyer." Haltingly he added, "I, uh, am here to work for General Hastings."

Ja'mae was suddenly stern with Mark. "Yes, I know. I know all things about my interns. I don't care who you work for or how you got your job, in the beginning, you will be reporting to me. That means that you *will* follow my rules."

Mark agreed as Ja'mae handed him an intern packet. On the front, Ja'mae had affixed his own set of rules of conduct.

"Rule One, you will be here on time every day ready to work. I don't want excuses about traffic, late parties, whatever."

Mark nodded along.

"Rule Two, the computers and other devices are not for personal use. No posting, snapping, chatting, etc., and don't even think about using your own phone for that either. No one will be posting a selfie with a confidential document in the background."

Mark was unfamiliar with most of those terms, and looked at the list with a confused frown, but continued to nod.

Ja'mae continued. "Rule Three, I am NOT your parent..." he stopped short, shaking his head. "You know, this list was created for teenagers and twenty-something college students who don't know how to wipe their own noses. You look like you might be older than *me*, so I'm assuming that I don't have to tell you how to behave in an office environment, especially one located in the White House."

"No, I certainly understand how to comport myself. I just really appreciate the chance to work here."

Ja'mae smiled slightly. "Well, just read the packet and be sure to check in with me at the beginning and end of each day until I'm satisfied that you're settled in. I'll sign you up for my next monthly tour of the White House, we even get to see part of the Executive Residence when the President is out of town. The man has a pantry full of Spam!" He mimicked a gagging reflex and giggled. "Can you imagine? All that money and the man loves to eat processed pig parts, how gauche!"

Mark allowed himself to chuckle. Ja'mae stiffened and jutted a finger into Mark's face. "But there had better never be a leak about that or anything else you see or hear in this office, do you understand?"

Mark's head was pushed back and his eyes bulged. "No, of course not. I would never..."

"Good. Now fill out all of the paperwork and later I'll take you to get your badge and start your security clearance."

Ja'mae swiveled and returned to his desk. Mark watched as he placed his keys in a desk drawer which contained some gum, a checkbook, and various beauty supplies. Standing in front were several college kids looking at their phones. Ja'mae looked up at them and produced a shoebox from under his desk. "Okay, that's it. Phones in the box, kiddies. Let's go."

Mark retreated to get to work on making his position official.

Every weekday, Mark would take the D.C. Metro transit to the Farragut West stop and walk several blocks to the White House employee entrance. He would arrive promptly at 6:30 AM and he actually beat Hastings to the office on a couple of occasions. After a few weeks in his father's basement, he found a relatively inexpensive apartment in a run-down section of Southeast D.C. His paltry wages didn't cover his expenses, but his father was more than happy to help Mark make up the difference on his monthly bills.

He garnered a few strange looks from fellow staffers in the beginning, but word soon circulated that he was just an intern. This was fine with Mark. The Beltway was full of Type A, cut-throat people who were always looking to get ahead by taking down a colleague, so the less Mark was noticed by others, the better chance he had of concealing his past.

His initial assignments from the General consisted of researching bills, drafting memos, reviewing press clippings, and any other menial work that made Hastings more productive. After a while, he was more comfortable with Mark and had him start sitting in on meetings to take notes. Mark would jot down the notes (in a sanitized form), summarize the important points for the General's approval, and then circulate them to the meeting participants.

This was invaluable to Hastings. When the General first came onboard as Chief of Staff, he had great difficulty with the concept that colleagues would disagree with what was decided in meetings and actually challenge his recollections as inaccurate. His word was never questioned in such a way in the Pentagon. He was quite gratified with his ability to now frame the conclusions of meetings to match his goals (within reason) and have a record to cite.

After a few months, Hastings was pleased to find Mark seated at his station typing away when he arrived in the mornings. It was at this point that the General felt that Mark was ready to accompany him to meetings with the President.

As they approached the Oval Office, he gave Mark his orders. "You keep your mouth shut and take notes, do you understand?" Mark nodded, intentional in his silence. "I need you in there as a resource only, not for your opinions.

If I want to know your thoughts on something, which is never, I will ask you when we're back in my office. You are just a piece of furniture. Have I made myself clear?"

"Yes sir, become one with the chair."

Thus began Mark's attendance at Hastings's frequent meetings with the President, always occupying a seat in the background. He was thrilled just to be present, but over time, he became somewhat disheartened by the counsel he witnessed from the President's Advisors. These people certainly had impressive careers and followings of their own, but they seemed to disregard the fact that they were appointed by the President to serve him; a fact that they ignored when placing their own policy prescriptions ahead of those of the President.

Davenport's ideas were unorthodox and often ran antithetical to conventional wisdom, but they were the policies upon which he was elected to office by the American people. These Advisors were frequently overruled by their boss, but through their actions and those of unaccountable bureaucrats, the President's policies would often be subject to harmful illegal leaks and clandestine opposition. This commandeering impeded the President's ability to conduct foreign policy in particular, a power vested solely in him by the Constitution.

It was at one of these meetings that the President was venting, his jacket discarded as usual so that the sweat stains on his shirt were visible. He tended to work himself up over his frustration with government and paced as he talked. His prematurely graying hair was wet and his shirt gripped his slender frame. This day, his annoyance with Washington was directed at Mark's boss.

"We're getting pummeled out there, Stephen. There are constant leaks, the Administration is still viewed as chaotic, I haven't heard a decent policy proposal from you in months..."

The General was prepared for this. "Sir, I have one suggestion that might interest you. It involves the Do Not Call List."

Mark reflexively looked up from his notes with surprise.

"What? What about the List?" Davenport sounded confused and exhausted.

"Sir, The Do Not Call List was one of the most popular initiatives of the Federal Government in the 2000's. The American people were overwhelmingly positive about the idea of preventing harassing telemarketers and other unwanted solicitations."

"I know what it is, Stephen."

"Right, but the List is now ineffective. Every day, people are being bombarded by unwanted phone calls again. The reason is that the technology has surpassed the intent of the original regulations and the regulators themselves are overwhelmed by the legion of complaints received on a daily basis. I propose that you announce an initiative to update these regulations to add teeth back into them."

Davenport was already considering the political implications. "Okay, how would you accomplish this?"

"You shift the burden of enforcement to the telecommunication companies. You bring them onboard ahead of time by allowing them to charge a nominal fee for such a service and by reassuring them that the target of the regulations are the bad actors and not them. Furthermore, you ban any entities or individuals associated with a violation of the updated law from future use of the Federally-controlled communication lines."

One of the President's aides chimed in, "It's questionable whether that would fly with the courts."

"Who cares about the courts?" Hastings was on a roll. "Look, anyone who opposes such a move is throwing their lot in with the hated telemarketers. Who's going to do that? And if there were to be a successful challenge in the courts several years down the road, you're still the President who stood firm with the American people."

Davenport nodded in agreement to what he was hearing.

Hastings continued, "And don't forget, there is a national security and healthy welfare aspect as well with these phone scammers." Mark winced but Hastings was close enough. "You bring onboard AARP..."

Davenport interrupted, "And Southern Poverty and Catholic Charities, whoever else advocates for the most vulnerable groups in our society." He had obviously already worked out how to complete the General's concept. "I love it. I want Camilla and the Legislative Team to review this proposal immediately. Has legal had a chance to vet it?"

"No sir, but I've had one of my staffers, who is a lawyer, take a look at it." Hastings turned and gestured toward Mark as he said this.

Although Davenport could see Mark clearly in his line of sight, he moved his head to the side to look at him as if to signify that he had never bothered to notice Mark before. Mark, not wanting to violate the General's "no-talking" rule, just nodded toward him.

"Well, have Counsel's staff take a look and coordinate with Camilla. It wouldn't follow a traditional legislative path, but she should still run point."

"Yes sir," replied the General with an upbeat tone.

As Mark followed him back to the General's office, he could tell the man's confidence and demeanor were buoyed. Mark was pleased to see this. "Good work in there," Hastings told him as he disappeared into his office.

Mark had stayed silent throughout the entire meeting and yet somehow had managed to garner the General's approval. He fully intended to continue such a successful plan of action.

The President rolled out his "Never Call List" proposal, as it was known, to great consternation and criticism around D.C. Some Constitutional scholars doubted that it was legal, lobbying groups for the telecoms and other business interests threatened to sue, and politicos largely disparaged it as pandering fluff.

Outside the Beltway, however, the reception from average Americans was downright ecstatic. Mark was correct that people were incensed at the flagrant violations of the intent of the old List which caused them constant disruptions. The public took to social media, radio shows, even human contact (as limited as it was in modern America) to cheer the initiative. Congress was flooded with supportive comments and Davenport, whose many flaws had included his appearance of being aloof and unsympathetic, was lauded as the champion of the little guy.

It didn't take long for the politicians on the Hill to jump on the bandwagon and voice their support. As Mark had suggested, the telecoms were brought onboard and the initiative had almost no organized opposition.

At the Rule-signing ceremony in the Oval Office, Mark was permitted to stand against the back wall behind the press. He watched as the President signed each individual letter of his name and passed out the corresponding pens to the various interest groups and lawmakers who had publicly supported the initiative. Standing next to the President, beaming, was Hastings. Mark watched him and smiled.

He looked around at the other junior staffers standing with him and noticed a Secret Service Agent a few feet away with a triangle on his wristwatch. He recognized it as a symbol of his sobriety program- the three pillars representing recovery, unity, and service. He edged his way over and whispered the not-so-secret greeting to him, "You a friend of Bill W.'s?"

The Agent took a long look at him and then realized his meaning. "Oh, yeah. Seven years sober," he said timidly as he sized up the inquiry.

"Good deal. I'm coming up on six months. I'm Mark," he said, extending his hand.

The Agent relaxed a little and shook it. "Charles Joeng, nice to meet you."

The two stood there awkwardly for a few seconds before Charles spoke again. "You're fairly new here, do you need advice on a good meeting near the building?"

"There are some meetings over by the Hill that I've been attending, but they're populated mainly by Congressional staffers, who I try to avoid."

Charles nodded his understanding. "There are some good ones that I attend in Federal Triangle. Lots of fellow Law Enforcement. Stop by our offices in the E.E.O.B. sometime and I'll give you the info."

"That's great, I really appreciate that." Mark thought, *Drunks helping drunks, that's how it works.*

As Mark was leaving the ceremony to return to his station, a few fellow staffers caught up to him. "That was incredible, I've never seen something gain support that quickly. Where did Hastings come up with an idea like that?"

Mark summoned all of the sincerity that he could muster. "My boss cares deeply about helping the President and is really in tune with the priorities of everyday Americans. It made perfect sense to him."

They were a little puzzled. "The *General* is in tune with everyday Americans? Never would've thought that a career soldier and Flag Officer would have such a common touch. Oh well, he's gold at this point."

Mark agreed and peeled off to return to work. He remembered vividly how his father would complain on his rare visits home about a few of his staffers who would claim credit for his legislation. These folks would blab all over the Hill about how they were the real power behind the throne. Soon enough though, those same people would find themselves marginalized and oftentimes jobless. In the very least, they almost never escaped his father's blacklist.

When Mark had seen the Never Call List initiative embraced by the President and then gain support from all corners of Washington, he had felt his pride swell and he was tempted to drop little hints to colleagues about his involvement in the creation. But he knew that this needed to be the General's victory, and he also knew that ego was his eternal enemy.

- 12 -

Following the victory, Mark's life grew exponentially easier as Hastings now gave him almost carte blanche to handle his work assignments without oversight. Mark's instinct to shun recognition for the initiative was spot-on. Word got back to him that the General had been casually making inquiries with Mark's colleagues to see what they thought about him, and not a single person could suggest that he was seeking credit for it.

As for him, Mark still kept to himself, perpetually frightened by the idea that a jealous colleague would discover his history and attempt to diminish him with it. When work became routine, he began to think about reaching out to old acquaintances on the Hill. He thought, *Can't hurt to network, right?* It turned out that White House staffers have many friends of which they were formerly unaware.

The first person he thought to contact was Arjun Chandra. Arjun had been a fraternity brother of Mark's at the University of Virginia and now lived across the Potomac in Arlington. Due to their college friendship, Mark had helped him secure his first job as a Congressional staffer. After Arjun had put in a few perfunctory years on the Hill, he had jumped at the first lobbying gig he could find. Arjun was born to lobby- slick hair, slick style, slick moral compass.

As the son of a Senator, Mark was a natural target for befriending by the ambitious future lobbyist. Arjun could be counted on to help Mark find a party any day of the week, which wasn't exactly beneficial to his academic performance. They attended many of the same classes together and Mark got his fair share of help in the form of lecture notes and study prep.

This is also where Mark began to cultivate his enjoyment of learning. He spent plenty of time partying and subsequently hungover, but he also excelled at literature, political theory, and history--East Asian and Russian in particular--and read multiple newspapers every morning, although oftentimes with a beer in hand. Regardless, Mark just wanted to see a familiar face and catch up, so he contacted Arjun and set a time to meet after work one day at the Cloakroom Bistro.

"Doc! Over here!" Arjun called to him from across the room. He was at the bar, of course, buying drinks for any staffer that he could identify. Mark was sure that all of these drinks would be covered by his company, ethics rules be damned.

"Hey bud, good to see you!" Arjun said as he hugged Mark. "What're you drinking? They've got some primo scotch here man. Drank some with the Majority Leader about a month ago."

Mark thought, *Ah the "name drop."* The modus operandi of the Washington lobbyist is to plant oneself at a Capitol Hill bar, purchase drinks for any politico who could remotely help with work (either now or in the future), and be seen with important people, or simply reference past times that one had been.

"I'm good man, I'll just have some coffee."

Arjun recoiled in surprise. "Coffee? What're you nuts? We haven't seen each other in like ten years and you want to drink coffee??"

"I've got more work to get to later tonight, so I can't." Turning down the drink and the revelry which was sure to accompany it was much harder than Mark had assumed it would be.

"Oh man, the West Wing Drone Syndrome, they're going to work you into a coma. You need to bail from there and come to the dark side, Doc." Arjun said this as he scanned the rest of the room looking for more important people to schmooze.

"Yeah, I really don't drink anymore so I'm not missing out," Mark said with a shallow voice.

Arjun's full attention returned to Mark. "What? Doc Rutherford, the Junior Year fraternity beer pong champion has hung up his spurs?"

"Just wanted a healthier lifestyle." Mark chose not to tell Arjun the whole truth as he had learned was his prerogative under anonymity.

"Yeah, well makes sense. I heard about the car wreck and the Senate race you lost." Arjun punched Doc in the arm and laughed as he said this.

Mark grew red with embarrassment and anger. It amazed him how people who had never gone out, stood on their own, and put their name on the line for anything were so willing to criticize and ridicule those who had. But then again, Mark had made it so easy for people to do so to him. He breathed deeply and thought, *Humility*. "That wasn't an easy time for sure," is how he chose to carefully respond.

"Right, but look at you," Arjun said, gesturing toward Mark with both arms. "You're in the White House now bud! How'd you do that?"

"I was just willing to do the work that others weren't."

This made Arjun assume a pondering look as he lowered his drink. "So, what *is* your title there?"

Title, not *job*. Title was everything in D.C. "I'm an aide. I work directly for Hastings."

"Oh that fossil? I heard he's on his way out after the next election." Arjun knew just how to belittle people while making himself look like someone in the know.

"Doubt it. He's got the President's confidence, especially after he spearheaded the Never Call List."

"No! That was Hastings? Wow, he scored big time with that one."

Mark stood a little taller hearing the praise for *his* initiative. "Yeah, the guy's on fire." Couldn't hurt to puff up his boss a little too. "So, who else is up here in D.C.?"

Arjun cocked his head and looked at the ceiling. "Uh, Tommy Grimes is lobbying, mainly his dad. Can't believe that worthless sack is being paid to essentially introduce his co-workers to his dad's Senate Committee members."

Mark rolled his eyes and thought, *Slimy Grimey. Where else would he end up but here?* As two college kids whose fathers were both Senators, albeit from opposing parties, Mark and he naturally became acquainted early-on in college. Mark did not like the guy; he cried every time he lost at something.

Arjun continued. "Sarah Tinsley is working for House Energy and Commerce. Uh… oh! Raleigh Simmons is over at the CIA. He left Army Special Operations, he's a spook now!"

Mark took note of that. "Oh, good to know."

"Yeah, I'll shoot you their contact info. Or maybe I'll bring it with me and come visit you at work to grab lunch in the White House Mess?"

Mark thought, *Ah, the worm turns. Of course Arjun would want to get something out of a "friendly" get together with me.* Being seen dining at the famous White House Mess Hall was a huge boost for a lobbyist in D.C., certainly to their ego if not their standing. Mark normally ate lunch at his desk or in the breakroom with the college kids, a little tech-savvy dweeb named César as his usual dining companion. He didn't even know if he was allowed unaccompanied into the Mess, let alone to bring a guest.

"Oh, yeah, that'd be fun." Mark watched Arjun finish his drink and started feeling antsy. "Listen, I've got to run, but I'll take a look at my schedule. In the meantime, could you send me Raleigh's contact info?"

"Sure Doc, I've got your cell."

"Thanks… and I go by Mark now."

He retreated from the bar and inhaled the cleansing air. Arjun had made him promise to set a time for lunch, which Mark had no intention of fulfilling. He was hoping for Raleigh's contact info though, that was a person who definitely qualified as one to whom Mark owed an amends for mistreatment.

For right now though, Mark needed to find a sobriety meeting to center himself.

It took Arjun less than a day to call about lunch and Mark had to apologize and explain that he didn't have the clearance to bring guests into the White House Mess. Not surprisingly, Arjun was not nearly as charitable once he figured out that Mark had nothing further to offer him.

"Sorry Doc, I mean Mark, Raleigh's contact info isn't exactly listed. I guess you could try to reach him over at Langley?"

Obviously, Arjun felt no duty at this point to hunt down the information for Mark, which, in spite of his prior claim, he clearly didn't have in the first place. Many people who worked at the CIA had no public listing, so Arjun's excuse had the added benefit of being true. Regardless, Mark was confident that he could track down Raleigh's contact info and began searching online.

Raleigh Simmons had been a hard-charging and athletic yet cerebral classmate at Virginia when Mark had first met him. As with most men who could qualify as a rival to him, Mark had disliked Raleigh from day one, and he had made his animus clear. It wasn't that Raleigh was smarter, and he certainly did not have a more distinguished pedigree, it was that Raleigh's character wasn't a façade like Mark's.

Raleigh had been on scholarship to the university and had worked various jobs for what spare cash he had. Mark distinctly remembered one night getting plastered with a group of fraternity brothers in a bar where Raleigh had worked and purposefully dumping over a table of beers to make him have to mop it up in front of them. Mark was sure that Raleigh would've beat him senseless if his buddies hadn't been there.

Thinking about his behavior made Mark cringe and the shame roused a craving to drink. *The same man will drink again.* Mark resolved to push forward and not let himself succumb to his past, even if the required process was painfully humbling.

As Mark had suspected, he could not find Raleigh through a public online search, so he logged onto his government account and called up Raleigh's name. "Raleigh Simmons" appeared with the title of "Analyst" over at the CIA. Mark didn't assume that Raleigh would engage in any type of meaningful discussion over a work phone, so he figured that he would have to find another way of contacting him. That would take some research, and he knew just the person to ask.

The next day as he entered the breakroom, he found his fellow intern, César, as usual sitting by himself eating a homemade egg salad. Mark took a deep breath and smiled as he approached him. "Hey César, how's things?"

The intern looked up in surprise as if he wasn't used to hearing from someone who wasn't barking an order at him. "Oh, hey Mark, things are going great. How are you?"

"Super my man. Just here to grub and then get back to it. Anyone sitting here?" Mark gestured toward the only chair left at César's table. The remainder had been poached by the other members of the intern crew and crammed into a single table in the corner.

"No, I'm just enjoying my lunch by myself. Please join me."

Mark took the seat and nodded his head awkwardly as he removed the contents of his lunch. "So, what things are you working on these days?"

"Oh, generally just gopher work, but when there are research assignments, I'm always at the top of the list," he said proudly. He leaned in toward Mark. "Mrs. Obodu even gave me her secure login for more sensitive information."

Mrs. Obodu, with the Office of Personnel Management, who had access to all Federal employee records. Mark was beginning to find César to be a much more interesting lunch companion. "Wow that's great. I know that I could use some help with some research..."

"Yeah, it's pretty cool. I had this one assignment having to do with counting whales. I'm like 'why do we need to know how many whales there are?' and they're like, 'because the President asked.' Only took me a couple of hours to find the right guy at the Oceanic Administration."

Mark was a little amused. *What a nerd*, he thought. "Oh, good deal. Like I said, I'm..."

"And my parents are coming to visit this weekend from Texas. First time to Washington. It'll be so great to see them."

Mark noticed César's head drop slightly.

He continued quietly, "It's been kind of tough being so far away from them. I don't have too many friends here."

Mark felt like an absolute jerk. Here was a kid, away from home, dropped into the harsh world of Washington, D.C., who just wanted to fit in and make friends. Mark had been annoyed by his earnestness and avoided him until now when Mark needed something from him. *Practice these principles in all our affairs*. Mark sighed with recognition. He smiled, "Tell me about your parents."

César's face lit up. "Oh, they're pretty cool. My mom is a professor at Rice University and my dad is an engineer with..."

"Oh jeez, César. Are you still whining about your parents?" One of the other interns had leaned back in his chair at the other table and shouted over. "We know, they're coming to visit you so you'll quit wetting your bed. Awesome."

The giggles from the rest of the table followed as César lowered his eyes. Mark couldn't believe it. There was a "cool kids" table in the West Wing much like the one that he had run in High School. He watched César's lip quiver as he swallowed the remainder of his sandwich. Mark's eyes narrowed as he turned his attention to the second table. He stood and walked over to it.

"That's not an appropriate comment for a fellow intern." Although Mark was still employed as an intern, he was viewed with a loftier status given his age and profession. The rest of the kids were quiet and focused on their food. "I think that you should apologize."

The antagonist rolled his eyes and said, "Sorry César, no harm bro."

Mark didn't like the kid's attitude, but the apology was made, so he began to return to his chair. The intern couldn't help himself. "Hey gramps, why are you here anyway?" His table mates chuckled.

Mark stopped. His anger swelled and his blood boiled. He turned back and looked at the kid who was wearing a smug grin. The mocking continued. "Why aren't you like, a partner with a firm or something?" he asked leaning further back in his chair.

Mark's instinct was to stomp this kid, or in the very least, pin him against the wall and scream at him. He forced himself to breathe. Anger, embarrassment, annoyance, these were the emotions that used to run Mark's life and what would push him back to drinking if he let them. For now, he was worried about these emotions getting him fired if he lost his cool. He felt his pulse calm. "Why are *you* here?" Mark responded.

"It's one of the top places to intern in the world, you know, like when you're in *college*."

"So you're in it for the prestige? To be able to put it on your resumé?"

The kid lowered his chair, looking much less cocky. "Well, yeah. It's not for the pay."

"Working here is a privilege. It is an opportunity to serve your fellow countrymen. It is not some title that was bestowed upon you because you're so uniquely qualified that the White House staff is somehow lucky to have you."

"Well duh, but I'm the one at the top of my class at Yale. And yeah, my dad went to school with Davenport, but..."

"The President."

"What?"

"Do not refer to him by name, he is 'the President,' do you understand?"

"Uh well, yeah."

"I'm giving you a warning." Mark's words were accompanied by a finger pointed directly at the kid's widening eyes. "If I ever hear of you disrespecting this office, the staff, or any of your fellow interns again, I will have you kicked out to Pennsylvania Avenue and then I will personally call your daddy to come pick you up. Am I clear?"

The intern was pale as a ghost. "Yes, sorry about that."

"Not to me, to your colleague over there."

"Sorry César, it won't happen again."

Mark held his finger not sure of what to do next. As naturally as he could, he lowered his hand and walked back over to his seat. He picked up his lunch and said, "So, what does your dad do?"

César was smiling from ear to ear.

That afternoon, after Mark had stood up for him, César brought Mark a flash drive with what Mark assumed was Raleigh's contact info. César was happy to help his new friend in any way that he could. Mark promised César that he would meet his parents when they were in town and then quickly turned his attention back to his task.

He scanned the drive that César had brought him. It was full of documents, many of which were marked "Classified." César had out done himself; this was Raleigh's entire Federal Employee file including his military service.

As Mark read, he learned that Raleigh had spent over a decade in the Army Special Forces. He was deployed seven times to hot spots around the world, including countries in which American Forces weren't known to operate. Raleigh led a squad in these regions which would support the local authorities to counter the terrorist threat there. There was a letter in the file from Raleigh to his Commanding Officer from a few years prior in which he had come to the conclusion that he was no longer in the business of protecting the world from terrorism, but instead, supporting local tribal leaders with dubious loyalties. He had wanted out.

The next document in the file was a Report that described his final deployment. Raleigh's squad had been tasked with helping to cement the position of a leader in Kandahar Province, Afghanistan. The principal had pledged his support to the central government in exchange for elimination of any challengers to his station. Apparently, in the course of his work there, Raleigh had discovered that this man was bedding the local tribal boys in his care, some as young as eight years of age. He had immediately reported this information to his superiors who had shown little concern for the leader's extracurricular activities. The mission had been afforded greater importance than the welfare of a few foreign children.

Raleigh however had not shared his superiors' indifference. Late one night, he and his squad had crept into the main house of the leader's compound to teach the child predator a lesson; Raleigh's training apparently included clandestine infiltration through lock-picking. The Army medics had been able to cauterize the hole left in the man by Raleigh's K-Bar knife, but the leader's genitals had been mutilated beyond the point of being salvaged. Raleigh had assumed full responsibility for the assault and would have been court-martialed but-for his insistence on calling multiple witnesses to appear at such a proceeding to bear account to the actions of the pedophile, and the Army's pre-existing knowledge of it. His statement to the investigator had read simply, "Virtue is bold and goodness is never fearful."

In lieu of a punishment, Raleigh had been strongly encouraged to retire and be picked up by the CIA. From what Mark could tell, this position was not what Raleigh had expected. He would not be an Operator, as most Special Forces veterans with the CIA were, but instead, he would be relegated to the position of Analyst, no doubt a result of their concern over his ability to follow direction in the field. The file concluded with several denied requests for a change of his position there.

Mark jotted down Raleigh's title "Analyst, Office of East Asia and Pacific." *How did he go from operating in the Middle East to a desk researching governments in the Asian Office?* Mark assumed that the higher-ups must be punishing him for pestering them with transfer requests. He now had Raleigh's exact location, but he still didn't have any personal contact information. He decided that he would have to approach him in person.

The Central Intelligence Agency was not a place on which most Americans could simply call for a meeting. Any such business would have to be of significant interest to a high-ranking Agency official for an individual to merit even an invitation onto its highly secure campus in the Virginia suburbs. Absent such a worthy justification, most meetings would be abruptly declined and petitioners directed to its milk toast website for requested information. That is, unless said petitioner represented a person with political power. Mark's position in the Chief of Staff's Office, as lowly as it was, still qualified him as such a person.

Mark reviewed the President's official public calendar to see what upcoming international event he could use as a pretext for a visit to the CIA. There was a reception at the

White House in a week for several South American countries allied against the drug trade. Some dinners involving European and Israeli dignitaries. A round table discussion in Canada on the future of renewable energy- he thought, *Someone was going to get fired for sure for putting that on Davenport's schedule*. Nothing stood out as a reason for the Chief of Staff's office to need a CIA debrief. Then Mark saw it listed two months down the road, "Summit with North Korean Chairman Kim Jong-un." *Of course*.

The President had successfully pressured China and other North Korean neighbors to force Kim to agree to some public demonstration of his commitment to abandon his nuclear program. North Korean leaders had for decades promised to demilitarize and reign in their aggressions toward other Asian countries and toward the United States, but without any real lasting effect. Past President's would hammer out "historic" deals complete with economic aid and easing of sanctions against the dictatorship only to have North Korea secretly continue its march toward becoming a nuclear state. Davenport concluded that it would take North Korea's benefactor, China, to achieve any concrete results, so he gave China an ultimatum- either help with North Korea or the United States would hit China with trade tariffs that would cripple its economy.

Traditionally, the Chinese would have found such threats to be hollow as the U.S. would suffer similar recriminations from China, but Davenport had made it clear from his governing style that economic pain was something he was willing to abide by as long as it produced lasting results. The Chinese also realized that U.S. tariffs would encourage American domestic consumption, which would have its own beneficial impact for the U.S. The Chinese leadership, which maintained its iron grip on its people only due to the country's economic health, decided it had no choice but to assist Davenport and the message was made clear to Kim that it was time for him to cease the saber-rattling and make tangible concessions.

Armed with the pretext of an impending Summit, Mark contacted the Office of the Directorate of Analysis and was referred to an aide to the Director. It was just an informal meeting, he assured the nervous woman, designed to bring his boss up to speed on East Asian issues prior to the Summit. He would be delighted to meet with the appropriate level managers and to relay to Hastings the information he was tasked with finding. The aide was a bit confused, but set up a meeting with the Director and several staffers from the East Asia Office nonetheless.

Mark now had his reason to visit the CIA campus, but he would have to think on his feet to get to Raleigh.

- 13 -

In the meantime, Mark had pressing matters in the West Wing. He was now accompanying Hastings to almost daily meetings with the President. In one such meeting, Davenport was on his own defending his re-calibrating intentioned trade policies regarding China, the European Union, and North American neighbors. In recent years, the U.S. had been taken advantage of by the nations in these regions as its focus shifted to global cooperation on terrorism and on encouraging purchase of the ever-increasing national debt. In challenging this status quo, the President brought to bear the significant market power of the United States in hopes of evening out the playing field.

The traditional "free market" advocates in his Party were once again railing against his staunch defense of the American worker and the companies which employed them domestically. The Secretary of State was no great free-trader, however, she viewed these disputes through the myopic prism of a diplomat who was concerned about pleasing her foreign partners and maintaining influence in international organizations such as the U.N. In these meetings, she was not shy about her criticism of the President's actions.

"You're going to upset Beijing to the point where American goods are essentially unaffordable there," she said with her haughty assuredness. "It's a country with over a billion potential consumers, not to mention the strategic political problems you're causing." She confidently ran her fingers through her short, platinum-gray hair to punctuate her point. The free-traders, agreeing with the Secretary, nodded their heads in rhythm.

Davenport was incensed. "You act as if I've demanded that China and Europe give special consideration to the United States. If anything, all I've done is force them to treat us more fairly."

The U.S. Trade Representative, who was a squirrely character with a nervous disposition, only seemed to find his voice when others had broached the issue first. "Mr. President, I have to agree with the Secretary. Your demands are too strict and China will retaliate."

"With what, a tariff on the goods that relatively few of their countrymen purchase now?"

The Trade Rep didn't like the attention, but couldn't shy away at this point. "Yes, but also with agricultural tariffs and with taxes on the properties and goods of American companies that produce over there. Those companies bring their profits home and will suffer significant reductions in such a conflict, which frustrates the purpose of your policy to provide tax amnesty to encourage these companies to reinvest their profits here."

"I'm supposed to abide by an unfavorable trade imbalance and disregard the needs of the workers here so that companies that use foreign labor and support foreign GDP don't get hit on their bottom lines? And these same companies may have no choice but to look the other way, but don't think that I've forgotten how those pirates in the Chinese government steal American technology to the tune of billions of dollars in annual losses."

The Trade Rep had obviously had enough of the spotlight, but the Secretary of State re-entered the fray. "I'm receiving tremendous pressure from our allies over this. If you continue to press them on trade, then don't expect their support at the U.N. or with countering Russia and China anymore."

The President was at a loss. He had won the election by winning in states that hadn't voted for his Party in decades because he had stood so strongly on the idea of supporting American industry. Now he found himself surrounded by Advisors who encouraged him to abandon the very policies that most endeared him to the public. The President leaned on his desk and dropped his head in defeat- seemingly not of his policies, but of his inability to win adherents within his own Administration.

Mark could tell that his resolve was waning. He looked at Hastings, who would naturally support the President's stances, however, the General viewed his role as Chief of Staff to be primarily administrative and not ideological and therefore rarely engaged in policy debates.

He looked down at his notes. As was his usual practice, he had documented the key points made by each participant, however, after months of witnessing Davenport's contrarian Advisors, these now appeared more as his overall impressions of the meeting. "Past Admin have capitulated, don't rock the boat"; "Corporations over workers"; "Foreign priorities, not American."

Mark began to question what he was really accomplishing in the White House. These "Advisors" were theoretically there to support the creation and implementation of the *President's* policies, not their own. In reality, the Executive Branch had become a revolving door for D.C. insider appointees who supported the interests of their wealthy benefactors and friends, both foreign and domestic, while in government and then cashed in afterward. The well-being of the nation became almost an afterthought in this process.

His internal discord drove him to instinctively pray for guidance. *We will lose interest in selfish things and gain interest in our fellows.* Mark looked up as the President's Advisors exchanged glances assuming that they had carried the day. He looked directly at the Secretary of State and asked a simplistic question. "Why are you advocating on behalf of foreign countries when advising the President?"

The room went silent. Hastings's head snapped toward Mark and his glare burned into him. The Secretary, astonished that a lowly aide would dare question her, looked at him with disdain. Davenport looked at Mark confused as to why he would speak, and then after contemplating the question, turned and stared at the Secretary expectantly.

The Secretary, beginning to realize that the President was entertaining the question, blurted out a response. "It's my job to inform the President of the positions of our allies and other important state-actors on key issues."

"Seems like he could get that from a Report or simply by reading the news. The media is so fixated on what our self-interested allies think of the President's strategic focus on a prosperous America that they devote entire news pieces to report on it, unlike say, what a construction worker in California or a line manufacturer in Ohio thinks. It's amazing how center-left news outlets became hard line free-traders as soon as the President proposed tough tactics to achieve greater fairness."

Davenport grinned. The other aides were flabbergasted. The Secretary stared indignantly. Hastings just continued to glare. Mark felt fearless.

The Secretary stammered, obviously groping for words to defend the conventional wisdom of her globalist foreign policy. "If we ignore the will of our allies then they will no longer support our foreign policy goals." She shook her head in disbelief, "This is how it's always been done."

Mark quickly retorted, "Yes, but support in lip-service only. They talk tough on Russia and China, while lecturing America on its foreign policy, and then turn around and cut lucrative trade deals to prop up these same oppressive regimes. All while demanding that America bear the burden of countering these countries militarily. Our 'allies' don't even spend the money necessary to protect themselves anymore."

Davenport was reinvigorated. "Exactly! Why can't you all carry that message back to the countries that claim to be so concerned about our policies? Stop telling me what more we need to do for them. America has been subjected to the worst of both worlds for too long." He closed the folder on the table in front of him. "Good, I'm confident in my earlier position, so take my intent and provide me the means."

The walk back to his workstation seemed like an eternity to Mark. Hastings had left the meeting the instant that it had concluded and was no doubt waiting to pounce on him. He wasn't sure if he should clear out his desk first or take the verbal beating and then do so. *Hastings may save me the trouble and simply dump my belongings over the south fence.*

He decided to walk directly into the lion's den and face the music. Hastings was in his office screaming at his secretary. He dismissed her and focused both bulging eyes on Mark. "I don't know what possessed you to open your mouth today, but you are finished. Gather your things and be prepared to answer any questions regarding your work assignments via phone and email from home."

Mark exhaled, "Yes sir, I understand." He was disappointed, but only in the fact that he had let the General down, not that he had supported the President in his mission. At least he could have that knowledge when he returned to Richmond on unemployment.

Hastings's anger subsided slightly with Mark's contrition, but he apparently still felt the need to admonish him further. "I went out on a limb for your father by giving you this job, I can't believe that you'd defy my orders and..."

His attention was diverted by a commotion in his outer office. Chairs screeched as people announced "Mr. President" in chorus. Before either of them could react, Davenport entered the room. The two instinctively snapped to attention.

"Stephen."

"Mr. President."

"Who is this kid?" the President said as he gestured sideways toward Mark.

"He's a soon-to-be former aide, sir."

"The hell he is. I've got what are generally considered to be the best minds in Washington advising me and all they can seem to tell me is that I can't do the very things that I was elected to do. I want him in all future meetings. If he has suggestions, I want him to advise you and you pass anything worthwhile on to me."

"Yes sir."

Davenport turned to leave and paused looking at Mark. "Oh, and kid, keep your mouth shut in the meetings." He winked and exited the room.

Hastings seethed at Mark. "Get back to work."

Mark sat at his desk and stared uncomfortably at his computer screen for half an hour before he succumbed to his desire to escape the General's presence. He fled to the breakroom where he found Ja'mae and César chuckling over cups of coffee.

César noticed him first. "Oh hey Mark, come sit down."

As he took a seat, Ja'mae observed him with a sour grin. "Well if it isn't the newest diva of the West Wing."

Mark winced, "Word travels that fast, huh?"

"Honey, telling off members of the Cabinet is front page news." Ja'mae shook his head, "I'm surprised you're still here."

"I am too, frankly." Mark began to rub his face contemplating the trouble he had been lucky to avoid.

César's eyes were wide. "Yeah, what were you thinking?"

Mark pushed his face out between his hands and stared directly at him. "I don't know, I just couldn't keep watching the President get pummeled by his own Advisors." He sighed, "I mean, I believe in what he wants to accomplish, which is ironic given the fact that I didn't even vote for the guy."

Ja'mae gasped and clutched his chest. The room was otherwise empty, but he inspected every corner before whispering, "Mark, we do not EVER mention acts of disloyalty around here. Dissent is punishable by career death!"

Mark shook his head, "I mean I didn't vote. I wasn't exactly in a... headspace where I cared about such things."

César was astonished. "You didn't vote?? I couldn't wait to turn eighteen!"

Mark began to question whether this was the best conversation for him to have at that moment. "You wouldn't understand. Sometimes life gets overwhelming."

"My parents immigrated here and had to go to great lengths to have the right to vote. They made sure that I understood how precious it is."

Mark nodded his head dismissively. "Right, it's important, I got it. My point is that I support the guy's policies and I think the majority of Americans do as well. We just need to help him to implement them and then get the message out on their effectiveness."

His two companions sat back in their chairs, avoiding his eyes. Mark was confused. "Don't you two support his policies?"

César was hesitant. "I do, but... I just think he could use different language to get his point across."

"Different language?"

"Yeah, my parents are from Mexico, immigrated here legally, so they support the idea of enforcing border laws, but they are offended when the President seems to malign all people from Mexico with his rhetoric. And, not that it's an excuse, but people who jump the border are, for the most part, just looking for a better life."

Mark sat back. When he had heard the President rail against illegal immigration, Mark had focused on the fact that the people involved were violating the law. Unwittingly, he had lost sight of the humanity of those same people.

César shifted uncomfortably. "I mean, people who are of Mexican descent aren't just a bunch of illegals."

And alcoholics aren't just a bunch of drunks, they can be in recovery too. Mark understood the feeling all too well. "Sorry man, I didn't think about how his painting with a broad brush would affect you like that."

César smiled. "Well, the President *is* right that there are plenty of bad actors that do come here illegally. In Houston, where I grew up, gangs like MS-13 bring drugs and violence across..."

"Okay," Ja'mae said, slapping the table, "Mark may have permission to have an opinion, but the rest of the interns do not. We should *all* get back to work before we end up in Mark's tenuous employment situation."

Mark shot him a frown.

"And don't worry Mark," he said with a wink, "your secret is safe with me."

- 14 -

The day of the CIA meeting arrived and Mark was unsure of how he would accomplish his goal. It wasn't as though he was wasting anyone's time *per se*--he would certainly be a part of the Summit preparations and had in fact devoted multiple days to researching the various issues at play--but the meeting would be somewhat duplicative. And after his recent transgression with Hastings, all a dubious staffer would have to do is contact the Chief of Staff's Office and ask why Mark was in their building, and he would be sent packing that same day. Officially, Mark was to meet with the Director of the East Asia Office and a few of her aides. He would have to be quick on his feet.

She was in the lobby when Mark arrived, standing on the iconic CIA emblem embossed in the center of the floor. "Hello Mr. Rutherford, I'm Jeanette Nguyen, this is Zhia Tao and Harry Dubois."

Mark needed to calm his anxiety, so he confidently shook their hands while looking them directly in the eyes. "It is a pleasure to meet you. The Chief of Staff thanks you for taking time out of your busy schedules to meet with me."

After the pleasantries were completed, the group made their way to a glass conference room on the second floor. Mark placed a legal pad on the table to prepare to take notes as the Director began the discussion.

"Mr. Rutherford..."

"Mark, please call me Mark."

"Oh sure, Mark, please call me Jeanette and the others at the table are pleased as well for you to refer to them by their first names." She said this as she nodded to the other two staffers. The dour Mr. Dubois did not nod back.

"We're happy to provide the Chief of Staff with any information that he may need at this time, however, we haven't even completed our Summit Dossier yet and therefore this meeting may be a bit premature."

"Oh, I understand that," Mark assured the group, "but I wanted to meet with you and learn anything that you may wish to convey early-on for my office to have studied prior to your official briefing."

Dubois was staring a hole in Mark. Jeanette spoke, "Oh, okay, well we've already compiled a preliminary Dossier of sorts for you to review and I'm sure that we could provide an overview of it today as well as answer any questions that you might have."

Dubois couldn't hold his tongue, "Why is an intern handling a meeting such as this?"

Mark froze as fear enveloped him- they had obviously researched him and discovered his lowly title. He looked at Jeanette instinctively to allow her to provide him cover.

"I'm sure that Mark is capable of conveying..."

"I doubt that *Mark* is supposed to be here." Dubois obviously believed that he had him dead to rights. "Come on Jeanette, this is highly unorthodox."

Mark composed himself as best he could. "I know that you're used to briefing more senior members of the White House staff, but I assure you that General Hastings..."

"I'm guessing that Hastings doesn't even know that you're here," Dubois said with an unbelieving frown.

Adrenaline flowed into Mark's veins as he looked down at the table to appropriately focus it. After a moment, he lifted his head. "I don't appreciate you looking into the background of West Wing staffers, is this a common practice of yours?"

The question was pointedly directed at Dubois, so his eyes widened and he was now the one looking to the Director for help. Seeing none, he realized he needed to answer. "Uh no, of course we don't..."

"Oh, so only I have been deemed unworthy of your time?"

"I'm not saying that, I'm just surprised..."

"To answer your question, I have an intern billet because I requested a low-level position to stay under the radar. I'm an attorney who is in addiction recovery. General Hastings knows this and has graciously allowed me to work for him as a service commitment. My work here isn't ego-driven, or for monetary gain, it is my opportunity to give back."

Mark's words were met with stunned looks from around the table. He looked at each of them individually as he said, "I do, however, attend all of the General's meetings with the President and am expected to provide my input. Now, if you have any further questions regarding my employment or the purpose of my meeting here today, I suggest that you direct them to the Chief of Staff of the President of the United States. Would you like to take a break to do that?"

The three Officers wore looks of amazement over his candid disclosure. Jeanette and Harry rushed to speak over one another. "No, no."

"I apologize for reviewing your..." Dubois trailed off as Mark looked at him.

Mark knew that he was in control. "It's fine. Now, can we proceed with the meeting?"

As the staffers completed their briefing, Dubois held his gaze down to his papers. "I want to apologize for suggesting that this was not an appropriate meeting for you. I would appreciate it if you could avoid mentioning that to the Chief of Staff."

Mark nodded. "It's no problem. I just appreciate you all taking time out of your schedules to provide this information to General Hastings and the rest of our office."

Jeanette perked up at the mention of his name. "Yes, how is Stephen? I haven't seen him since we worked together on the Quadrennial Defense Review four years ago."

Mark instinctively gulped, then hoped that no one had noticed it. "He's hanging in there," he said.

"Yeah, can't be easy with this President." Her eyes widened, "Not to say that I don't have the highest respect."

"He's got his hands full for sure. I'll certainly pass along your regards to the General." The staffers began to relax as they saw an end to the meeting when Mark spoke up. "Oh, one more thing, I was hoping to ask a few follow-up questions to one of your Desk Officers if I could. Is Raleigh Simmons in the building?"

The three exchanged surprised looks. Jeanette responded, "Uh, he should be, but he's really not the person..."

"I'm sure that you've all covered most of the information here, I would just like to ask him about a few more things." The Director equivocated, clearly grasping for any excuse. Mark quickly added, "I understand that he's a fellow Virginia grad, I wanted to meet him."

She hesitated and then responded, "Okay, I'll have him come up immediately."

Within five minutes, Mark saw Raleigh walking down the corridor with two superiors, including Dubois, strenuously whispering to him. He could tell that they were threatening him with dismissal should he veer from the company line. His hair was long and shaggy and he was still sporting the beard of an Operator, no doubt his rebellious way of showing that his mind was still in the field.

As Raleigh entered the room, his look of annoyance gave way to one of surprise. Before he could say anything, Mark jumped to his feet and thrust out his hand. "Mr. Simmons, I'm Mark Rutherford from the Office of the Chief of Staff."

Raleigh was still in shock as he reached out with a callous-covered hand to shake Mark's. Mark looked at Dubois, "I'll just meet with Mr. Simmons privately if you don't mind."

Dubois's face looked pained, but he nodded his head and signaled for the other staffer to exit with him.

Mark took a seat as Raleigh glared at him. "Doc, what the hell are you doing here?"

"Hi Raleigh, sorry to pull you away from your work."

"Yeah, well they said that some donkey from the White House wanted to talk to a Desk Officer, but I didn't think that they meant a literal ass."

Mark chuckled as Raleigh took a seat.

Raleigh continued, "I hate to disappoint, Doc, but I'm not allowed to tell you anything meaningful."

Mark just smiled. "Please, call me Mark."

Raleigh squinted his eyes at Mark revealing creases in his weathered skin and slowly nodded as if he could tell that there was something different about his old college acquaintance. "Okay... Mark."

It took Mark only a few minutes to explain his life-changes and to make his apologies to Raleigh about his past behavior. Mark knew that Raleigh was not one to cry over being mistreated, so there was no airing of grievances on his part. As Mark finished, Raleigh's curiosity shifted to the reason for his visit that day.

Mark explained, "Well, as your bosses I'm sure informed you, I'm working for General Hastings and a major focus over the next month will be the upcoming Summit with North Korea."

"It's staged theater."

Mark was taken aback. "President Davenport pressured the Chinese to force Kim Jong-un to the table."

"To appear as if he's going to do something about North Korea's nuclear program. Kim will sign some papers, Davenport will declare victory, and when push comes to shove, Kim will still have a nuclear program because he knows that the U.S. will never be willing to do what is necessary to prevent it from becoming a nuclear state."

Mark was slow to process this, but finally asked, "Well what would be necessary?"

"You either take out North Korea's nuclear capability or you take out Kim Jong-un."

Mark shook his head, not wanting to believe what he was hearing. "But the President has elicited unprecedented assistance from China through diplomatic means. Either Kim abides by the international mandates or..." He found that he couldn't complete his sentence.

"Or what? For decades now, every U.S. Administration has attempted to use diplomacy to solve this issue. Some used the carrot, some the stick, some both. And yet here we are still dealing with it in the 21st century."

"The President has threatened to destroy the North Korean regime if it doesn't comply."

"How, by starting a massive conventional war against one of the largest armies on the planet? Or by launching traditional, mass-fallout nukes against a country that borders a close ally on one side and an important trade partner on the other? Not to mention Russia and Japan are in the neighborhood and probably wouldn't look too kindly on a nuclear cloud across their skies. And please don't mention the United Nations sanctions, that useless sack of doorknobs couldn't count to two if you spotted them the 'one'."

It all sunk into Mark's brain. Logically, there was no reasonable way to use military force to destroy North Korea's nuclear program. All he could manage at that point was, "Well, I have faith in the President to come up with something."

"Yeah, your boss has guts, I'll give him that. And he's crazy enough to scare most countries into compliance, but I doubt he's willing to consider either of those two steps. That's really what it would take."

As Mark exited the building and into the night, he felt disillusioned by what he had just heard. *Are we accomplishing something with this Summit or are we just rearranging the deck chairs on the Titanic?* Through his preparation for the meeting that day, Mark had convinced himself of the importance of a successful Summit and

Raleigh's valid points cast doubt on the likelihood of an effective solution there.

An unsettling feeling engulfed him, as if the diminished meaning of his work were corroding his confidence in the underpinnings of his sobriety. He took a deep breath and meditated on his thoughts. Eventually, he managed to shake it off; he knew that he couldn't allow problems to fester and manifest in unhealthy ways. He fixed a time in his head to study his recovery texts and attend a meeting, but this threat that he had experienced to the soundness of his sobriety alarmed him.

- 15 -

To describe Mark's relationship with Hastings as "strained" was an understatement. The General was now obligated to keep him onboard, but he didn't want Mark involved in anything that wasn't required. Mark knew this and focused on performing his work professionally and without pretense. He continued to attend all meetings with the President and prepared his notes per usual, leaving to Hastings the decision of whether to share any information that he felt would be beneficial.

One important meeting took place after a Special Counsel had issued a Report on alleged Russian involvement in Davenport's Presidential election. His unorthodox and chaotic campaign (and staffing therein) had created situations where junior members had run amuck and had made incidental contact with people later found to have ties to the Russian government. The Opposition Party latched onto these contacts and alleged all forms of collusion by Davenport and his inner circle. The exasperated President denied any wrongdoing, but an investigation was commenced nonetheless.

For the next two years, the Opposition Party swore that it had in its possession conclusive tangible evidence that the President had in fact colluded with Russia, which was repeated and amplified on a daily basis by the sympathetic media. Upon the completion of all the questioning and probing, which naturally shifted the focus of the Administration away from official duties, the investigation resulted in a couple of staffers facing unrelated charges (mainly for lying to investigators) and a Report which concluded that the Russian government had in fact engaged in activity designed to disrupt an American election, but not to support any one candidate.

Mark was most astonished by the fact that the Special Counsel had unwittingly highlighted the improper actions of the Law Enforcement and Intelligence leadership of the former Administration to weaponize the resources of the United States Government against Mr. Davenport's campaign, even going so far as to spy on him and his officials. A contemporaneous report from the Department of Justice Inspector General concluded that the faulty evidence relied-upon by the FBI as a basis to probe the campaign had in fact gallingly originated from a *foreign agent* hired by the Opposition Party.

Despite maintaining publicly for years that it had proof to support its charges, the members of the Opposition Party finally had to admit when placed under oath that there was in fact no such evidence; it was all a hoax. Instead of being ashamed, the Opposition offered no apology or even admission as it simply rushed into its next investigation of the President. Regardless of these revelations, Davenport was still left with a decision over how to deal with the Russian activity.

"I had nothing to do with any work by Russian agents, why the hell am I stuck having to answer for something the Russians did? This is merely partisan nonsense, I'm not going to legitimize it by highlighting a bunch of accusations against some foreigners who I've never met, let alone colluded with."

Most people in the room nodded their heads. Mark had noticed that this was becoming a more commonly-employed safe method of remaining in the volatile executive's good graces. Mark's recent brush with doubt over his sobriety emboldened him, so he instead stared purposefully at the President. His intensity was not lost on Davenport, who returned the look.

"Oh for crying out loud, what?" he finally said. Hastings, realizing that Davenport was speaking to Mark, swiveled quickly and looked at his assistant with consternation. His face conveyed a not-so-subtle warning that Mark was in danger of losing his job if he were to respond, but Mark was well beyond caring about whether or not he kept his job. He was either there to make a difference or he was happy to resign.

"Well sir, seems like you could handle two problems at once here." Davenport's expression did not change, so Mark took this as an invitation to continue. "It's become quite clear that the predominant effect of Russian engagement with the United States over the past decade, either government-sponsored or simply government-sanctioned, has been overwhelmingly negative. Law Enforcement Agencies are expending enormous resources in combating all forms of illegal activity by Russian nationals including gambling, drugs, human trafficking, theft, etc. Russian agents have been actively sowing seeds of discontent on both sides of the political spectrum in an attempt to tear us apart. You warned the Kremlin to cease such political meddling and the response was a chuckle and a shrug. Why not solve both threats to our country while proving to the

American people that you take such illegal actions seriously?"

"I told you, I'm not going to legitimize..."

"I get it, it's unfair that you've had to deal with this issue."

Davenport's eyes widened as he was not used to people disagreeing with him let alone interrupting him to do so.

"But it's there. The American people are skeptical of both political parties when it comes to this controversy. Even with a Report that exonerated you personally, your Administration is going to continue to be derided for any perceived weakness in dealing with the Russians. If you use the publication of this Report to double-down on your earlier demand, you'll make it clear that you have no tolerance for Russian interference and that you're willing to take harsh measures to deal with any and all foreign threats to our society."

Davenport was nodding. Mark knew that he had him at the word "harsh"; such actions defined the loose cannon persona that he treasured.

He continued, "You send a very public demand to Moscow that it not only cease any sponsorship of interference in American political affairs, but that it also shut down any activity of its citizens of a clandestine or illegal nature in the United States."

The Secretary of State had heard enough from the junior aide. "Do you think that we're sitting on our posteriors over at State? We've pressured the Russians to do this already. They scoffed and pleaded ignorance."

Mark didn't divert focus to respond to her. "When, not if, the Kremlin issues a denial and condescending response, you follow up with an Executive Order- all future visas for Russian nationals will be on hold indefinitely. In announcing this policy, you simultaneously issue a list of current visa holders whose papers have been revoked and order them out of the country immediately. I guarantee that Federal Law Enforcement Agencies can provide you with a list of personae non grata who they would be happy to see permanently removed."

Davenport smiled, but Mark wasn't done. "You then repeat your ultimatum to the Kremlin and include a demand for specific evidence to substantiate Russian involvement in these areas and require proof of concrete steps taken to end the activity. If your demands aren't immediately met, to *your* satisfaction, you announce that you will expel another round of Russian nationals every week until they are."

The Secretary was apoplectic. "They'll start expelling our diplomats, businesspeople, academics!"

"So? What great national goal is being achieved by having a few American citizens in Russia and at what cost to the rest of the nation? Russia has devolved into a Third World country with an inflated sense of self-value. The leadership retains control by maintaining the façade of global relevance. Its economy is in the tank, it manufactures almost nothing of substance, its population is dying off, and the only thing keeping its corrupt autocratic system afloat is that the few stay rich and the drunken citizenry buys into the lie that the country still matters. Time to pull back the curtain and let the people see the truth."

The Secretary stared speechless with her mouth agape. Obviously, Mark's ideas ran counter to every instinct that she had groomed over an extensive diplomatic career.

"And best of all Mr. President," Mark said smiling, "you show those smug gangsters in Moscow who really wields power in this world."

Davenport grinned as he envisioned that scenario. He looked over at the State Department and National Security Council (N.S.C.) staff. "I want a pro/con breakdown of this proposed policy by the end of next week. And don't give me some garbage list of pointers that concludes that this simply can't be done or I'll remove anyone associated with it."

Several aides raced out of the room as the Secretary and other senior officials exited shaking their heads.

He then turned to Hastings. "I want Mark to be a part of the Summit Team for North Korea in two weeks."

Hastings opened his mouth as if he wished to debate the issue further, but instead he simply replied, "He'll be there, Mr. President."

"We may want to travel through Russia to get to the Summit, though," Davenport laughed, "because it may be impossible to get a visa after I do this."

Mark chuckled and then predicted, "That won't happen, sir, Russia needs foreign money. If they block entry to American citizens, they'll wither and die from the fallout. You watch, if you follow this course and Russia doesn't freeze entry on American visas, you'll know that you have them."

As they returned to the office together, Hastings turned to Mark. "You'll be sick that week and have to stay home."

"Yes sir." Mark responded without any sign of protest or even disappointment.

Hastings stood in his doorway watching him. He shook his head, confounded. "Come into my office. Tina, push my schedule back by ten."

Mark took a seat across from the General and humbly awaited the consequence of his actions. Hastings thought for a moment before speaking. "I don't understand you, Mark. In some ways, you're the perfect worker, always value-added. On the other hand, I'm amazed at how you can violate the trust that I've placed in you. I judged your outbursts in Davenport's presence to be an ego-driven need to be 'important', but then I just informed you that you will not be accompanying the President to the Summit in two weeks, in spite of his instructions, and you are serenely accepting of it. What is your motivation here?"

Mark, the newly-sober pursuer of good, was pained to hear how he had failed the General. He recognized his transgression. "Sir, first off, I owe you an apology for defying your orders. You took a great leap of faith in bringing me onboard and I feel terrible if I let you down."

As always, Mark felt a relief to have cleared his conscience. To stay clear, however, he knew that he needed to now make his actions match his words. "I didn't join your staff because I needed a job, I did it because I needed a purpose. For all of my adult life, well really my whole life, I've been consumed by the pursuit of selfish desires. This led me to ruin. Now, my life is devoted to service, it's what keeps me sober and gives me meaning, and I can't fake my way through it. I just feel like I have an obligation to speak up, and if that means that I am dismissed by you or the President, then I'll have to accept that."

Hastings's face was still disapproving, but he nodded his head. Mark wasn't sure, but he thought he perceived a recognition by the Military Officer of Mark's concept of a greater devotion to service.

"Well, at this point you're Davenport's darling. You've been judicious so far with your opinions and I'd advise you to keep it that way. Better prep for the Summit, there is a briefing on Friday involving N.S.C., State, and the CIA East Asia Office."

Mark's eyes widened. He nodded his head but knew that he had better be otherwise engaged during the time of that meeting. Besides, he had already received that briefing.

Mark left the General's office feeling uneasy about his exchange with Hastings. *Was I really 'just trying to help' or was I fawning my ego?* He realized that he needed to be more proactive about his sobriety if he were going to rely on it so resolutely for his daily strength. He decided that a visit to Charles Joeng in the E.E.O.B. was in order.

He went over to the building and made his way down a set of stairs to the key-coded door used by the Secret Service. He knocked on the door and explained to a female Agent that he was looking for Charles. He was invited in and found Charles performing inventory in the weapons depot known as the "Armory."

"Oh hey Mark, how are things?"

"Good Charles, I just wanted to check in about my program." He joined the Agent at a table that he was using and the two sat in silence while Charles filled out a form.

After a few seconds, Charles looked up in anticipation. "Uh, so what's up?"

Mark sighed. "I'm a little worried about my motivations here in the White House. I don't know if my intentions are pure, or if I'm..."

Charles cut him short. "Whoa whoa, you said that you wanted to discuss your program, so present this all in terms of your recovery, not your job. If you're spiritually fit, the rest tends to follow."

"Oh, sorry. Well, I feel like I'm consistent with attending meetings and reading materials on my own, but I'm still feeling a little shaky about where I'm at in the program and how I practice its principles here."

"Okay, meetings and reading are good, where are you on the Steps?

"Well I went through them fairly quickly in rehab and I guess I'm mostly done with them."

"You may go through the Steps a first time, but you're never truly 'done' with them. It's a good idea to periodically perform the first nine Steps and then ten through twelve are all about incorporating those first Steps into our daily existence- maintain your spiritual connection to your Higher Power, take inventory of your wrongs and promptly correct them, work with fellow alcoholics, and practice these principles in all of your affairs."

"Yeah, I think I'm doing those things. All except the work with others."

"Well, what does your sponsor say?"

Mark shifted a little. "I don't have one. Who in the White House has time to add more meetings?"

Charles laughed, "You'll have plenty of free time if you relapse and get kicked out of here. I can be your temporary sponsor if you like? We can meet in a breakroom and have coffee once a week."

"That'd be great, thanks for offering."

"Sure thing."

Mark felt relief at just the thought of having a more seasoned member of the program helping and guiding him. *Charles is right, if my program becomes compromised, then my whole world will fall apart in due time.*

Charles checked the clock. "Might as well start our work now, how is your communication with your Higher Power?"

Mark stared blankly. "Uh, I mean I pray."

"Uh huh, I bet it's pretty one-sided right?"

Mark shrugged and silently nodded.

"Communication with your Higher Power is about establishing a relationship through conscious contact, not just foxhole pleas for help. First thing I want you to work on is defining what your Higher Power is and what It means to you."

Mark smiled slightly, "Homework? Well, I guess I asked for it."

Charles chuckled. "It's not just mindless work, this is your opportunity to get a grasp on who God is and how the two of you relate. But keep in mind, your Higher Power existed before you embraced sobriety, so this is about deepening your *understanding* of who God already is, not just creating a conception of a God that is convenient for your needs. God is either everything or He is nothing."

Mark nodded, "Yeah, I like that idea. I started to do that, but I guess I should complete that now."

He sat back and looked around at the weaponry in the room. "What kind of sidearm do you carry, a Glock?" He knew a decent amount about guns--he grew up in the south after all--but he stepped lightly as he was exiting his comfort zone.

Charles looked at him amused. "A Sig Sauer."

"Can I take a look?"

After a pause, Charles grabbed one off of the rack and double-checked to be sure that it was empty. "Here, it's unloaded but always handle a firearm as if it were."

Mark felt the weight and looked down the sights. "It's heavier than the Glock."

Charles looked up from his paperwork a little surprised. "Yeah, it's unique to the Secret Service, we like it that way. Now hand it back before someone sees you with it."

"Not until you promise to take me shooting sometime." He smiled at the hollow demand.

"Okay, do you have your own firearm?"

Mark looked over the weapon case. "My dad keeps one in Virginia that I can borrow."

When Mark returned home that night, his new assignment was front on his mind. He pulled out a pad of paper and wrote "Higher Power" at the top. He stared at it for a bit, grasping for definition, but came up with only sobriety-related concepts. He racked his brain, *Charles said that I need to understand my Higher Power, not just create one to fit my comfort zone, so there obviously are historical resources that can provide description.* He exhaled and looked around the room, settling on his phone. *Maybe a verse would help.*

He opened the Verse of the Day, *It is for freedom that Christ has set us free. Stand firm, then, and do not let yourselves be burdened again by a yoke of slavery.* His brow furrowed as he thought, *Freedom from the slavery of alcohol, that definitely sounds like the work of my Higher Power.* He knew that Jesus preached and practiced the sound ethics reflected in the A.A. life, but what else was He? *Might as well check the internet again.*

He typed in "What was Jesus about?" and reviewed the postings. After reading several links, a common theme was presented. Jesus claimed to be the son of God, come to earth to teach us to act righteously, but also to bridge the natural chasm which exists between a perfect God and an imperfect/sinful humanity. He instructed us to seek God's will in our lives so that we would know how to act in specific situations by applying the greater ethical standards that He had established, and when we inevitably fall short of these standards, to ask forgiveness from those harmed, as well as from God, and continue on our path of progress.

It ended with the concept that His crucifixion was the sacrifice that united humans to God. Mark nodded his head as he read this, but couldn't comprehend the part about Jesus dying for humanity. *I already communicate with God, why would I need Him to send His son to die?* He shut down his phone shaking his head disapprovingly.

After weeks of meetings and other preparations, the Summit Team departed for Malaysia, the neutral site where the discussions were to take place. As was his nature, the North Korean dictator did not trust a visit to the United States and the American President was not willing to honor

Kim with a state visit on the Korean Peninsula unless and until an initial agreement had been reached.

Mark attempted to appear calm as he took his seat on Air Force One for the lengthy flight. After an hour of reading and then re-reading the Summit prep documents, he wandered to the aft through the traveling Press Corps to grab a cup of coffee. Sitting in the rear near the reporters was the Press Secretary, Omar Khalili, furiously barking orders to his staff.

"It's obvious that The Herald has an established narrative for the after-report on this Summit, and it is *not* positive. I think they're still pissed about the fact that I had promised a one-on-one with the President and he begged off at the last minute. I need you to go give their reporter some attention and try to talk her back down."

As the staffer ran off, Mark noticed Omar's empty coffee cup and replaced it with a full one. The Secretary absently thanked Mark, pushed his thick glasses up the bridge of his nose, and returned to his computer.

Mark hovered. "So, just having an interview canceled will change a news outlet's coverage?"

Omar looked up at him in disbelief. "Seriously? They'll sink this President because they don't like their seat assignment." He refocused on his computer. "They can be incredibly petty and self-absorbed, but Davenport is a conservative and he also excels at picking fights, so he especially has a constant target on him." He started typing and said distantly, "I keep telling him that you don't pick fights with those who buy their ink by the barrel, or whatever the digital equivalent is to that, regardless of whether the press is fair or not."

"Okay, but what did you mean by 'an established narrative'? We haven't even held the Summit yet."

The Secretary scoffed and looked at Mark out of the corner of his eye. "Reporters will often draft stories based on their preconceived impressions and will make predictions as to the outcome of events. Take the last election for instance- it was a midterm, which is traditionally bad for the incumbent President's Party, but the various news outlets ran constant stories about how there was going to be an historically poor showing for his endorsed candidates. Regardless of whether or not this prediction was accurate at the time, simply repeating ad nauseam the idea that it would come to pass naturally aided in a self-perpetuating result."

Mark nodded his head in tentative agreement, "Right, I mean the President's Party did take a drubbing last election."

"But see that's just it! The Party turned over the House, which was to be expected in a midterm, but they actually *gained* seats in the Senate. But what did you hear as the post-election analysis from the press? That the President took a beating, just as they had predicted, the facts be damned. They invest in their aspirational prediction and then are either too proud or too biased to admit that they were wrong."

Mark remembered the impression that he had formed from the news reports at the time that the President had suffered a significant setback from the election, but given that he was half in the bag during that period, he didn't dare venture an opinion on the matter.

Omar grumbled, "The last President was *their* guy, so when he had two disastrous midterms, there hadn't been any speculation that his unpopularity was going to lead to a loss in the election and so the results were portrayed as being unremarkable."

Mark felt for the guy. "Sorry Omar, let me know if I can be of help."

He exhaled and rubbed his face, "It's just disappointing, journalism is worlds away from what I thought it would be in the ethics-focused classrooms of college. I've always been center-right in my personal political leanings, but I was inspired by what I heard from a reporter who was a guest lecturer in one of my seminars. He conceded that his news organization was left-leaning, as most of them are, but he told us, 'I decided early in my career that I would never suppress or change a story if the only reason was concern over political implications, if you do that, you're no longer a journalist.' I wish that belief was universally-held."

Upon landing in the Pacific Rim country, Mark cut a wide berth around the Press Corps to head toward the Summit site. Almost all discussion points had been hammered out ahead of time, so most of the two-day meeting was ceremonial in nature. The President sat with the North Korean leader and talked tough on human rights, Asian security, and of course, nuclear non-proliferation. Kim focused on smiling and acting the part of the confident dictator.

During the proceedings, Mark took note of a woman who sat motionless about five feet behind Kim. He leaned into Hastings and asked, "Who is that woman just sitting there behind Kim?"

His boss whispered back, "That's Kim's sister, Kim Yo-jong. She attends all official events with him." He thought for a second and then added, "Involuntary obligatory participant."

The climax of the Summit involved the two men signing multiple agreements on humanitarian support and military de-escalation dependent upon North Korea's abandonment of its nuclear program. The two men raised a triumphant glass at the state dinner signifying the close of a successful event.

As the President prepared to board Air Force One on his return to the United States, he had a surprise prepared. He approached the gathered press with an announcement.

"Although I did not agree with the partisan calls for an investigation of my campaign perpetrated by the Opposition Party, I do thank the Special Counsel for his conclusion that there was no evidence of intentional collusion with foreign actors by me or my staff. What I did find troubling in his Report were the conclusions about foreign interference in American affairs. The Report focused primarily on political meddling, however, the greater negative effect on the United States by Russian nationals has been a pervasive and long-lasting scourge on our country."

"For far too long, Russian criminal activity in our country has run amuck. These people have engaged in crimes ranging from human trafficking and drug smuggling to theft and cybercrimes. Law Enforcement is overwhelmed in dealing with these criminals and America has suffered at their hands. Now, we see clearly the true extent of intentional Russian interference in our country- activity which is in the very least tolerated by its leadership, and in many cases, directly sponsored by it. In the past, I have called for the Kremlin to reign in the illegal actions of its

171

citizens, both state-sponsored and otherwise, and the reaction of Moscow has been one of denial and disinterest. Today that changes."

Davenport turned toward the group of twenty or so staffers gathered by the plane and motioned for Mark to come forward. Confused, he slowly approached the President who was holding a large black binder and an official pen.

"I am signing an Executive Order, effective today, which will freeze all future entry visas to Russian citizens. Additionally, the State Department has prepared a selection of 1,000 Russian nationals who will be immediately and permanently expelled from the country. If Russia fails to produce evidence of improper meddling in our political system as well as evidence of other crimes committed by its citizens on American soil, to the satisfaction of the American government, another group of Russian nationals will be expelled on a weekly basis until it does. At the conclusion of this production of evidence, Russia will then agree to punishments and future changes in its conduct and the actions of its citizens."

With that, the President signed the document and handed the pen to Mark. He whispered, "You keep this."

Mark didn't remember the return flight to Washington, as far as he could recall, he floated home on a cloud.

- 16 -

When Mark landed and checked his phone, his whole world had changed. He had about a dozen texts and voicemails exclaiming amazed congratulations from friends and colleagues. When the delegation reached the White House grounds, he headed to his workstation which appeared abnormally barren. With the Summit completed and the Special Counsel Report aftermath essentially handled, he realized that his schedule was practically empty for the next few days, at least by West Wing standards. Plenty of time for him to check in with all of his congratulatory "friends."

There were texts from people to which he replied with a simple, "Thanks, hope you're doing well." A message brimming with pride from his father, to which he would respond with a call, and a voicemail from Arjun acting like they were now best friends. Before he could text a reply to that message, his phone rang. *Speak of the devil.*

"Hi Arjun, thanks for the voicemail."

"Doc! What the hell, man??"

Mark cringed at hearing that name. "Yeah, that was quite an honor for sure."

"Dude, you have got to let me see that pen!"

Mark quickly realized that Arjun continued to view their relationship through the prism of a couple of frat brothers chatting over a keg. "Uh, yeah I've got it here. I'll be sure to show you some time."

"Well how about tonight, bro?"

Mark looked at his calendar and realized that it was a Friday. He also felt a pang of guilt that he hadn't been to a recovery meeting in over a week. "Oh, I don't know, I just got back and I've got some things to take care of."

"Screw that noise! You're coming out tonight and showing me that pen. I want to hear all about it!"

Mark swelled a bit and thought, *Couldn't hurt to hang out with a few friends.* "Okay sure. I've got a meeting with the President here in about two hours, but I should be able to come out tonight."

"Cool bud. Meet me at the Pulpit around 9:00. There are some peeps that you've got to meet and some ladies that would definitely like to meet you."

"I'll see you then."

Mark Rutherford's social calendar had just gotten interesting for the first time in years.

In the early afternoon, Mark accompanied the General to the scheduled meeting on the Summit. As was his m.o. as a successful businessman, Davenport had always wanted a post mortem on important events to get an immediate reaction on what went right and what went wrong. In reality, Mark assumed that the President had these meetings simply to know if he should be pleased or upset about the underlying event.

As Mark and his boss approached the Oval Office, he locked eyes with a man leaving the room, trailed by two bodyguards. Mark's blood chilled as he waited for his brain to produce an identification. He turned toward Hastings as the man walked past. "Isn't that Thomas Fleuric, the billionaire? What is he doing with the President?"

Hastings looked at him with a disapproving frown. "Don't ask stupid questions. Either you know the answer and shouldn't need to ask or you don't know and shouldn't know."

Feeling humbled, Mark returned to Earth from his orbit. Still, he couldn't shake the feeling of unease.

The various senior staffers took positions on the couches and chairs surrounding the President's desk as Mark and the other nobodies sat in the background. Congratulations and hearty handshakes were exchanged all around.

The President smiled and started to talk. "Before we begin, I want to make an announcement." With that, he cocked his head to the side and looked at Mark. "Why are you sitting back there?"

Mark's eyes grew as he looked about with confusion. Davenport continued, "Mark, you're being elevated to the position of Special Assistant Counsel. Come join us."

Mark was stunned and his mouth hung open. He looked over to Hastings who gave him a sly grin and motioned for him to take the seat next to him. Mark regained his wits. "Uh, thank you, sir. What an incredible honor this is." He quickly walked up and took the seat next to Hastings as if to thwart the offer being timely revoked. He smiled and looked around the room as the other attendees smiled and nodded at him, all except the Secretary of State.

The President slapped his hands together, "Good, well for now, you'll still be reporting to Stephen, but we'll figure out where you fit in later."

Mark looked at the General, "My pleasure, sir."

As soon as the meeting was over, Mark practically ran back to his station. His plan was to grab his belongings and get to a place outside of the White House where he could gloat without reservation. The first call was to his father, who was astounded.

"Wow, I've never heard of a promotion happening so quickly, this is wonderful news!"

"Thanks Dad. I can't believe how this worked out."

"Did you take a moment to thank your Higher Power?"

Mark, realizing that he hadn't, sheepishly replied, "No, but for sure I'll do that."

"Uh huh. Keep in mind that a mindset of gratitude, like all tenets of the program, is meant for our benefit, not God's. It keeps us centered, positive, and humble."

"Got it." Mark was already distracted.

"Okay, why don't you come to Alexandria for dinner tonight? We could go to the evening meeting in Old Town that you like and then eat and listen to live music at Murphy's."

"Uh, I've actually got plans tonight. Meeting up with an old college buddy who is a lobbyist in town."

There was silence on the line until his father finally broke it. "An old drinking buddy?"

"All my old buddies are drinking buddies, Dad."

The Senator laughed, "Well I know that feeling. Just be smart. *Remember that we deal with alcohol- cunning, baffling, powerful.*"

Mark smiled, "Yeah, I've read the Big Book too. I'll be careful."

Later that night, he arrived at the Bully Pulpit, one of the places to see and be seen on Capitol Hill. He checked himself out in the front glass and frowned disapprovingly as he realized that he needed to upgrade his wardrobe for his new position. Undaunted, he swung the door open and waded into the boisterous crowd.

"Doc!! My man, pots and pans!" The bar was loud, but Arjun was practically screaming at Mark from across the room. No doubt a combination of excessive drinking and the derivative importance of being affiliated with a Presidential Advisor.

"Hey Arjun," Mark said as he approached. He raised his hands in a prohibitive fashion even before his host could offer him a drink. "Just a cappuccino for me."

"Aw Doc, it's celebration time!"

Mark leaned in. "Call me Mark, remember? And no alcohol."

Arjun nodded. "No problem, Do... I mean, Mark." He ordered the coffee drink and turned back smiling wide. "Hey bud, I brought a few peeps you've got to meet. Some guys from the Hill, some d-bags from Brookings," he rolled his eyes as he said this, "and a couple of lady-admirers. Come on over."

Mark stood up straight, stuck his chest out a bit, and followed him.

"Ladies! This is the President's closest Advisor, Mark Rutherford."

The women shook Mark's hand and introduced themselves. After enthusiastic urging from Arjun, Mark employed his best false-modesty in describing to the two of them the events leading up to the scene on the tarmac in Malaysia. Both women began to edge each other out to get closer to him.

Arjun of course had to interrupt. "Okay, okay, you're the bomb, we get it Mark, but you'll have to excuse us a moment ladies."

The women wore confused looks as Arjun put his arm around Mark's shoulders and guided him away. "I went out with the one on the left for like a minute, but feel free to hook up with either one. Right now though, I've got a couple of guys that I'd like you to meet."

Mark looked back over his shoulder at the women with whom he would much rather be meeting and then back at Arjun. "Oh yeah, who?"

"My bosses. They're pretty impressed with you and I said that I'd introduce you."

Mark was kicking himself. *Of course Arjun planned this entire night for his own gain.* Arjun led him to a side stairwell and up to a cordoned-off area above the noisy bar where two men sat together.

"Mark, this is Davis Holmes and Julius Johnston. They're the owners and managers of our lobbying firm."

The men stood and reached out their hands as Mark did his best to smile. They exchanged pleasantries and then returned to their seats at a poorly-lit table. They each had straight brown liquors in front of them, probably a very smooth scotch like Mark would have once enjoyed.

Julius noted Mark's gaze at his drink. "Would you like one? I'll have the bar bring one up for you."

Mark's focus returned to him as he looked up at the finely-attired man. "No, thanks. I've got a cappuccino coming."

Davis joined in, "Good man, always on the clock when you work in the West Wing, right?" He winked, which combined with his cheap suit and short, round stature, gave him the appearance of a door-to-door salesman.

Mark nodded in response as he instinctively took a half step back. The room momentarily went silent until Julius spoke, "So Arjun tells us that you are the newest Advisor to President Davenport. Congratulations, we need all of the good people we can get to help that knucklehead."

Davis snorted. "Oh you snowflake, he's the best thing to happen to this economy since Reagan. Aren't you the one talking about renovating your kitchen now with all of your extra income?"

"The best economy since Clinton," Johnston replied in exaggerated fashion. "Well regardless, I'm sure that young Mr. Rutherford here is keeping the man in check." He waved a bejeweled hand at a chair, "Have a seat, Mark."

Mark found his footing as he joined the table. "The President is an impressive man and his instincts have made him a success in business and now politics. I just try to be a helpful part of what he's accomplishing."

Julius flashed his bright-white teeth. "That's a very diplomatic answer." He paused. "My colleague is correct, though, I am renovating my kitchen, and I just purchased a sailboat, and am looking at a beach house in Ocean City. The benefits that I reap from the hard work of Administration employees such as yourself."

"Oh yeah, you've got to see his boat, Mark!" Arjun was so loud that Mark almost jumped out of his chair. "You should take him sailing around Annapolis, J.J.!"

Julius looked up at him annoyed. "Arjun, why don't you go check on Mark's cappuccino."

Arjun, realizing his clumsiness, said sheepishly, "Oh, sure Julius. I'll be right back."

"Take your time."

As Arjun disappeared, Davis leaned in. "We just think it's unfair how miserly the government is with its pay scale. You're a young attorney, you've got debts and expenses I'm sure, it can be tough to get your head above water in a town like D.C."

Mark naturally thought of his daughter. He certainly wished he could afford to contribute toward her future.

Julius saw the contemplation in his eyes. "If there's any way that we can be of service in that sense, we would certainly like to help."

Mark had allowed his mind to wander, but he quickly snapped out of it when he realized that they were suggesting something highly illegal. These two men knew his resumé, knew about law school, maybe even knew that he was newly sober when they offered him a drink. Mark needed to extricate himself from this conversation and this place. "Uh, listen, it was nice meeting both of you." He stood and forcefully extended his hand. Both men stood reactively and shook it. "But I've got to get back to my friends downstairs."

Mark walked away from the table without looking back. The two men grinned at each other as they watched him leave.

Mark's evening was cut short by the obviously planned attempt to influence him. He realized what a mistake it was for him to be in a bar in the first place, let alone meeting with morally-bankrupt lobbyists. He explained to the group gathered at the bar that he was tired and needed to head home. As he was preparing to leave, the two ladies each stuffed their cards in his hand. One had a note scribbled on the back that made Mark blush.

As he rode the Metro back to his apartment, the impromptu meeting with the two lobbyists began to bother him. He picked up his cell and called his little buddy.

"Hello... this is César."

It was only 10:00 PM on a Friday, but Mark had obviously caught him fast asleep. "Hey César, it's Mark. I need you to research something and deliver to me a written memo, but don't retain anything electronic on it. Research the lobbyists Julius Johnston and Davis Holmes... and their clients."

He awoke Saturday morning and mulled over the idea of meditating and praying, two key components of his spiritual maintenance which had gone neglected in the last couple of weeks. After his second cup of coffee, he checked the time and decided instead to leave early to meet up with Charles for the drive out to Manassas, Virginia, for their planned outing to the gun range. He departed the Metro in Old Town and borrowed his father's .38 revolver, but what he really wanted was to try Charles's Sig Sauer semi-automatic pistol. At the range, he broached the subject.

"Mark, I could maybe let you fire off a few rounds, but I could lose my job for letting you handle my weapon."

"Aw come on, no one here knows who we are. And it's not like your bosses are going to know."

"Just keep it low profile when you're firing, okay?"

"Sure." Mark fired off six rounds and then placed the firearm on the bench aimed downrange.

Charles watched. "Nice grouping. You obviously have some experience at the range?"

"Yeah, I used to go shooting in college and such, pretty common for southern boys. Some of those guys were just goofing around, but I learned to calmly squeeze the trigger and place the bullets where I want them to go." He snickered, "But it's much easier without any booze in me." He reviewed Charles's gear. "So, you carry this pistol with you in your waist holster, correct? What else do you carry?"

"We're cleared to carry many different types of weapons."

"Well, I mean in particular when you're guarding the President."

"Oh, on POTUS detail? I'll have the Sig on my waist and then numerous high capacity ammo magazines. Some old timers carry a spare weapon, but, for the most part, we've phased out shoulder holsters and secondary firearms in favor of extra ammo instead."

"Gotcha. So how do you draw?"

Charles looked around to be sure that no one was watching. When he was confident that it was clear, he placed the gun in his waist holster, and in one quick motion, pulled it up to his line of sight and placed the remaining rounds into a tight group on the target.

Mark watched intently. "But you wear a suit when on duty, so how do you have quick access to the firearm if there is an emergency?"

"Well, if shots are being fired, it's just one fluid motion like you just saw, brushing back the coat jacket and firing.

But if it's just a perceived threat, then we push our jackets back out of the way and hover our hand back behind the grip, while moving to get in front of POTUS of course."

"Oh, makes sense." He reached out and balanced the Sig in his hand, "I like the feel of the semi-auto, I might have to get me one."

When Mark returned home in the afternoon, he checked in on the news coverage from the Russian Executive Order. At first, the reaction was fairly negative, along the lines of what Omar had been describing. Liberal pundits became reborn supply-siders lamenting the potential loss of jobs from the interruption of Russo-American commerce. Analysts tried to find a constitutional violation in the expulsion of foreign nationals, even though such power is vested solely in the Executive with almost complete discretion. One commentator ironically accused Davenport of being mentally unhinged while frantically yelling at the camera.

As the hours had passed, however, more reasoned voices appeared. A former Director of the FBI, and prominent member of the Opposition Party, praised the President for having the guts to remove a known criminal element. Policy Institutes issued press releases endorsing Davenport's tough stance on the corrupt Russian regime. Even Progressive groups timidly supported the rebuke of foreign interference. This was as close to a home run as the President could expect.

The response from Moscow was predictable. A handful of American diplomats, academics, and businesspeople were expelled and a threat of future retaliatory expulsions was issued should the United States follow through on its plans for continued removal of Russian citizens. However, a crucial mistake was committed by the Russian Ambassador while speaking to an American news network. The diplomat had harshly criticized the President for his actions and predicted a future replete with global instability, but he then took it a step further and suggested that Russia might freeze all entry visas from the United States.

Within the hour, the Embassy had walked back his comments on future visas and had recalled the Ambassador. Not many people connected it, but it was just as Mark had predicted: if foreign businesses felt that Russia was becoming unpredictable in its policies or a threat to American capital, those businesses would likely pull out on any planned investments and potentially cancel existing ones. A freeze on American entry into the country would certainly qualify as such. The Russians couched the recall of the Ambassador as a "protest of American policies," but the White House knew better. In reality, the Russian government had to make it clear to the international business community that it was distancing itself from the Ambassador's comments. The Russians had caved.

Within the first week, Russia began delivering to the United States Government evidence and people it claimed had been at the root of the election interference. The Department of Justice and Intelligence Community confirmed that the people who were handed over were suspected of involvement, although as expected, key government agents were not included. On the criminal front, the Kremlin had less power to hand over senior mobsters, after all these men were close allies of those in power, but scores of criminal syndicate members were delivered after days of negotiation. The criticism of Davenport's policy and the innuendo of his supposed Russian collusion all but disappeared.

- 17 -

At this point, Mark couldn't be any higher. He strutted around the West Wing like he owned it. He wouldn't lower himself to perform menial work anymore, and instead, philosophized with other senior members of the Administration in endless meetings. With so many victories under his belt, he decided to call and check in with Raleigh to bask in his due praise.

"What did you think of the move with Russia?"

"I'm floored that Davenport would do something like that to his Russian pals." Raleigh apparently had to try to stick it to Mark somehow.

"Ha ha, yes even in the absence of evidence to suggest collusion after a two-year investigation by top Law Enforcement officials, I'm sure that your base assumptions hold greater validity."

"Absence of evidence doesn't equate to innocence."

Mark shook his head. The modern political equivalent of insisting that man never landed on the moon; the experts must be wrong or are part of the conspiracy. Davenport had his veracity issues, but it was appalling to Mark to watch his detractors hypocritically practice comparable deceit in their criticisms.

"Yes, one of the great pillars of our system of justice, guilty until proven innocent. I think I remember that from my first-year criminal law classes."

Raleigh laughed. "Okay, okay. In all seriousness, that was a masterful move on the President's part."

Mark's ego reached new heights. "You mean on *my* part."

"No kidding, you recommended this course of action?"

"Every word of it. The President wasn't sold on it at first, but I convinced him otherwise. Why do you think that I have this fancy new title and same crappy workstation?"

"Nice Mark. You're going to get real popular real quick."

"Yeah, I was already ambushed by Arjun Chandra's bosses at Johnston & Holmes."

Raleigh groaned. "*Those* guys. They've been on the CIA's radar for quite some time. We're certain that they've been involved in helping their clients evade American and U.N. weapons sanctions for years now, but they're smart, they always use intermediaries for their dirty work. Arjun should be very careful working for those two."

"Yeah, I got that sense with them."

"Anyway, congrats on the one-two punch on North Korea and Russia. The next step is to watch for Russian money to enter the U.S. as a proxy. The PATRIOT Act has useful language for monitoring international transfers of over $10,000."

Mark grabbed a pen and made a note to review the PATRIOT Act and other international money transfer provisions.

Raleigh continued, "But the actions taken so far are good conceptual policies."

Mark was confused. "What do you mean 'conceptual' policies? Davenport already implemented them."

"And they will slowly erode away. Do you think that the American government has the will to halt all Russian entry into the country every time we want to remove their criminal element? They'll send new ones to replace the old and the game will continue."

"You don't think that this will have any lasting effect?"

"Uh," Raleigh hesitated in his critique, "don't get me wrong, Mark, it will be incredibly disruptive to Russian criminal activity. And I'm sure that the political interference will be far less obvious in the future."

Mark felt a little better. "Well then, that combined with our new Nuclear Anti-Proliferation Treaty with North Korea and things are looking up." Raleigh fell silent, it was deafening to Mark. "I mean, I know that you were skeptical, but it's got to do some good, right? Or do you think I'm wrong about that?"

Raleigh exhaled. "It's probably not going to last. The systems that Kim agreed to dismantle are old and antiquated and he likely had already replaced them with new ones. It was a last-minute addition, but I'm sure that the pre-Summit briefing mentioned his new focus on intercontinental missiles."

The official briefing that Mark was compelled to avoid. He rubbed his face as he absorbed the pessimistic analysis.

Raleigh continued, "I wrote that report. He's dumping enormous sums into perfecting a missile that can strike the west coast. What the CIA has additionally concluded, but won't admit to in writing, is that he wouldn't be developing weapons that could reach the continental United States and tip them with conventional warheads. They would have to be nuclear to have any meaningful effect, miniature nuclear technology to be precise."

Mark completed Raleigh's line of thinking. "Which would necessitate a continuing nuclear program."

"Right, the smaller payload allows the nuclear program to continue clandestinely underground. I believe that it's already dangerously close to viability."

Mark started grasping at solutions. "What about enhanced sanctions to prevent this?"

"It's pretty much too late for that, and past sanctions simply haven't motivated Kim, he could care less about the welfare of his people." He lowered his voice, "Frankly, I think we should eliminate the guy. If it were a viable option, I'd volunteer to lead a team to do it myself, but there's no way the brass here would even consider something like that. So we're stuck with the status quo as Kim draws dangerously close to having the capability to strike the United States."

Mark shook his head, "And the dance starts all over again, nothing ever changes."

"I know that it's not what you want to hear, but the Agency believes all this to be true, even if they don't expressly admit it. Sorry bud."

Mark hung up the phone and stared at the wall. He had assumed that they were making permanent, world-improving changes with these new initiatives, not just putting lipstick on the proverbial pig.

Within days, the reports returning from overseas were less positive than the initial ones. The Russians had adapted their strategy in much the fashion that Raleigh had predicted, except the individuals expelled by the United States were proving to be resourceful as well. Hundreds had joined together to sue the Federal Government for a violation of claimed Due Process rights and dozens more were seeking re-entry from other countries. In North Korea,

Kim set a date to test a ballistic missile thought to be capable of reaching the continental United States. The Russian policy at least bore some fruit, but the North Korean Summit proved to be mostly a charade.

Mark sank into a depression. His sobriety was based on selfless work and service to his fellow man; it was what provided him a purpose, and the seeming failures of the work in which he had placed so much stock dealt a devastating blow to his faith in the program. He hadn't been to a sobriety meeting or even considered his spiritual condition in weeks and these developments further suppressed his motivation to do so. The hope that he had found in the program seemed to be slowly draining away.

For the next few days, he went to work, returned home, and otherwise barely left his empty apartment. The dishes stacked in his kitchen sink and the overflowing trash cans began to fill the air with a stench. His place began to eerily resemble that of his last days in Richmond.

As he returned home from work that Friday, he had a text message from Arjun. "Hey man, I'm meeting up with those two ladies at the Grill. You should come!" He read the text repeatedly. He shrugged, *Why not?*

Mark entered the Capitol Grill to meet Arjun and his entourage with less spring in his step than he had the week prior. He approached the bar where they were standing and laid his hands on it.

"Yo Mark! You look like hell man!" The master of the obvious had spoken.

"Yeah, just a long week."

"Well, you came to the right place to fix that, my man! What can I get you, a decaf or something?" Arjun found this hilarious.

Mark shifted his gaze from Arjun down to the brown liquor in his hand. The look did not go unnoticed.

"Oh, you want a drink, drink?"

Mark stared. He thought about the months of work that he had put into his sobriety, the life-changing practices that he had adopted, and the relationships and wreckage that he had repaired. Then he thought about the significance of it all. He thought, *What good is this effort if it's all ultimately meaningless in the end?*

He then uttered the two words that topple many a recovering alcoholic, "Screw it."

Arjun flashed a devilish smile and handed him a scotch. Mark savored the harsh liquor as it slid down his throat. The commotion of the bar faded out as he waited for the alcohol to hit his brain. Even as he felt the warmth engulf him, the words of Big Book haunted him, *cunning, baffling, powerful.*

Instead of relief, he felt regret. The warnings that he had heard spoken repeatedly in the recovery rooms to describe the feeling of relapse rang in his head, "There's nothing worse than a belly full of booze and a mind full of A.A." His smile sank as he stared at the empty glass. Simple regret couldn't turn the clock back for him now to stop him from taking that first drink. His alcoholic mind could think of only one thing to cure his dismay- more alcohol.

With quiet desperation, Mark ordered a second and then a third. As his thoughts dulled, he turned his sights to the ladies who had been clamoring for his attention. He slid his arm around one and suggested that they take the party back to his place, by way of a liquor store. Arjun was told to stay behind to take care of the tab.

He awoke the next day around noon as his companion was dressing and heading for the door. She offered for him to join her for lunch, but he waved her off and promised to meet up with her again sometime soon.

After she left, Mark's apartment was oppressively empty again. He sat on the side of his bed for what felt to him like an eternity trying to contemplate where his life was at; a task made all the more difficult by a pounding headache. The shame washed over him, not just the shame of his plummet back into the world of drinking, but all of the shame that he had previously resolved through his work in the program. He knew that his renewed spirit and freedom from remorse was predicated on his continued sobriety and meaningful living. All of this felt lost to him. He knew of only one other way to deal with guilt, shame, and dismay. The drink.

He dragged himself to the corner store for a bottle and drank steadily that day until he passed out. When he came-to in the middle of the night, he started up again until after sunrise. He repeated this despair-driven process all day Sunday as well. The messages on his phone began to accumulate as a familiar feeling of impending doom descended on him. Monday morning was the culmination of the dread.

As he woke, his whole body ached and trembled from the excessive amount of alcohol in his system. He vomited until only blood and bile were produced and tried to drink fluids and eat plain foods to get himself to a passable state. After a shower, he held a razor in his shaking hand and stared at the reflection of his weekend beard. He finally admitted the danger in attempting a shave, and instead, he dressed and reached his office an hour late.

Hastings was already in a meeting, so Mark quietly shuffled to his desk and took a seat. He exhaled as he felt like maybe he could escape detection for the day. Tina approached to hand him a stack of papers.

"Here are the weekend headlines, here is the revised schedule... whew! You smell like you got into it over the weekend Mark!"

His stomach knotted as he looked at her. "Yeah, had a couple of buddies in town. We really tied one on." Lying was a sickening necessity.

"Oh yeah, you've got to watch out for those 'old friends'." She used air-quotes as she said the last part. "They come out of the woodwork when you get a job in the White House."

She smiled and returned to her desk. Mark realized that she had no clue of his sobriety history and he began to breathe easier.

"But you might want to hit the bathroom and use some of the mouthwash and such in there."

Mark hurried to the bathroom and drenched himself in air freshener and mouthwash. He returned to his workstation and trembled in pain. He thought, *How am I going to get through an entire day like this?* He retreated to his familiar concept of simply hiding and buried his head behind his monitor.

He skipped all of his morning meetings with the excuse of project deadlines, and at lunch time, he looked at the clock and felt like he had been in the office for a week already. There was no way he was going to make it through the remainder of the day in his condition and he decided that he needed some hair of the dog.

He rushed out of the building trying to avoid any contact. One fellow staffer saw him and tried to call him over at the gate, but Mark just waved and pointed at his watch as he hurried toward the street. Once there, he jumped on the Metro heading far from the Federal buildings downtown to find a nondescript chain restaurant where no one would recognize him.

He sat at the bar and scanned the restaurant. There were plenty of people in suits, but no one who resembled a Washington insider. He ordered an I.P.A. and breathed deeply as he anticipated the relief. As he drank the beer, it went down to his queasy stomach like broken glass. After draining the pint, his shaking subsided and the pain in his chest disappeared. He felt calm and ready to complete his workday. Then the bartender asked if he wanted another. "Sure," was Mark's response.

He shook his head to himself after ordering the second beer and wondered how he could even consider sitting at a bar and drinking in the middle of a workday. He had needed one beer to calm his jitters, but now he was instinctively adding more alcohol on top of the residual already in his system.

"Oh, would you like to add a shot of whiskey for two dollars more?"

"Okay." Mark was stunned. His brain had instantly measured the "value" of adding a shot of booze to his system and ordered it without considering the consequences. Despite months of recovery work, his alcoholic mind was still present and now had regained control of his will.

Mark finished the drinks and carefully made his way to the Metro. His head was buzzing as the new and old alcohol mixed and took over. He was about to board his train back to work and was strategizing how to avoid people the rest of the day, when he finally concluded that it would be smart to just go home and sleep this off. *Best to just play it safe*, he rationalized.

He called Tina and asked her to let Hastings know that he was going to be off site at meetings for the remainder of the day. He mustered as much authority and clarity in his voice as he could manage in hopes that she wouldn't speculate to the General that Mark was absent due to a hangover. He didn't exactly work for the General anymore, but the outcome of a confrontation over a relapse would be embarrassing in the least and career-ending at worst. *Besides*, Mark assured himself, *this isn't really a relapse, just a slip*.

Mark felt giddy as he exited the Metro station at his home stop and undid his tie. *I can get home, order some food, lay on the couch all afternoon, and wake in the morning refreshed!* Then he passed the corner liquor store on the walk to his apartment. He stood in the doorway looking at the bottles. His mind enticed him, *Why not enjoy your afternoon? You've already been drinking today anyway*. Mark's body relented and he purchased a fifth to take back to his apartment.

195

At first, he sipped on the liquor and tried to temper it with swigs of water in between. After an hour or two, the water glass was empty. By midnight, Mark was just drinking straight from the bottle; less to clean up, made sense to him.

His body woke him up at 5:00 AM to a splitting headache and seizing tremors. He vomited periodically and then shuffled back to his couch to shake and seize. By 7:00 AM, he regained his bearings and thought about next steps. *How could I let this happen again?* kept running through his brain. He couldn't miss a second day of meetings; Hastings would send a search party after him at that point. He would have to grit his teeth and suffer through the excruciating day.

He walked into his office avoiding all eye contact and discussion and sat behind his desk, distraught over his predicament. Even if no one smelled the stench of booze on him, questioned his now four-day facial growth, or commented on his disheveled clothing, he would have to painfully sit through meetings unable to say anything. He was sure that there was no way that he would get away with it.

Tina looked at Mark with concern and simply kept her distance. Her lack of eye contact was not lost on him. Hastings walked out of his office and greeted Mark. "You boycotting the Gillette Corporation or is that some new look for you?" He gestured to his own non-existent beard while saying this.

Mark looked up from his hunched posture and smiled, "Yeah… just trying something… new."

The General just looked at him. He must have witnessed many a hungover soldier attempt to assume his post in the morning. "Come into my office."

Mark took a seat as Hastings closed the door. He sat behind his desk and stared into Mark's bloodshot eyes. Mark assumed the role of the workplace drunk- he had been hiding like a child who had broken his mother's favorite lamp and now he cowered in anticipation of the punishment.

"You don't work for me anymore, so I'm not going to fire you, but as the head of the President's staff, I can't let this go on."

Mark nodded silently and tried to think of a way out.

"I'm assuming that you missed work yesterday because you were drinking again and you're obviously unfit for work today. If Davenport smelled you..." He just inhaled loudly and let that sink in. "You will leave here immediately and you won't return until you're clean. Do you understand?"

Mark nodded in relief.

"Get out of here and don't ever return like this again."

Mark left almost all of his belongings on his desk and practically ran out of the building. The shame was stifling even as his mind celebrated and plotted how to spend the rest of the day in a booze-filled haze. He wanted to collapse but kept it together on his commute home.

He spent the rest of the day fighting the urge to use alcohol to relieve the pain. He laid on his couch and convulsed in between trips to the bathroom to dry-heave. At 5:00 PM, his mind convinced him that he had performed his penance and learned his lesson and that it was a respectable time to drink again. *But just beer this time so that I can function in the morning*, he told himself.

By 10:00 PM, he had finished most of a six-pack and was trying to plan his way forward. A week earlier, he had been a trusted Advisor to the President of the United States and now he was just a useless drunk again. He dragged himself to bed and held a pillow tightly over his face, resigned to the idea that he had lost all hope.

Wednesday morning, he returned to his station early and clean-shaven just to show that he was capable of performing his duties. He was shaky and slow in his meetings, but passed as presentable. He had resumed the lifestyle of the functioning alcoholic.

Over the remainder of the week, his coworkers reacted to his changed behavior. Whereas before he had been reserved but willing to thoughtfully engage in discussion, now he was downright silent but petulant in his infrequent debates with others. The President's faith in him diminished by the meeting.

Over the next several weeks, he flailed about in his daily life. Charles texted him numerous times about meeting, but Mark always had an excuse regarding some urgent issue. He would frequent the bars promptly at 5:00 PM dropping his name and title to impress the ladies. Arjun and a pocket flask were his constant companions. He would pick up random women and dispose of them in the morning, hoping in vain for some form of personal validation from the experience. His smell of liquor and taste of decay accompanied him at all hours.

On one night out with Arjun, Mark was feeling overwhelming self-pity, and as is common for alcoholics, he incorrectly judged his enabler to be a friend and not a problem. Through slurred speech, he confided in Arjun about his daughter.

With the North Korean regime resuming military testing and build up, Davenport wanted an immediate follow-up Summit to impress upon the dictator there that he meant business. Whatever the "miscommunication" was from the first meeting, he hoped that it would be clarified and resolved finally in the second. The date was set for a little over two months out.

Given his diminished status, Mark had come to the realization that he was on the verge of being excluded from the Team for this Summit and decided that he had better come up with some ideas for the President if he were to get back in his good graces. He called Raleigh to set up a meeting at the CIA.

When they sat down in the familiar conference room at Langley, Raleigh had briefing books with him. He placed some materials in front of Mark and lingered on his face. "You look different Mark, they working you long hours or something?"

"Yeah, they're task-masters for sure." Wanting to move the discussion along Mark said, "Now, I'm trying to get a handle on how to advise the President on this new round of talks."

"Well, if you ask the folks here, they'll tell you to move for more sanctions in the U.N. or perhaps try to beg China to cut off aid. Not much exciting in these papers."

Mark threw his briefing book aside. "Great, so just tell the President that he should do what every Administration before has done and hope that the results are somehow different?"

Raleigh was taken aback by his anger, but nodded agreement. "Yes, that's in essence what you'll get from the leadership."

Mark was exhausted from the resumption of his dual-life and lacked the patience for more non-answers from Agencies and Departments. "So why am I here then? What is the point of all of this? We're not actually achieving anything."

"Welcome to my world. I receive information about some belligerent new program that Kim is developing, I write it up in briefing format, it is completely ignored, and the conclusions and recommendations stay the same. All the while, Kim is coming imminently close to achieving the capability to attack us where we live."

Mark attempted to moderate what he was hearing. "You keep mentioning a potential attack on the U.S. and tying it to a nuclear weapon, but he wouldn't gain anything tangible from attacking us, so wouldn't he just use his status as the head of a nuclear state as leverage?"

"Well, that would be bad enough, but..." Raleigh exhaled. "Look, I'm not supposed to divulge this information because it's considered 'unverified', but we have a... source who is well-placed inside of the North Korean regime. This person has recently revealed that not only is Kim on the verge of producing a viable nuclear weapon, but his intent isn't to use it in a play for relevance, but as a show of strength. And he intends to use it against the United States."

Mark's eyes bulged. "Why haven't we been told about this??"

Raleigh lifted his hands in caution. "It's single-source intel and therefore deemed insufficient by the leadership here. And I have to admit that I am in the minority in trusting the information from this source. I can't divulge the exact station of this person, but let's just say that it is so high up, that I think we have to err on the side of believing it."

Mark rubbed his face. He knew that Davenport, the political outsider, was never going to receive an unfiltered intelligence briefing like the ones Raleigh had been giving him. He dropped his head and thought about when he could have his next drink.

Raleigh watched his posture in silence and finally shrugged, "Wish I had better news, Mark, but things aren't getting better, they're getting worse. And nothing changes unless you change it."

It was Thursday, so Mark knew that there would be a sizable crowd at the Pulpit. Arjun would provide the drinks as usual, he assumed. It wasn't like Arjun was coming out of pocket, he would use his company credit card and meticulously collect his receipts; he never missed an opportunity to expense a cost. They met at the bar and Mark downed a scotch with one gulp.

Arjun raised his hands. "Whoa, easy man. Remember you almost passed out at the bar last week, don't want you to get in trouble."

Mark had little concern for his well-being at this point, but survival in the jungles of Washington was still a priority. He nodded his head but still ordered another. "Make this one a double."

He was halfway through that drink when Arjun leaned in. "Hey, my bosses wanted to meet with you again."

He hung on the bar and shook his head, "Yeah, well I don't want to meet with them."

"I'm sure that you appreciate the booze and the ladies that I've been providing you, Mark. It would be rude not to sit down with them."

Mark understood. He straightened himself up as Arjun led the way upstairs.

"Mark, good to see you again. I assume Arjun has been taking care of you?" It was Davis. Or Julius. Mark couldn't really tell through the alcohol haze. The white guy, so, Davis.

"Yeah, we're having a nice time. Just out on the town to let off a little steam. Got to do that every once in a while."

Julius chimed in, "You've been letting off quite a bit of steam the past few weeks."

Mark's stomach clenched. *Of course these two have been keeping tabs on me.*

Davis read his mind. "It's okay, Mark. We're friends! And we're very discreet." The two smiled as he continued. "Can I get you another drink?"

Mark relaxed at the idea of more escape. "Sure, I'll take another."

Arjun was sent to fetch the drink so that the three could talk. Julius leaned in. "Mark, allow me to commiserate with you. Arjun has been telling us about your frustrations at being thwarted in your work. It's a common problem in this town."

Mark let his mind wander. *Yeah, this swamp is the problem, not me.*

Julius resumed, "You can't change this town, no one can. That's why you should focus on accomplishing things for you. For instance, taking care of your loved ones."

Mark froze. Arjun had told them about Bella.

Davis now leaned in. "There's no judgment here. You just need to consider where you'll be after this President is gone. With your less than stellar past and current," he shot a glance at the cocktail in Mark's hand, "issues, I think that you would find it somewhat difficult to secure gainful employment in the future. However, we understand your *present* value, and if we were to come to an understanding now, you could come lobby for our firm later on, a wealthy man with a generous expense account."

A fresh drink was handed to Mark as he stared at it. He thought, *How did I come to this? Why am I listening to these two?* But alcoholics don't make the decisions, they have decisions made for them. He took a swig and leaned back in his chair. The two lobbyists took this as their cue.

Julius went first. "Mark, we make money when our clients make money and they make money when the country is purchasing weapons. If there is a lasting peace, then the country doesn't need new weapons systems, and nobody makes money." He said this as if it would be a national tragedy.

Davis went next. "But if the next Summit were to prove fruitless, well, it would only be prudent for America to start planning for the next conventional war." He was quick to add, "In Asia hopefully, not here of course."

Mark thought about the dog and pony show that the last Summit proved to be and realized how easily the next one could wind up the same way. *Afterall, what's the difference?* "I'm already pessimistic about the sincerity of the North Korean leader," he said.

Both men smiled. Julius said, "If it does turn out that way, then it would be beneficial to our clients. At that point, I'm sure that we would be able to help with your family expenses, at least until you're free to join our firm."

Mark had heard enough for one night. He swallowed his drink and stumbled out of the bar. He made his way to the Metro and held up a pillar while waiting for his train. His anger rose in him, *The program work was a lie, there's no great "purpose" to be found there. If I can't find any meaning in service then I'll just look out for me... and for Bella. This is how I make it up to her, this will make things right. All I have to do is keep my job through the next Summit and then I can be left alone to drink, and be paid handsomely for it.* He feebly tried to convince himself that money would be an adequate substitute, but he couldn't shake the realization that he was treating Bella in the way that he had hated his father for treating him.

As Mark staggered out with barely a word, Davis looked at Julius. "Looks like we have a golden opportunity with this one."

"Yes, but we'll have to be sure that he stays quiet. A lush like that starts blabbing around town and we'll be wearing prison stripes for the rest of our lives."

"So he does what we want and then we ensure that he disappears without a trace. Happens with drunks all of the time."

- 18 -

Monday morning, Mark lined up to enter the East Gate as usual. He placed all of his belongings into trays and walked through the metal detector to an unfamiliar "beep." The Secret Service Officer asked him if he had anything that would set off the machine. He lazily checked his clothes and froze when he hit something hard in his coat pocket. In his morning haze, he had slipped his flask into his jacket. Sensing his shift in demeanor, the Officer asked him what he had in his pocket.

"Nothing I just forgot..." he said, as his eyes darted around.

"Sir, I'll need you to step aside please for a search."

The Officer began to speak into his shoulder mic when Mark saw Charles walking past him. "Charles!" The Agent stopped and looked over at him. Mark said, "I forgot to congratulate you on your certification."

Charles walked over and Mark turned completely toward him to obscure the Officer's view. Mark palmed the flask and slipped it to him in his handshake. "Well done, buddy." Charles was already confused by Mark's congratulatory words, but the object he had in his hand stunned him. Charles met Mark's eyes and could see the desperation. Mark mouthed the word, "Please."

"Oh thanks, Mark," he said as he moved the flask to his front pocket.

"I meant to, uh, tell you before..." Mark said, trailing off.

Charles looked at him full of pity. "Yeah. Thanks." He turned and walked through the Law Enforcement entrance to the White House.

Mark's relief quickly turned to shame.

He went home that night and ordered Chinese, but he doubted that he'd eat much. He sat in the dark and just stared at his tumbler of scotch. He couldn't stop drinking, it was his body's natural state, and at that point, he couldn't harness a reason to stop.

The doorbell rang and woke him from his trance. He picked up his wallet to pay for the meal that he didn't want and headed for the door. As he opened it, his father stood there.

"Hi Mark," he said with a slight smile and gentle tone.

Mark had imagined his father eventually confronting him about his return to drinking. He pictured yelling, disappointment, perhaps even threats of cutting him off, but he never imagined a scenario where he would be smiling.

Mark was at a loss. "Hi… Dad."

"Is it okay for me to come in?"

Mark waved him in and sat on the couch. He knew that his father was there because he was drinking again, but he still looked over at the table that held his scotch and wished he could hide it somehow.

"How are you, Mark?"

Mark's ego jumped to defense. "I'm fine," he said dismissively.

His father looked around the disheveled apartment. "Oh, I hadn't heard from you in a while and thought I'd just check in."

Now it was his anger's turn. "Figured you'd come by to tell me what to do? Play daddy again?"

His father shook his head and said, "No, just be here for you."

Mark exhaled and could taste the liquor on his breath. His temper subsided as his spiritual instincts directed him to pray for clear focus. As he completed his simple prayer, he came to the realization that even in his relapse, God was still there, hand extended. Mark asked for all of his defenses to be lowered. "I've been better." He looked down in shame. "I started drinking again."

"Yeah, I'm not an idiot."

Mark looked up at his father who was grinning. Mark grinned as well. "I thought you'd be upset with me, or judgmental, or something."

"I'm upset *for* you. I know your heart and where you want to be in life and this isn't it. I'm just here as a fellow alcoholic offering to help in any way that I can."

Mark couldn't believe his father's compassion. Regardless of the man's personal feelings--which would naturally be disappointment and anger at Mark's failure in the face of the opportunity given to him--his father was only there out of service to his fellow alcoholic, and his son.

Mark eased a bit. "Nothing I'm doing matters. I'm an Advisor to the President of the United States and all of the work, this 'service' that I thought was so important, never actually accomplishes anything enduring. If I can't make a difference serving in the White House, then where could I possibly find purpose? I just don't see any ultimate meaning in any of the recovery work."

His father shook his head. "Do you know why we work with fellow alcoholics in this program?"

Mark began to recite the language of the Twelfth Step. "To carry the message to other..."

"It's to stay sober. I've worked with many alcoholics over the years and do you know what my success rate is? One hundred percent."

Mark looked at him skeptically but held his tongue.

"I have stayed one hundred percent sober throughout that entire time. I can't control the actions of other people, I can't force people to get sober or stay sober, but the work that I do, that service, keeps *me* sober and provides an opportunity for others to achieve sobriety as well. It is up to them and their Higher Power whether or not they take that opportunity. That is how I stay sober, *One day at a time*."

Mark repeated the recovery slogan, *One day at a time* in his mind. "I always thought that those sayings were so stupid. I don't want to be sober for a day, I want to be sober for the rest of my life."

"We have those sayings for a reason. If you maintain your spiritual condition, through *daily* work, you have the promise of sobriety for that day, and you have the same promise for the next day, and the next. You don't get overwhelmed by the enormity of a lifetime and forsake the present, which is obviously what you did."

Mark understood his point but still felt lost. "I just don't understand, to what end?"

"In terms of the program, that *is* the end. The Big Book describes the *road* of happy destiny, not a destination. Read

209

page sixty-three, it discusses our new purpose- *What we can contribute to life*. It's not a list of tangible accomplishments, but of a way of living."

Mark appreciated the point, but couldn't shake his residual emptiness. He exhaled and shook his head.

His father watched his unease. "Look, if you're grappling with existential questions involving your place in the universe, the program work isn't an end unto itself, it's just the beginning. Don't forget your spiritual connection, that's where you'll find the deeper answers. The purpose is provided by you and God... and only if you're sober."

Mark sank back into the sofa. In the very least, he knew that drinking would never provide any greater purpose to his life, to the contrary, it would in fact prevent any hope of finding it. He may not understand where his destiny lay, but it was obvious that it wasn't at the bottom of a bottle. He exhaled as he prayed for strength and walked to the sink to pour out the remainder of his scotch. His father gave him a hug, then Mark thanked him for coming and walked him to the door.

As his father left, he turned and said, "Next time that you're feeling overwhelmed, reach out to somebody. We're all in this together."

- 19 -

The detox from alcohol that night was painful but manageable, especially since Mark felt confident that this would be the last one of his life. He laid in bed shaking and after several hours, he checked his phone in frustration. Waiting for him was the latest Daily Verse. It read, *Be still and know that I am God.* He repeated the verse as his body eased; he knew that his life was in his Higher Power's able hands. He whispered, *"His will be done."* When he awoke, he felt his body purge the last of the alcohol from his system as his mind cleared. He was energized with the renewal of the hope of the program.

That week, he returned to his schedule of early arrival and quiet, dutiful work. His presence in meetings was thoughtful and cooperative. His appreciative colleagues took note.

Once he was successfully on top of his day-to-day work, he prepared himself to head over to see Charles about reestablishing his recovery program. As he arrived, he quickly checked the Daily Verse, *First, Love the Lord your God with all your heart and with all your soul and with all your mind and with all your strength. The second is this: Love your neighbor as yourself. There is no commandment greater than these.* He focused on the line, "Love your neighbor as yourself"; surely, part of his recovery involved forgiving himself and learning to love who he was. After all, sex and alcohol had provided him no self-worth.

Mark was allowed entry to the Secret Service H.Q. by an Officer and he found his sponsor in the Armory. Mark knocked on the open door, "Hey, can I come in?"

Charles smiled, "Sure, I've always got time for you. Looking to get your flask back?"

Mark turned red with embarrassment. "Yeah, sorry about that. And no, I don't want it back."

"Good, because I tossed it. What's up?"

"I just wanted to apologize for putting you in that situation and to thank you for helping me. And I was hoping that you'd continue to work with me."

"Happens to the best of us, bud. I'm proud of you for rebounding."

"Thanks. I got overwhelmed by my role here and lost focus on my sobriety. I just didn't feel like I was making a difference anymore."

"You're making a difference in *your* life, and in so doing, you have the opportunity to make a difference in the lives of others. But only if you maintain your sobriety."

Mark nodded. He looked around at the arms that Charles was cataloging. "You're doing this again?"

"It's a way for me to be a servant. The Secret Service provides an essential law enforcement function, which requires constant administrative oversight. It's not the glamorous side of our work, so people aren't leaping at the chance to do it, but it has to be done."

Mark looked over the ammunition lining the case. "Why are some of these magazines bright blue on the shaft?"

"Oh, those are blanks. After Columbine, every Federal Law Enforcement Agency was required to have blanks and sim rounds for active shooter training. It creates in each

Agent what's called 'stress inoculation' so that we learn to cope with and overcome the pressure of countering a live threat before we have to face one in real time."

Mark nodded and turned his attention to a plastic box on the ground with a skull and crossbones painted roughly on it. "What in the world is this?" he asked chuckling.

Charles looked and smiled. "That is what we called in the Marines the 'Last Resort'. It's a container with frag grenades, smoke grenades, flash bangs; munitions that explode, stun, obscure, etc. If all hell broke loose in the field, you would just start tossing whatever was in the box. Same principle here."

"I hope it never comes to that."

"Yeah, you should," he said as he returned to his work.

Mark furrowed his brow. "You have to inventory what's in there?"

"No, that is *definitely* outside of regulations." Charles looked back over at Mark. "In fact, it doesn't exist."

Mark nodded his understanding. He left the E.E.O.B. and returned to his office to review for the "Summit Plan" meeting which was to take place the next morning, the gathering of all interested parties in the President's foreign policy council for the purpose of determining what the goals and preferred outcome would be for the upcoming Summit. Mark had been reading the background materials for weeks and stared at the binder that he had kept from Raleigh's last informal briefing. The milk toast recommendations became less meaningful the more that he read them. He began to be resigned to the fact that the theme of this Summit would be to "aim low."

His attention was redirected when Hastings emerged from his office with a stack of papers. "Tina, I need..." The General stopped as soon as he realized that his assistant was out.

Mark stood and said, "Is there anything I can help with?"

His former boss looked him over cautiously and shook his head. "No, I'm on a conference call but I need to get these in front of POTUS ASAP. Can you just alert me when Tina returns?"

Mark nodded, "Sure, but I'm happy to take them for you."

The General thought for a second and then heard something on his speaker that gave him a start. "Um, fine thank you," he said as he handed over the papers, turned, and began replying loudly to the members of the call.

Mark took the short walk down the hall to the Oval Office and was in the process of handing the documents to one of the secretaries outside when the door opened.

"Mark, what've you got there?" the President asked as he handed a folder to the secretary.

Mark bolted to attention. "Sir, just some documents that General Hastings asked me to bring to you."

Davenport motioned for the secretary to bring them into the Oval. "Come on in Mark, I'll sign them while you're here."

Mark entered behind the pair and stood off to the side of the imposing "Resolute Desk," pretending to admire the various national treasures which adorned the office.

As the President reviewed and signed the paperwork, he asked, "So what are your thoughts on the upcoming Summit?"

The question was posed as if he were making small talk about the weather. Mark's eyes bulged as he panicked over what to say, with his instincts telling him to keep things light and positive. He slowed his brain and considered his principles, *Rigorous honesty*. "Given the current limited goals of this meeting, it doesn't appear to me that there's a reason to have it, sir."

Davenport stopped mid-signature and looked up at him. The secretary excused herself, clearly recognizing that it would be best to remove herself and avoid being caught in potential crossfire. The President reclined in his chair and said calmly, "Okay, what makes you say that?"

Mark steeled his nerve as his brain grew alarmed at the secretary's hasty retreat. "I believe that American foreign policy is geared toward a conventional 'carrot and stick' approach, which has been successful in dealing with regimes that respond logically to such tactics. However, I don't believe that the North Korean leader is a rational actor, and therefore traditional diplomatic maneuvering has and will fail with Kim."

The President nodded his head, "Yeah, the guy acts like a mongoloid."

Mark wasn't sure what to say to this assessment. "Uh, right, so the U.S. would need to be unconventional in its approach."

"Okay, so what are you proposing?"

Mark recalled his discussions with Raleigh about the need for a radical change, but lost his nerve. "Perhaps extreme pressure from the world community? But focused on China as the key to North Korean cooperation."

Davenport scoffed. "China has proven to be an unreliable partner in countering North Korea, and our 'allies' have shown no interest in joining us in applying pressure on China to take necessary actions. We'd be on our own."

"Understood, but this strategy would require building bridges that have been… damaged in recent years."

The President's eyes narrowed. "You mean, go kiss the rings of foreign leaders to get them to act in a way that they claim to already support?"

"No sir, not to beg for help, but to endear yourself to their peoples before then inducing their leaders to act. Like how the *Pravda* newspaper in the Soviet Union used to advocate for a change in policy. Obviously, the editors of the paper couldn't come out and openly criticize the regime, so they would devote the first three paragraphs to praising a particular policy and then start the fourth with a subtle, 'however' followed by a suggested change."

The President rolled his eyes and looked away.

Mark continued hesitantly. "And I think that such a posture would go a long way domestically as well."

Davenport's attention returned to him. "What exactly are you saying?"

"Sir, to achieve meaningful changes abroad, we must be united at home. I think that some of your statements cause… *division* in our country and that conversely, you could use your pulpit to be a unifying force."

Mark internally cringed awaiting the President's response.

"I call it like I see it, it's what garnered me the support to be President in the first place. If some pantywaists can't handle that, then I don't need them."

"Well, frankly sir, *we* need them, as a *nation*. Major change like this doesn't happen without broad support, and broad support comes from a unified populace."

Davenport threw his arms up. "Why are you here then? If you have such strong disagreement with how I run things."

"I support your policies, sir, just not always your methods."

Davenport dismissively checked the antique clock by the Rose Garden window. "Well regardless, what you've suggested is not exactly an appropriate proposal for a Summit Plan meeting, now is it?"

Mark looked down, realizing that it wasn't. His brain kept repeating, *Nothing changes unless we change it*. He hesitantly opened his mouth to speak when the President beat him to it. "If you think of anything more pertinent, I'll be willing to hear it tomorrow."

"Yes sir. Thank you."

The next morning, Mark awoke with the Summit Plan meeting dominating his mind. He had tossed and turned all night contemplating his options for proposals and began to be dismayed. He admitted to himself that even if the U.S. were to rally its self-interested allies to apply pressure to China, which was highly unlikely, then China would just pick them off one by one by offering plum trade deals. Raleigh and his words resonated in his mind.

He made his way into the office and slumped down in his chair. After several minutes of thought, he picked up the phone and called Raleigh.

"Hey Mark," he chuckled, "wasn't sure you'd want to hear anything more from me. Most politicos get their fill after *one* meeting and return to seeking out the 'safe' opinions."

"Raleigh, I just need to be certain, you stand by your earlier assessment about our only valid options with North Korea, correct?"

Raleigh paused in appreciation of the significance of the question. "Yes, and I would say that it is the true assessment of the American Intelligence Community, not just mine. They're just afraid to go on the record because the natural follow-on conclusions would be so controversial."

There was silence on the line until Mark said, "Okay, got it," and abruptly hung up the phone. Raleigh just stared at the receiver.

As the time for the Summit Plan meeting approached, Mark walked into the briefing room and took a seat in the back so that he could maintain a full view of the proceedings. The President entered and all participants took their seats to begin the meeting. The Secretary of State was first to speak.

"Mr. President, I was as dismayed as you at the announcement of North Korea's plans to test an intercontinental missile so soon after our last Summit. I have aggressively warned the regime about your extreme displeasure at this development and I have good news- the North Koreans have agreed to postpone any such tests for an additional year."

Mark thought, *How convenient, until after the President's reelection campaign.*

The Secretary portrayed some false modesty at the applause from the room and then added, "In exchange for a reduction in sanctions in the meantime of course."

Davenport just listened. He seemed accustomed to disappointment at this point. He finally spoke, "You really suggest that I reduce my own sanctions to achieve a delay in the implementation of a technology that could only be used for the purpose of attacking the continental United States?"

Mark broke the two-person dialogue. "With a nuclear warhead don't forget."

The Secretary exhaled; she had obviously assumed that Mark was marginalized given his position in the background. "You don't know that for a fact."

Mark scoffed, "Are you seriously suggesting that Kim would pour his resources into a technology capable of striking the Western United States and arm the payload with a conventional explosive?"

"I'm saying that it doesn't matter at this point because he has begun dismantling his nuclear program."

"He's almost certainly already upgraded his program within a different facility underground. The CIA is convinced of this and you know it."

The CIA attendees furiously scanned their briefing books to see if they had in fact expressly admitted to this conclusion.

As Mark watched the commotion in his periphery, he said, "All you're accomplishing with this effort is to push the problem once again onto the next Administration while pretending to achieve a meaningful result."

Davenport smirked. "Tough talk Mark, but I haven't heard any valid alternative from you."

"Sir, sanctions against North Korea have not and will not dissuade Kim from his goals. All they have done is cause greater misery to his people while his capability to strike the United States grows more imminent. I would propose that you present a final demand that Kim completely dismantle his nuclear program, cease work on his new missile technology, and allow confirmation of this by the United States and other NATO countries, not the feckless U.N."

It was the Secretary of State's turn to scoff. "Anything else you'd like? They're obviously not going to agree to this, so then what?"

"Then you very publicly park submarines in the Sea of Japan and give him a deadline before you strike."

The room exploded in frantic murmurs. Given the conversation that had transpired between them just the afternoon prior, the President gawked at the suggestion. The Secretary of Defense, a grizzled Army veteran who generally kept quiet during discussions of diplomacy, felt compelled to speak up at the suggestion of military force.

"Mr. President, I strongly advise you to avoid any brinkmanship that would potentially lead to a necessity for a use of force on the North Korean mainland. We need to ease tensions, not escalate them."

Mark had anticipated this. "Sir, we are not engaged in forward-projected dominance here, but instead, we are acting in proactive defense of ourselves and our allies by meeting the danger where it exists. The North Korean regime has been aggressively militant toward that cause through its pursuit of weapons and programs whose only purpose would be to strike America." His brain briefly considered divulging the information from Raleigh's secret source, but he quickly dismissed the idea, recognizing the compromising position in which it would place his friend. "I don't call for the use of military force lightly, but if you are unwilling to compel Kim to halt and dismantle these offensive programs, then we are accomplishing nothing with our work here."

The Secretary of Defense turned back to the President and allowed the two opposing statements to stand on their own. About as positive a response as Mark could hope for.

The Secretary of State, however, would not allow it to settle. "Mr. President, you are already seen as unpredictable and aggressive in your foreign policy. The effect has been beneficial to your goals regarding trade and security."

Davenport grinned at the admission of his apostate diplomat.

She continued, "But if you were to position the country on the brink of war, you will be forced to either act rationally and be perceived to have lost your nerve or you will be forced to engage in hostilities that will almost certainly create an ongoing conflict. You don't want to lose the credibility that you've so carefully cultivated to date."

Mark raised an eyebrow to what he had just heard. "Mr. President, the United States has spent hundreds of billions of dollars over multiple decades in dealing with this issue and pressed sanctions that punish the people instead of the regime. The Secretary of State essentially just admitted that Kim will never voluntarily dismantle his programs, so if we don't have the will to act to force disarmament, then the humane course moving forward would be to simply acknowledge defeat and shut it all down in consideration of the welfare of the Korean people. But if you are going to act, the options for meaningful change are to either compel dismantling of its offensive capabilities or to eliminate the regime and allow a free people to decide the fate of the country."

The murmuring began anew as Davenport leaned in his direction. "Wait a minute, you mean take out Kim? Not the nuclear and missile programs?"

"The weapons programs are ideas; they are capabilities built over time. The technology has likely shifted to a mini nuke program hidden in deeper, more unreachable locations. You need to eliminate the proponent of the programs- the regime is our enemy, not the people of North Korea."

The Secretary of State shook her head, "Even if you were certain of where Kim would be at any given time, you'd never be sure if you could actually take him out."

Mark raised his arms toward her. "So your vote is to give up? Because what we've been doing for umpteen decades now obviously isn't working and all you've been suggesting is more of the same." He looked around the room. "This is it. We must decide now if the United States is to ever act to end this unceasing threat before it's too late. If it proves necessary, I am even suggesting a tactical nuclear strike."

The President waived his arms. "That's enough. I'm not going to use nuclear weapons to kill one man. And Mark, you're correct that any strike against a weapons program, no matter how successful, would not be a permanent solution and therefore would result in greater fallout than gain for me." Davenport looked scornfully at the Secretary of State. "Besides, I have no international support to remove Kim."

Mark leaned forward, pleading, "And in 1938 there was no mandate to remove Hitler, can you imagine if a courageous leader had acted unilaterally to end that menace? The lives of tens of millions of people would have been spared, the course of history would have been changed for the better. Don't you think that it would be worth the condemnation of the few to improve the lives of the people of Korea and to end once and for all this urgent threat against the United States?"

All eyes turned to the President as he absorbed Mark's words. The silence hung thick in the room. He looked at Mark and made a pained expression, "Of course I agree that Kim is a threat, and growing more imminent by the day." He exhaled. "But I have no consensus to remove him, and if I did, we don't know who or what would take his place. So I'm left with no other option than to agree to the course of action suggested by the State Department and N.S.C. We will postpone the North Korean problem as best as we can and hope that things change in the future."

Mark absorbed the verdict as he made his own decision. *The courage to change the things I can.*

He returned to his office and called Raleigh. "Be prepared for a meeting on the Summit in one hour. I'll come to you."

"Okay, it would be helpful if you would call the Director and tell her that you are requesting these meetings with me. I'm starting to take some flak over it."

"She's still here I'm sure. When people are called to the White House, they linger for as long as possible to maximize their exposure. I'll inform her in person."

When Mark arrived at Langley, his demeanor was as serious as it had been earlier on the phone. Raleigh met him in the lobby and started walking him up to the conference room. "So I gather that the meeting didn't go as you had hoped?"

"If you mean 'are they satisfying themselves with the same ineffective diplomacy as always?' then the answer is 'yes'."

"Sorry to hear that, but it's essentially what I predicted."

Mark stopped at the conference room door and looked at him. "What would happen in North Korea if Kim were to be eliminated?"

Raleigh gave a confused look and then started to swivel his head around to see if anyone was in earshot. "I've never shown you the lower floors like I promised." He spoke loudly while pressing a finger to his lips. "I apologize, let me show you around."

Mark was momentarily confused, but quickly understood that the conference room was no longer as secure as he had previously assumed. "Yeah, I'd like that."

They headed down the stairs and arrived at what appeared to be a storage room. Raleigh shut the door behind them. "Why are you asking me about a post-Kim North Korea? You just said that the President is punting the issue."

"Just answer my question first."

"Well, unlike in years past before the internet and proliferation of cheap information technology, the people of North Korea now know that Kim is a savage despot and there is no love among the populace for him. His paranoia prevents any type of natural heir to his position, so succession would be an open question, but we have hope

224

that there would be someone in line to seize power with the interests of the people of North Korea in mind."

Mark paced while Raleigh awaited the reason for these questions. Mark finally blurted out, "They all know that this threat will continue and will grow beyond our capacity to deal with it absent some type of decisive action on our part. I argued for a demand of demonstrable abandonment of the North Korean aggression, or an end to the regime, and the President demurred. He made it clear that he would not entertain those options and chose instead to push for further delay." He looked at Raleigh. "This Summit is ultimately futile, as are all of our policies toward North Korea."

Raleigh sighed. "Okay, but what does that have to do with you?"

"The President agrees that the regime is the problem, but acknowledges that his hands are tied, so I'm going to do what I know the President would want done but can't. At this next Summit, I'm going to assassinate Kim."

Raleigh's laugh turned to concern when he saw Mark's face. "Mark, you can't kill the leader of North Korea."

"You think I *can't* or *won't*? You said so yourself that you believe that he is nearing the capability to obliterate an American city. I am NOT going to sit idly by while that happens. If you doubt my determination, I can assure you that I am resolved."

Raleigh stared directly into Mark's eyes, sizing him up in the way only a Field Operative could. He finally spoke, "I told you that I'd love to be given the opportunity to eliminate Kim," he lowered his head, "but I'm never going to have that." He exhaled, "You, on the other hand, will." He looked up at Mark, slowly nodding his head. "I'm in."

For the next hour, the two discussed potential scenarios for Mark to assassinate Kim. No preparations had been made for such a conversation, so most of it revolved around concepts and ideas which would need to be further researched. With their nebulous ideas in place, they agreed to meet again in one week.

As Raleigh reached for the door, he asked, "Wait, have they determined where the Summit meeting is to take place?"

"Oh, it's going to be in the Inter-Korean Peace House in the Demilitarized Zone Joint Security Area between the north and south."

"Good, we have extensive intel on the D.M.Z. fortifications, so I'll be able to map out in detail how this would work." He reached out his hand to Mark who shook it. He continued, "Do NOT talk to anyone about this. I'm not worried about what will happen to me if we are discovered, but I do worry about someone ratting you out. This is a noble cause. If things get dicey and you need to alert me to an alternate meeting location, just tell me to meet you at our 'old hang out' for a beer. That will mean the parking lot in Fort Marcy off of the George Washington Parkway."

Mark nodded his understanding while contemplating the irony of "meeting for a beer."

Raleigh placed his hand on Mark's shoulder. "And if at any point you decide that you can't do this, just let me know and it's off. No judgment on my part."

Mark headed back to Washington pondering Raleigh's description of their plan, "A noble cause." He exhaled and hoped maybe his Daily Verse would help him assess the "nobility" of his new cause. *Then Jesus said to his disciples, 'Whoever wants to be my disciple must deny themselves and take up their cross and follow me. For whoever wants to save their life will lose it, but whoever loses their life for me will find it.'*

He swallowed hard, realizing that this action would likely cost him his life. He also stared at the language, "Loses their life for me..." In his headstrong rush, he hadn't even considered consulting his Higher Power first.

- 20 -

Over the following week, Mark's entire focus in life turned toward his new task. Studying the North Koreans was an activity which could take place in the open, so he began to examine the makeup of Kim's regime using his secure terminal. Through the years, names had come and gone as the tyrant's consideration was that if no one stayed around long enough, then no one could conspire against him. This gave him a lasting yet superficial security.

The exceptions to this rule were trusted family members and his immediate guard. The State Security Department members, who guarded him at all times, were loyal because they were eager beneficiaries of the largesse of the regime. Although Kim's people were the most impoverished in the world, he and his comrades lived in opulence. The members of his guard had sold their souls for a decadent life while their fellow countrymen lived in squalor.

His family members, although now dwindling in number, did enjoy the same lifestyle, but hardly had a choice in the matter. There were only two left of note- his uncle, who was the head of a military program, and his sister who had accompanied him during the first Summit. Her husband had been executed by Kim years before and her teenage daughter was kept by him in a school run by his cronies. Hers was a forced loyalty.

Mark looked at the clock and shut off his computer as Charles would be awaiting him in the E.E.O.B. He found him sipping coffee at a table in a breakroom as he joined him. "Hey Charles, sorry I'm late. Been swamped with this upcoming Summit."

"No problem, bud. Better you than me."

Mark thought about the comment and then looked up at him. "You're of Korean descent, correct?"

"Yeah, I even speak some of the language." He looked at Mark leerily. "Why?"

Mark shook his head, "I was just wondering how an event like this affects you personally?"

"Oh. Well my grandparents came here during the war as part of a program to relocate loyalists who were threatened by the communist regime. They were angry about the tyranny that had taken everything from them, but they were also grateful for the freedom that they found in the new land that they cherished until their deaths. I would be lying if I said that they didn't have an influence on my decision to join the Marines and now the Secret Service. They instilled great patriotism in me."

Mark nodded. "And what if the United States had the opportunity to remove that regime, what would they have said then?"

"I think they would have celebrated such an event, although..." he paused, "I think they would have respectfully suggested that it should be the Korean people to create such a result."

"Oh, you mean like a pride thing?"

"No, more like a destiny. It's called 'Juche', which means 'self-reliance'. It's a very pervasive concept in our culture. The goal of a unified peninsula is known as 'Joseon', and about the only thing that both north and south agree on is that this must be an independent Korean determination."

"Oh." Mark was a bit disheartened.

"But anyway, that's way above my paygrade. Let's talk about how you're doing. How many hours have you been sober now?"

Mark allowed himself to laugh, "Oh shut up."

After wrapping up with Charles, Mark ate lunch and then grabbed a ride from the executive car service over to Langley. As strange as it sounded to Mark, Raleigh had suggested that their meetings continue there to hide in plain sight as irregular rendezvouses off site would draw more attention than a meeting at the CIA. Raleigh had set up a table and chairs in the storage room and had come prepared to discuss details.

"I've examined the Peace House and the security plan for both sides, at least the typical plan that the North Koreans would follow for such an event. The building was constructed for meetings and ceremonies, so it is relatively small with a simple layout. The front area is wide open and can accommodate ceremonies, press conferences, photo ops, etc. Through the doors directly behind that is the formal meeting room where you'll have a main table with dignitaries and then side tables for staff. Security will surround the meeting participants on both sides of the room. The two sides will enter the room from their respective anterooms located on opposite sides of the meeting room."

"The anterooms are essentially the staging areas and housing for extra staff, equipment, weapons, etc. The Secret Service will maintain a heavily-armed quick response force known as a C.A.T. Team in there. The doorways into the meeting room have monitors on them, and to enter, a participant will need to have a badge with an embedded code signal. If a person attempts to enter the room without a proper badge, an alarm will sound and both principals will be rushed out of the room and into their anterooms. So, issue one would be to figure out how you get a coded badge into the meeting room."

Mark shrugged, "Okay, I've got to get cleared for the meeting room while Kim is present."

"Or just get your hands on a badge."

"I'll figure out the protocol to see if I will need to do that."

"Okay. Issue two is that only POTUS, essential staff, interpreters, and Secret Service will be allowed beyond the side tables located next to each anteroom. You'll have to figure out how to get into the room and then make your way to the main table."

"That won't be easy. If you were to lean the wrong way in a Summit meeting, they would pounce on you."

"Right, but issue three is the real problem, how you would kill him. You'll never be able to carry in anything that resembles a traditional weapon. Nothing that can shoot, stab, explode, etc. Assuming that you won't be within striking distance anyway, that leaves agents like toxins that transfer through the air, which might work, but releasing them could kill everyone in the room."

"Yeah, and I couldn't just pull out a bag full of ricin and blow it in his direction."

"No, but the CIA has developed some creative delivery devices over the years." Raleigh produced a few photo pages and placed them on a table. "Pens, gloves, cigars," he said laughing. The attempt on Fidel Castro's life with a poison cigar was legendary at this point.

"I wouldn't be able to hold anything in my hand if I got close to him, which is a big 'if' to begin with. And anything on my skin could kill me beforehand or unintentionally transfer to non-targets."

"Yeah, except for if you wore jewelry, a ring for instance."

Mark was puzzled. "What do you mean?"

He pointed to one of the photos. "There's a device that the CIA developed back in the 80's that is essentially a syringe hidden inside the jewel stone of a class ring. The Operator removes the stone, which is hollow, turns the syringe toward the palm, and injects the poison into the target."

"Did it work?"

"Not really. They only tested it through zero toxin dry-run simulations and there were significant problems. One was the fact that the needle was short and girthy and drew a great deal of blood, so the recipient obviously knew that they had been stuck. There's no element of deception to avoid detection and allow for escape by the Operator, and if the target is going to be aware of the strike, might as well just blow them up or use a sniper."

"Uh huh. What were the other problems?"

"Well the fact that it took a great amount of force and time to push the poison from the reservoir into the target. To deliver it, the Operator would essentially have to slap the person hard and be able to hold the needle in for a few seconds. With the influx of cash and loosening of oversight after 9/11, many of these old ideas were given a new life.

The Ring was one that was updated for a faster-acting injection, but the mechanics didn't really change. Not exactly a plausible scenario for your plan."

"No, it's not. And we can't count on me being next to Kim, let alone be able to slap him. What else?"

"There are traditional means such as choking, beating, that type of thing."

"No, the Koreans aren't going to just leave me alone in the room with the guy."

"Well, you'll have no weapons so how are you gonna kill him??" Raleigh turned and crossed the room. "I know, maybe you could talk him into committing suicide."

Mark didn't appreciate the sarcasm, but he knew that he needed to keep Raleigh onboard with the plan. "Sorry, I know you didn't ask for this, and I know that you're trying your best."

Raleigh turned back around. "I've spent a week straight thinking about this and I don't see how you could actually accomplish it. You'll be so close but..." He leaned back against the wall in frustration and stared at Mark, watching him for several seconds. He cocked his head to the side. "You know that I want this guy dead, I'd happily slit his throat just to see him smile. He deserves to die for all of the atrocities that he's committed and the threat that he poses to America. That type of evil is what inspired me to join the military in the first place and what has kept me in the game even after being relegated to a desk. But I don't understand *your* motivation here."

Mark walked over to the table and took a seat. "You know about my God-centered and service-based sobriety program, that's what attracted me to this work, but the lack of tangible results shook my faith in it and caused me to question the meaning of it all. I feel like if we could finally resolve this issue, it would prove to be some greater purpose that's been missing in my life."

"So, you're 'on mission from *Gad*'?" Raleigh said this like Dan Aykroyd's character in *The Blues Brothers*.

Mark laughed. "No, I'm not getting signals from God through my TV telling me to kill people if that's what you mean."

Raleigh chuckled.

Mark added, "But I seek His guidance in all of my actions. I always have to ground myself in His will and humbly accept His direction as I understand it."

Raleigh said, "That's a lot of pressure, to understand what God wants. Glad it's you and not me."

The hair stood up on Mark's neck as doubts filled his mind. *He's right, how can I ever be sure?*

Raleigh watched him and finally said, "Okay, regardless of your motivation, we are in agreement on the greater cause here, but why you?" He turned serious. "If you were to go through with this, you know you probably wouldn't survive."

Mark shrugged. "Who else is going to do it? I'm uniquely situated. Besides, if I'm willing to advise the President to send Americans into harm's way to accomplish this goal, then I should be willing to make the sacrifice myself."

Raleigh nodded his head in understanding.

Mark said, "But situated or not, I'm not going to have this opportunity if we can't figure out the means." He sat up and looked at the picture of the Ring left on the table. It had a hideously large emerald-colored stone. "So, what kind of toxin does it use?"

"What, the Ring? Actually, it's just anthrax, but an extremely potent strain as well as a sodium pentothal solution that is designed to immediately incapacitate the target. The anthrax can generally kill a person within a day."

"Anthrax?"

"Yeah well since the delivery mechanism couldn't be improved, they didn't bother with updating the toxin.

"Don't we all have inoculations for that?"

"I did when I was deployed, you don't. It's not exactly on the recommended vaccine regimen. And the inoculations are short-lived, a target would have to have taken the preventative three doses for the weeks leading up to the exposure incident to effectively neutralize it."

"And if Kim had this inoculation?"

"The sodium pentothal would still render a target unconscious and their heart would all but stop, but they would theoretically survive. For certain, they'd be incapacitated and appear to be dead."

They sat there for a minute until Raleigh broke the silence. "It's not like that matters though, if you were to try to approach Kim, the Secret Service would shoot you before the Koreans had a chance."

Mark thought about Charles and how proficient he was with his sidearm. "What would your instinct be if I said that we could use any device in this scenario?"

Raleigh looked up from the table. "A gun."

With that, Raleigh escorted Mark out to the front and resumed his daily menial tasks. As Mark rode in the car back to Washington, he called his dad. "Hey, remember how you said that you owed me a birthday gift or two? I was thinking about a Sig Sauer pistol."

As he reached his workstation, César was waiting for him. "Hey Mark, or Mr. Rutherford? I'm sorry I'm not sure what to call you now!"

Mark, already on edge, was at first annoyed, but César's smile conveyed his pride in knowing that a friend of his was climbing the ranks of the West Wing. "You can still call me Mark." He smiled, "What can I do for you?"

"Oh, I just wanted to be sure that you got my research on Johnston and Holmes. For lobbyists, they sure seem to be connected to a lot of shady stuff."

Mark cringed and quickly looked around. "Hey, let's have this discussion over some coffee."

"Oh sure. When you said that you wanted to learn more about them, I couldn't figure out why, but I heard you talking to your friend Arjun on the phone a while back and he must be Arjun Chandra? One of the lobbyists who works for them? Anyway, you might want to warn him about working in a place like that."

Mark raised his hands to signify a halt, "Okay buddy, save it for the breakroom."

He grabbed his phone and practically pushed César out the door. As he exited, General Hastings emerged from his office, watching him intently.

- 21 -

The words on the screen began to blur as Mark tried to focus for another hour of Korean history. What started as normal research for his "project" had become an in-depth review of the state of the North Korean regime. Kim was a horrible, self-serving dictator, a terrible man who deserved to be eliminated. There was no debating these facts, but Mark couldn't shake the idea that the Korean people should be the ones to be given the opportunity to free themselves. Although, he wondered if this wasn't an excuse to absolve himself of the responsibility of relinquishing his own life in the cause.

And then he asked himself, *What cause?* As it stood, he would be thirty feet away from the man, in an anteroom, separated by a signal alarm and layers of security, and without a weapon to use. There was essentially no "cause" at this point.

He rubbed his face and looked at one of the open browser tabs on his internal Top-Secret Server, "Kim Yo-jong," the tyrant's sister. She would be in attendance at the Summit, acting as Kim's captive hostess. Her information: "English-speaking, widowed mother, ties to the State Security Department." She not only had Kim's confidence but also that of at least part of the elite group that guarded him.

Apparently, it wasn't always that way. She was educated in Switzerland with Kim. The intelligence suggested that she had been exposed to "Christian ideology," seemingly too much for Kim's comfort as she had been sent away to a reeducation camp for two years after he had succeeded his father to the seat of power. She had started numerous orphanages based on the concept of "Wholehearted free service to the poorest of the poor," modelled after the work of Mother Teresa. Kim Yo-jong had become too well-liked and too altruistic in her motives.

At the Summit, she would be by his side for sure, even if Mark wasn't. *This is going nowhere, time to check in with Charles.*

They sat down at the same table as always except Mark slumped into his chair. "You look a little frazzled, Mark."

He rubbed his neck. "Yeah, I am."

"Are you taking any breaks from work? Getting exercise?"

"I run several times a week." He lifted his eyebrow, "Oh, and I got a Sig Sauer. Been out to the range a couple of times."

Charles smiled, "A Sig, nice. It's good that you're trying to maintain a balance, but you're obviously still out of sorts. Why don't we start with the Serenity Prayer."

Mark shook his head. "Why? I've been reciting that for months now and I don't feel serene. How is repeating a prayer supposed to take away the problems of the world? I mean, I'm trying to save the people of North Korea..."

Charles gave him a concerned look. "Mark, you're not responsible for the fate of the Korean people. I know it may feel like it, and I respect how much of you that you're investing into the work, but you can't look at it that way."

Mark, realizing how close he had just come to tipping his cards, nodded in agreement. "Yeah, you're right, I'm just taking this Summit too personally."

Charles sat back. "Do you know the significance of the Serenity Prayer in our program?"

"Yeah, it's designed to help us keep calm when we're getting crazy, it keeps us from running to alcohol to deal with things."

"That's the *result*, yes, but do you understand the meaning behind the words?" Mark looked at him blankly. Charles quoted, "*God, grant me the serenity to accept the things I cannot change.* You are admitting that there are things that are out of your control; this is a big admission for egotistical drunks. Then you are asking God to help you identify such things and to accept their existence peacefully. *The courage to change the things I can.* You are asking God to help you act in an appropriate fashion to handle issues within your control. *And the wisdom to know the difference.* You are asking God for guidance in how you categorize and approach these two types of issues that we face on a daily basis. This is what it means to *Take life on life's terms*, not to get steamrolled by life, but also not to take on all of its problems."

Mark realized that in all of the times that he had recited this prayer, he had never truly contemplated the specific words. "So, *I* don't need to be the one to create the solution to the world's problems." He shook his head. "I'm such a fool."

"No you're not! You're a selfless servant trying to make this a better place, good for you. But keep your expectations reasonable." Charles paused. "And start with things that you *should* change, like with your immediate friends and family."

Mark stared at Charles and thought about his family. "I've got to go." He got up and walked back to his office to gather his things.

On his Metro ride home, he began to contemplate what the fallout would be like for those he loved and cared about-his father, George, Julia, General Hastings; they may not understand his actions, but hopefully they would respect the intended results. His thoughts then lingered on Bella. He decided that he needed to reach out to George, so when he arrived home, he gave his brother a call.

"Hey Mark, how are you??" George said excitedly.

Mark smiled. *It's inspiring how George still exudes kindness in spite of his condition.* "I'm good George. How are you doing man?"

"Oh, pretty good! My P.T. is coming along so well that I've become pretty self-sufficient. Still can't walk though, so I cancelled my entry for the Richmond marathon this year." He laughed.

Mark laughed as well. "Well, you'll get 'em next year. I'm so happy to hear about your improvement."

"It's coming along. But enough about me, tell me about life in the White House for my big brother!"

"Oh, it's not as glamorous as it may seem."

"Yeah, that's what I tell people about my wheelchair."

Mark found himself laughing again, then it hit him, George seemed a little *too* chipper. Mark also had not heard from Linda since she had confronted him in the bar in Richmond. "Uh George, are you sure everything is okay?"

George stutter-breathed as tears came down, "Linda left. I can't really blame her. Who wants a useless husband to take care of?"

Mark fumed. He considered altering his assassination plot to include a housewife from Richmond. "That woman isn't worth one of your tears, George. I'm so sorry that she did this to you." As he listened to George gently weep, he imagined the pain he must be experiencing without Bella. "Where did she go with your daughter? Is it far away?"

George sniffed. "Huh, no Bella is here. Linda ran off with some guy she met online. I don't know if she's coming back."

Mark lit up. "Bud, you're set! Screw her!" He quickly realized that he was not being helpful. "I mean, sorry she left and all, I know that can't be easy."

"I guess you're right. She hadn't been very pleasant since my accident. I just thought that I was lucky that she stayed around."

"You don't want someone sticking around who doesn't truly want to be with you." Mark's guilty conscience stabbed at him from inside. "George, I also owe you an apology for the things that I've done to you. Things that I..." The will was there for him to be honest and tell his brother everything, but he knew that telling him was a greater wrong.

"Mark, you're a great brother, stop stressing about things in the past. I'm just so happy for you now." Mark exhaled in relief. George added, "Besides, who else would have sent me money to help after my accident?"

Mark cringed as the relief dissipated. "Please don't thank me… it's the least I could do." He shook the guilt away. "Well, the good news is that now you have your daughter all to yourself."

"Yeah, she's wonderful. But now I have to pay for a caretaker, and Linda takes half of the money that comes in, I just don't know how I'm ever going to afford to pay for it all. Dad is helping all that he can, but he doesn't have much of a business anymore."

Mark thought, *And until recently, he had been stuck subsidizing me.* Mark's resolve returned to focus. "George, I'll take care of it. I promise you."

He hung up the phone and made a cup of instant coffee. It was late for caffeine, but he couldn't sleep anyway with the crushing weight of culpability. He felt he had to provide for George and Bella, that was his living amends; a way to make an atonement through unilateral action when an apology is impossible. Their problems took precedence over everything now. *But how can I make this right?*

He thought about his longshot plan to kill Kim and how little chance of success it really had. His brain added, *Charles showed me that I don't have to change the world to make a difference at home.* He had to admit to himself that he couldn't both attempt his plan and take care of his family. He would either be in jail or dead--the latter scenario being the most likely--and his wage-earning days would be over.

And how will I earn money in the future? The only people likely to offer me employment when this position ends... his eyes opened wide, *are the sleazy lobbyists.*

He arose early with little sleep and called Arjun.

"Hey Mark, haven't heard from you in a while! Want to go to a Nationals game? We have great seats right behind..."

"Arjun, shut up."

"Oh, okay. What's up?"

"Tell your bosses that I want to meet tonight. You won't be there."

"Uh," Arjun's voice betrayed his hurt feelings, "okay I can do that. But..."

Mark had to be clear about the seriousness of his instructions. "It will be just them, alone. 8:00 PM. Do you understand?"

"Yeah, I'll have to check and see if they can meet you."

"They will be there exactly on time or I will walk and none of you will ever hear from me again. Do you understand?"

"Yes, I'll let them know."

"I will call you at 7:30 PM and give you the location to pass on to them."

Arjun started to respond as the line went dead.

At exactly 7:30 PM, Mark called Arjun. He answered on the first ring and Mark instructed him to tell his superiors to meet at the south entrance to the Torpedo Factory in Alexandria. Half an hour would be just enough time for them to drive there from their offices on K Street.

At 8:02 PM, Davis and Julius hustled up to the door where Mark was standing. "You're late."

Julius was not amused. "You get somewhere in D.C. in thirty minutes! What the hell is all this about?"

Mark handed the men each a coffee and motioned for them to follow him. "We're just three businessmen enjoying

243

a beautiful night in Old Town, walking down to get a view of the Potomac."

The two lobbyists caught their breath and strolled with him at a leisurely pace. Mark loudly identified various historic landmarks as the three made their way to Waterfront Park. When they were alone, Mark spoke. "I've considered your proposal and I agree."

Julius smiled widely. "Well that's good to hear. We'll have to work out..."

"I've worked it out. It will go down exactly as I describe it to you and you will either agree to the terms or not. If you disagree, we will never have contact again. That includes your errand boy, Arjun."

Davis looked around as he spoke, "Quite the change in heart all of a sudden, how do we know that we can trust you?"

Mark swiveled his head as he spoke loudly to the empty park, "I am approaching these two gentlemen without their prior knowledge. This is my plan; I take full responsibility."

Their eyes went wide as they rescanned the park for other people.

Mark looked at them condescendingly. "Satisfied? You're both lawyers, this would be basic entrapment. But if you're not comfortable, I'll walk right now."

Mark knew that what he had said was not incontrovertibly true, but he counted on their greed trumping their discretion. The lobbyists looked at each other and then nodded their assent.

Mark took a deep breath. "I will give you the international instability that you seek. It will be an incident at the next Summit that will cause unprecedented hostilities by the North Koreans and resultant military build-up by the Americans."

Davis shrugged, "Okay, what is it?"

"An attack on a world leader."

Julius responded, "You're going to kill Davenport? I'm in."

Davis rolled his eyes at him and then turned back to Mark. "Even if you were able to assassinate Kim, the resulting instability would be unpredictable. The Korean peninsula could even end up reunified with him out of the way. What good would that do us?"

"I said 'attack' not assassinate. Imagine the reaction of the North Koreans if an Advisor to the President of the United States were to make an attempt on Kim's life."

Davis nodded, "There would be reprisals, skirmishes, maybe even a full-blown war."

The two lobbyists practically salivated. Julius frowned, "And what would you gain from this?"

"Five million dollars."

The men were already stupefied by the direction the conversation had taken, but a sum of money that large still made them gasp. However, Julius was obviously a master of tempering expectations while preserving a deal.

"Mark, we were considering maybe a half a million or so. We would lose money over the lifetime of a lobbying contract if we had to pay out that amount."

"Please don't insult my intelligence. I've seen your handiwork on behalf of your arms dealer clients. The feds may never have been able to prove your involvement, but you've arranged for much larger payouts by those corporations. You can arrange for the purchase of a life insurance policy on me through one of your offshore companies."

The two lobbyists looked disconcerted with his inherent knowledge of their practices.

Mark continued, "And one of your clients in fact owns an insurance carrier, so the paperwork should be easy enough to handle."

Davis was confused. "But if you're dead, then how will you collect the money?"

Julius shot him a look of annoyance.

Mark answered him, "I won't, but my daughter will."

Julius had obviously already connected those dots. "A five-million-dollar policy... we'll look into it, but it should be doable."

Mark said, "Here is the relevant information for the policy," as he handed Julius a sheet of paper. "You will purchase the policy in the name of Theresa Harris Rutherford, my deceased mother. Back date the original paperwork to roughly thirty years ago listing herself and me as the policy owners and her as the sole beneficiary. Add an addendum dated to roughly four years ago whereby I changed the beneficiary to Annabelle Elizabeth Rutherford of Richmond, Virginia. There will be no requirement of a death certificate, a verbal government declaration of death will be sufficient proof. Can't count on the Koreans to provide a certificate if I end up in their hands and I'm not going to allow it to be tied up in the courts."

Julius nodded as he read the same on the paper. "But you understand that there will be a suicide exemption, can't have us purchase a policy like this then have you just off yourself."

"Yes, I understand why you would retain that." Mark took a deep breath. "You are both aware that if this were ever to be discovered, we would all go to prison for the rest of our lives, so I don't need to tell you how sensitive this is. No discussions outside of the three of us. You have one week to have everything in place, and at that time, you will anonymously deliver to my estate attorney the executed policy. I will tell her that I found this old documentation and ask her to independently confirm its validity. Her name and address in Arlington is included."

Both lobbyists nodded at this.

"If I need to communicate with you, I will set it up through Arjun. After you leave here tonight, tell Arjun that he should not contact me again, but if I reach out to him, he is to do exactly as I tell him. And whatever you do, don't answer any of his foreseeable multitude of questions."

Julius grinned slyly, "We won't speak a word to him."

"Good, the rest is up to me from here on out."

- 22 -

With roughly two weeks to go before the Summit, Mark wanted to meet with Raleigh so that he could work out the final details of his secret plan. He obviously wasn't likely to be able to kill Kim, but he needed to at least get close enough to cause a reaction from the security teams. He would leave behind a note with a call to arms against the despot- it was of little comfort, but maybe his death would at least lead to some greater good.

His phone chimed with a text from Julia. "Hey Mark, I'm in town for meetings. Got time to catch up?" He shook his head and deleted the message. He refocused on Raleigh and called him to set up a visit, nauseous over his deception.

After a few obligatory minutes in the conference room, they made their way to the storage room. Raleigh spoke first. "I've got to tell you, I don't see how your plan will work."

"I do. I'm in tight with the Secret Service and I've got access to their H.Q. and friends on the inside. I'll secure a signal-equipped badge to gain entry to the meeting room. Once inside, I'll take a gun off of one of the Agents."

A mixture of amazement and disbelief filled Raleigh's face. "You're going to just take a weapon from a trained Agent? I don't think so. Besides, they'd air you out before you could even aim it. Don't forget that the President will be located in the same direction as Kim when you're pointing the barrel at him."

Mark pictured himself being "aired out"- riddled with gunfire so that the holes in him allowed the air right through. He shuddered at his likely fate. "Just let me worry about that." The guilt seized his voice.

Raleigh looked confused, but also smiled proudly that Mark was willing to continue in the face of such odds. "Okay, I trust you. It's probably best that I don't know too many more details anyway, just in case. If they suspected me, the CIA would be very aggressive in seeking information. You just tell me what you need."

Mark's shame gripped him, but he held himself together. "Tell me about Kim's guards and how they would react to a crisis like this."

"The instant that they sense a danger, the guards closest would cover Kim while the rest would fire on any active threat."

"Okay, but this is a Summit meeting with the American President. Obviously, they will be instructed to act with extreme prudence."

"Well yes, if there is simply a perceived threat, such as a radio alert or an alarm or something, they'd quickly escort Kim out of the meeting room and into their anteroom. The same for POTUS. But the anteroom is more fortified than the meeting room, they'd just hunker down in there, blocking access from both sides until they were positive that the threat was cleared."

"But they have to act quickly, who all would be left in the meeting room? Maybe I could use one of them to gain entry?"

"Probably several people. Any American aides and interpreters who didn't slip inside the anteroom would be left in there and the same with the North Koreans. There would be at least one or two security personnel from both sides inside to determine if the threat had passed."

Mark thought about Kim's sister. "What about Kim Yo-jong?"

Raleigh chuckled, "Mrs. Rogers?" Mark was puzzled at the statement. Raleigh waved and shook his head, "Sorry an inside joke."

"Joke about what?"

"We call her that because it's a reference to what got her on the outs with Kim years ago. You see, she established these orphanages while her father was still alive."

"Yeah, I read about that."

"Oh, well the brother took over power and went to tour one of them. He shows up and apparently his sister is standing out front all proud and her brother looks up and sees a quote above the door- *Love your neighbor as yourself.*"

Mark's eyes widened as he completed the verse. "These are the greatest commandments."

Raleigh saw his reaction. "Yeah that one! What kind of fool puts a western religious quote on a North Korean state facility?"

To Mark, this was not some foolish mistake, but the purposeful actions of a woman so committed to her God that she was willing to forfeit her privileged existence for the good of her people. Her faith was stunning.

Raleigh continued with his story. "The neighborly connotation was too much. We started comparing her to Mr. Rogers at that point, but I guess Kim didn't 'want to be her neighbor.'" Raleigh found this to be hilarious. "Kim doesn't take kindly to perceived competition for the allegiance of his people, so needless to say, she was personae non grata for a couple of years while they apparently washed that stuff out of her brain. He also had her husband executed as punishment for good measure. Frankly, she's lucky to still be alive."

Mark said, "But now she's with him at all Summit meetings, so she's obviously trusted again."

"About as trusted as anyone in his circle. She may be crazy religious, but she's not ambitious, so that saved her hide."

Mark nodded. "So, would she be left in the room in an emergency?"

Raleigh frowned. "Maybe. She's symbolically very important to the regime, so I would think that she would be a priority. Of course, nothing comes before Kim's safety." He leaned in toward Mark to whisper, ignoring the fact that they were alone in a storage room. "I guess at this point I can tell you, remember the secret 'source' I was telling you about?" He trailed off, nodding his head.

"She's the source?? But how?"

"It was NOT easy, but the CIA over the years has positioned numerous plants and contacts inside N.G.O.s and humanitarian organizations, and Kim has allowed his sister to maintain limited contact with them. So eventually, we had an asset smuggle her an internet-equipped satellite device called 'Oz' and that's how we established a communication line." He sat back and shook his hands like a magician as he finished his lengthy explanation.

Mark shook his head in disbelief. "Why wouldn't the CIA trust her analysis of Kim's intentions?"

"We've got to be cautious, I mean, look what happened with the intel on weapons of mass destruction in Iraq. Those were unverified, single-source reports that eventually led to a war."

"Okay but this isn't some random North Korean bureaucrat, this is the sister of Kim Jong-un."

"Yeah, and we were excited to be in contact with her, but after months of essentially exchanging pleasantries, she suddenly blurts out this highly sensitive, earth-shattering info about Kim's nuclear hostilities. We know that she received the communication device willingly, but we had to take a step back and evaluate whether she had been compromised."

"And what was the verdict?"

"'Inconclusive' is how my bosses termed it. There's not exactly an easy way to check a source like that. I personally believe that she's still the one communicating with us, or else why hasn't she been removed or killed? And if it's disinformation, I can't see how that message benefits Kim. The information came after the last Summit and it expressed concern about Kim's next moves. I think that she saw how Kim was actually emboldened by the outcome of the last meeting and she therefore reached the conclusion that he is preparing to attack as soon as he perfects the capabilities."

Silence enveloped the room as Mark's mind raced. Raleigh, watching Mark's reaction, started to shake his head. "No, no, no, I am NOT letting you contact her."

Mark returned his attention to him. "Why, because I might upset the delicate relationship of the two countries?" he asked sarcastically.

"Uh, you might blow up the Summit? You might get caught?"

Mark looked at him incredulously.

Raleigh sighed, "Okay, I get your point, but keep in mind that you wouldn't be certain of who you were actually talking to. What would you hope to accomplish anyway?"

"I'm just..." he paused, the weight of his secret plan crushing down on him, "I'd like to keep my options open."

Raleigh frowned, sympathetically assuming that Mark was contemplating a way to avoid going through with killing Kim. He nodded his head and whispered, "Always good to have options."

Mark's eyes moved up to Raleigh's as he refocused on the more immediate issues. "Okay, I'll consider further how I could use this line of communication. Right now, let's finish discussing the scenario where the meeting is disrupted. There will be some aides, interpreters, and a few security personnel from both sides, people who are armed and trained to eliminate the threat."

"Yes, and not Kim. Your window would be shut at that point."

Mark stared distantly. "So, it would have to take place before the meeting or somehow after the disruption." He looked down at his watch and stood. "I should go. Can you secure for me schematics of the Summit site and get me this Oz?"

Raleigh solemnly nodded his head. "Yeah, it obviously won't be missed since the higher-ups decided to shut down the project indefinitely. The next session had been scheduled for three days before the upcoming Summit, so she should be logging on that night."

He led Mark up the stairs to the lobby and out of the building. As they shook hands he said, "You look worn out. Take it from me, you can't let the gravity of a mission dominate your thoughts." He started back in then turned around, "And for God's sake, get in some more target practice."

Mark returned home that evening and sat on his couch. Nothing felt right; he wanted to help his family, but he knew that this plan was shameful. Using Raleigh, faking a threat against Kim which would only embolden his militarism, enriching the despicable lobbyists...

He got up from his couch and walked over to his refrigerator. Hanging on it was the photo of his daughter. His mind considered loftier goals, *What kind of world am I leaving for her?* His original motivation had been service, not money. *Maybe I should tap into some inspiration.*

As he scanned the room for his Big Book, his phone rang, and when he retrieved it, he read the name "Julia." He winced over the idea of having a conversation with her at that moment, but he finally relented and answered.

"Hey Mark, how are you??"

"Hey Jules, doing okay." He didn't quite know how to tell her about his recent relapse.

"Yeah right ya drunk, I heard you were suckin' the liquor teat again." She chuckled.

Mark smiled; she had obviously heard already from his father. "Yeah, I got a little sideways, but I'm back working on my recovery."

"Good for you! I'm only in town till tomorrow, so get your butt over here so we can have some coffee."

"Jules, it's 8:00 PM."

"Oh, I'm sorry it's so late, do you need someone to help you down the stairs, grandpa?"

Mark laughed, "Okay, okay I'll come meet you."

He grabbed his Big Book for the Metro ride to Crystal City where she was staying and met her in the empty coffee shop in the lobby of her hotel. They hugged and sat at a table.

Julia pulled her chair in. "Sorry about givin' you a hard time, but where I come from, when people fall off the wagon, you give 'em grief not pity."

Mark could relate. "No, I needed well-intentioned friends willing to give me a kick in the can, but my dad beat you to it."

She smiled, "Yeah, he told me. So I take it you're back on track?"

"I'm done with the drinking if that's what you mean. For me, alcohol poses as the tempting solution to all problems, but in reality, there's no problem that a drink can't make worse."

She furrowed her brow, "Any new *big* problems you want to tell me about?"

Mark shook his head, "Not like that. Still only got the one kid."

She mimed brushing the sweat from her forehead and chuckled. "So, what's been troublin' you?"

He exhaled, "I just lost hope in my program, and without hope, alcoholics have no motivation to stay sober."

"Yeah, makes sense. Do you still feel this way?"

"Not hopeless, no, but I still have trouble finding the ultimate point of it all. I mean, I did the Step-work of the program to get sober. The program taught me to connect with my Higher Power and to serve my fellow man to stay sober. I reached the height of most people's conception of service, but it still feels so superficial."

"It sounds like you've got it right, what am I missin'?"

He stared at her, contemplating how to restate. "I'm working in the upper echelon of our government and I can't seem to..."

"Hold on, back up. I'm sayin' that you seem to have the *priority* right."

Mark was lost. "What do you mean?"

"What you just said and what you're actually focused on are two different things. You need to have your thoughts and actions match your intentions." She leaned toward him. "Mark, all of this is because of God. Your sobriety, your service, your meanin', it's all due to His work in you and now it drives you to serve Him. Service work is a reflection of the grace He has given you. Findin' your true meanin' in the results is just lookin' at it backward."

Her breakdown made it all so clear to him. Sobriety was the grace given to him because of his relationship to God. Service maintained his sobriety and was the natural manifestation of his gratitude. *The relationship is what matters.* This epiphany caused him to look at her expectantly. "How do you know this? You have this relationship with God?"

"Yes, it drives who I am. Like any human, I fall short in followin' His direction, but when I'm doin' His will, I know that I'm on the right path." She glanced away. "My relationship with you was wrong, I was tryin' to find love through the physical instead of the spiritual, but He didn't abandon me and He always accepts me when I return to Him. The irony is that when I fight His direction, *I* am the one who suffers from my own poor choices." She smiled. "But I don't have to wallow in that, I reconcile with Him and keep movin' forward."

Mark said instinctively, "*Progress not perfection.*"

"Right, we're never goin' to be perfect, but He is. He forgives our mistakes and His will directs our progress."

He immediately thought of the Third Step- *Turned our will and our lives over to the care of God.* Mark was astonished at the similarities of their spiritual conditions. "How do you know about following God's will? I mean, I was a broken alcoholic."

"We're all broken. I was broken too, in my own way. You don't have to be livin' in the gutter to need God in your life, at least to have what I would consider to be a life worth livin'."

Mark's eyes narrowed. "Yeah, that's what I've been searching for. How did you find this?"

"I asked Jesus to guide my life, to wash away my sins and remove the barrier between me and God. To make me whole with Him, which happened through Jesus's sacrifice."

Mark shook his head, "I read about that, but I didn't ask for God's son to die just to talk with God."

"Whoa, pump your brakes, that is *God's* requirement for reconciliation, not yours, and He even provided the means to be with Him by allowin' His son to die in your place. You just have to accept what was already done for you."

Mark nodded. "Okay, how do I do that?"

"You ask Jesus to be your life savior, in the same way that you asked God to be your savior from your addiction. *All who receive Him, who believe His name, He will give the right to become children of God, who were born, not of blood nor of the will of the flesh nor of the will of man, but of God.*"

He looked down briefly and thought and then looked up, "What's your purpose in life though, to go to Heaven?"

"No!" Her exclamation startled Mark. "I mean, yes you eventually go to Heaven, but this isn't just about redemption after death, this is about havin' God with you every day of your life. It's written, *If the Spirit of Him who raised Jesus from the dead is LIVING in you, He who raised Christ from the dead will also give life to your mortal bodies because of His Spirit who lives in you.* It sounds like that's what you're missin' in your relationship- you communicate with Him for the work in your program, but you miss out on bein' a child of His, with all of the power and peace that come with it. You have the right to be called a child of God by acceptin' the son-ship of Jesus. You assume his place by lettin' him assume your faults, *reborn* in His likeness."

After hugging goodbye, Mark's head was spinning as he rode the Metro back to Washington. He thought about Kim Yo-jong and the respect that he had for her fearless actions, no doubt a reflection of the confidence and power she found in her relationship with Christ, a belief that provided meaning.

He focused on the Big Book in his hand. He opened it to page sixty-three as his father had mentioned in his recent visit. *As we felt new power flow in, as we enjoyed peace of mind, as we discovered that we could face life successfully, as we became conscious of His presence, we began to lose our fear of today, tomorrow or the hereafter. We were reborn.* Mark wondered how much of his relapse had really just been a fear of the unknown, a fear that existed in him because the only One who could truly know all things, and therefore provide the direction, was God.

He looked back down at the text and focused on what he knew. Jesus had encouraged all people to serve, to love, to seek peace; all the goals of Mark's program and all of the things that he wanted in his life. But these were actions born of the relationship with God, a communion that can only be achieved by accepting Jesus's sacrifice. His pulse quickened as he realized that he was finally truly understanding his Higher Power. Mark closed his eyes and asked God for this ultimate meaning, the relationship to Him through the one who had personified and inspired the work of the program on Earth. Jesus.

The weight of worldly expectations fell off as he felt peace flow in from his new relationship with God.

Mark Rutherford was reborn.

- 23 -

Mark awoke the next morning, opened his window, and breathed in the air. It was an incredible relief to him knowing that he would always have a purpose in life through his new relationship with Christ. He felt true serenity. As he sat down on his bed, his conscience prodded him to the realization that he needed to address his secret plot. After only a moment, he shook his head and thought, *There's no way that I'm going through with something as depraved as this, I better call Raleigh and tell him that it's off.*

As he picked up his phone to call, he saw the Daily Verse on the screen. *A person may think that their own way is right, but the Lord weighs the heart. Commit to the Lord whatever you do and He will establish your plans.* He nodded his head and thought, *Time to let God direct my actions.* He quieted his heart and lowered himself to his knees to commune with Him.

He started, as always, by thanking God and then he humbly sought His guidance. He started to tell God that he was going to cancel this plot and then he realized that he needed to place his problems before Him and then patiently await the answer. He asked God for guidance on how to provide for his family. He prayed for the Korean people and their need to forge their own path. He sought wisdom on how to deal with the lobbyists. He focused his thoughts on nothing more than to do what was right, in all things, *Thy will be done.*

Instead of a cancelled plot, he arose with the seeds of a new plan.

He called Tina and informed her that he had business off site that morning and that he would be late in reaching the office. Since he only tacitly remained under Hastings's purview, she just made a note of it. His next call was to Raleigh.

"I don't know about meeting at my location, Mark, the brass has been asking all sorts of questions. I don't mind the heat, but we may have company if I list you as a visitor today, so it would probably be best to meet off site. Besides, you're the one handling the cooking, maybe I should just come to your kitchen."

Mark shook his head at the ham-handed attempt at subterfuge, but Raleigh was smart not to be too descriptive on the phone. "I have an idea for the main course, just be prepared with the list of ingredients to make it work. I'll be there at noon, and don't forget to bring your little dog Toto, too."

They met in the lobby and started walking through the security gates. As Raleigh had predicted, there were security personnel watching and talking into communication devices. He tried to act nonchalant. "Happy to review any final info that the President may need, Mark. Shall we head to the conference room?"

Mark looked at him and could tell that their secondary meeting room was no longer secure either. "Actually, I'd like to see more of the building as we talk. I was at the

Pentagon last week, in the E Ring. Does this building have a *Ring*?"

Raleigh signaled his understanding but said, "Uh, well why don't we take the elevators to the top floor and you can ask my Director about that."

The two walked toward the bank of elevators as their tails disappeared into the stairwell. A mention of the Director had obviously made them anxious to notify her immediately and to prepare the entrance of the West Wing guest.

They boarded the elevator and Raleigh selected the sub-basement. He looked at Mark in purposeful silence. As they exited the lift, he led Mark quickly. "They're not following closely, nor have they instructed me not to meet with you, they just want to know what we're discussing. We can briefly disappear down here before they come looking. Maybe there's another storage room we can use."

"Take me to the Ring. That room should be safe."

Raleigh thought about it and nodded his head. "Yeah, that will work. I will need a buddy of mine from the Security Protective Service to let us in."

Mark hadn't considered this. "You have friends in Security?"

"Sure, I know a few S.P.O.s as they're known. They're mostly former cops or ex-military. We have drinks every once in a while and make fun of the wannabe Operators in the building who've never left the safety of their desks."

The two were keyed into the room by Raleigh's contact and left alone. It was much smaller than the storage room they had been using. Raleigh opened his sling bag and handed over a file. "Here are the schematics of the Summit

262

room." He then pulled out an envelope-sized electronic device. "And here's the Oz."

Mark looked it over. "That's it?"

Raleigh shrugged.

Mark flipped it back and forth in his hand. "I guess I just thought that something this high tech would be more substantial."

"Well, it works like a tablet. Just be *really* smart about what you say to Dorothy, it may actually be the Wicked Witch on the line." He added hesitantly, "And if you can, could you drop it in the inter-department mail over to me before you… depart?"

Mark looked at him as the word hung in the air. He turned his head and nodded as he locked the items into his briefcase.

Raleigh checked his watch and asked, "Okay, anything else left to work out?"

Mark sighed. "I just want to thank you for everything, Raleigh, and please accept my apology if things don't," he grasped for words, "if I let you down."

"Mark, you're a good man. You're doing what you think is right. You could never disappoint me."

He wrapped Mark in a bear-hug that startled him. Raleigh backed up and wiped away the moisture from his eyes. "Okay, so is that it?"

Mark grinned, "No, show me this infamous Ring."

In the Director's office, a group was standing with her awaiting the arrival of their White House visitor. She checked her watch for a third time. "It's been over five minutes, they obviously didn't come here. Get the Security Protective Service to see where Simmons took him."

Within a few minutes she received her answer and the group headed with several S.P.O.s to the sub-basement. They walked around garnering surprised looks from long-forgotten archivists and administrators.

"Well, they're not wandering the halls, what room could they be in?"

A S.P.O. stepped forward, "Ma'am, apparently one of our personnel gave them access to a Special Projects storage unit shortly after they exited the elevators."

"Old Cold War technology? Take me there now."

As the ever-expanding group reached the door, she had the S.P.O. scan his badge and she entered. As she did, she watched Mark slam a case shut and look up at her. Raleigh was standing only a few feet behind him in the cramped room.

Instinctively she shouted, "What do you think you're doing??"

Raleigh cleared his throat, "Director, you know Mr. Rutherford, Special Assistant Counsel to the President." He leaned forward and opened his eyes wide to impress upon her the significance of Mark's new title.

"Uh, right. Mr. Rutherford, how are you?"

Mark embraced Raleigh's emphasis of his new title. "Director! So good to see you. Raleigh was kind enough to give me a private showing of some of your fun gadgets from the Cold War days. Pretty impressive stuff."

She slowly scanned over the case next to Mark. "Oh, I'm glad you were able to take a look."

"Yes, thank you. I'm sorry, I'm confused as to why you're here, did we have a meeting scheduled?"

"No, I was just unsure of why you would be in the sub-basement. Of course, a Presidential Advisor is always welcome to tour the campus, we just ask that a representative of our Government Affairs Office be present as well, Mr. Rutherford."

"Oh, I apologize, I kind of sprung this on Raleigh. And please, call me Mark."

He backed away from the case where he had been handling the Ring and was escorted to the second-floor conference room where Raleigh provided him a more conventional Summit briefing. Afterward, Raleigh walked Mark out of the building and saw him to the executive car for a final word.

"We shouldn't have any further contact here. If you need me, call me over to the White House."

Mark nodded his understanding.

Raleigh exhaled, "Good luck. I'd tell you to go have a drink, but go do whatever it is you do now."

As Raleigh returned inside, the driver walked over and started the car. "Back to the White House, sir?"

"Yes, by way of a doctor's office. I have a prescription to fill."

Mark entered his apartment that night and activated the Oz. The tablet powered-on and displayed a line-by-line series of written exchanges between the CIA and "KYJ," which he figured he could safely assume was Kim Yo-jong.

As Raleigh had suggested, the interface was uncomplicated and the software was common sense.

He started to review the exchanges from the beginning, which had commenced ten months prior. As he read, he thought, *Raleigh wasn't kidding about the elongated "wooing" stage.* The sessions hadn't moved considerably past an attempt to gauge her views on Kim's regime until the last exchange. He also noticed in the timestamps that the sessions lasted exactly five minutes. *This must be her self-imposed time limit, designed for her safety,* he surmised.

He focused on the last communications, which had started in customary fashion, but had quickly turned to Kim's intentions. Kim Yo-jong, if it was in fact her, had warned the CIA that her brother would, "Do great wrong." The CIA, apparently assuming that she was speaking in generalities, had replied with a vague hope that they could work with her to avoid such an event. Her response had been urgent in its tone, "The missiles are active and the nuclear program is almost complete. He intends to use this on America." This had obviously thrown the CIA for a loop, as they considered the information for over a minute before typing another vague response. She had pressed further, "You must do something, these weapons are not for bargain, but for death," and finally, "You must act soon." Mark read and re-read the exchange, and came to the same conclusion as Raleigh, *This is almost certainly her and she's pleading with us to take the threat seriously, but I need to be sure of this when I attempt to communicate.*

He hid the device in a drawer as he contemplated how he might use this channel. Running through his head was her consistent sign off, "Peace be with you."

- 24 -

The weeks went by as the White House finalized its preparations for what was essentially a ceremonial meeting. Mark entered his office on the Monday morning before the Summit, only four days until the delegation would be leaving for Korea. His extracurricular work had kept him preoccupied, so he had been distracted from his daily business. He woke up from his distant thoughts when General Hastings called him in.

"Mark, close the door please."

He did as instructed and took a seat.

The General looked down at his desk for a few seconds and then met Mark's eyes. "You won't be attending this Summit."

Mark's mouth dropped as his heart skipped a beat. "What? How could this possibly be??"

"The President is frankly ambivalent toward your participation. He still respects your counsel, but your ideas were so radically different on how to deal with the North Koreans this time that he worries that you might be at odds with what he is trying to accomplish in this meeting."

"What? I would never cause a scene." Mark's conscience knifed at him from inside.

"I don't doubt that, but I have my own concerns, and as the President's Head of Administration, I need to have a greater confidence in you as well."

"I'm not drinking if that's what you're worried about."

"No, I'm happy to see that you've dealt with that." The General looked down again. "I'm concerned about your association with the lobbyists Johnston and Holmes."

Mark's eyes nearly popped out of his head.

The General continued, "I heard you discussing them with César."

Mark's heart re-started and he was thankful that the General hadn't seen the look on his face. "Oh, I was just curious what their business involved. I have a friend who works there and I was worried about him."

"That very well may be, but I will need you to discuss this with the Office of the General Counsel to be sure that you're clear of any conflicts moving forward."

Mark was relieved that his true involvement with them had not been discovered, but he was now off of the Summit Team. "General, this is ludicrous."

"It may be. It may be nothing, but my job is to protect the President, and with his indifference toward your presence, I just don't think that you should attend. But don't worry, you're still safe in your position and you'll have your own office soon, assuming that the informal probe clears you. You'd just miss this one event."

Mark shook his head.

Hastings said, "Besides, this is turning out to be a lackluster meeting anyway. I promised Jamie that he could attend an overseas trip and I'm giving him your spot."

Mark sat in silent disbelief as his plan collapsed in his head.

The General added, "You know, he mentioned to me that you were telling people that you didn't vote for Davenport in the last election. He was worried about your reputation with you advertising something like that. He's looking out for you."

Mark's eyes narrowed, *Yes, I'm sure Ja'mae had my best interests in mind.* He walked back to his desk and dropped into his chair, internally cursing Ja'mae's conniving and cursing César's loud mouth. He shook his head, *Maybe this just isn't God's will after all, maybe my will is driving this.* With this thought in his head, he decided to check his phone for a Daily Verse. *And we know that God causes everything to work together for the good of those who love God and are called according to His purpose for them.*

Work together for His purpose. *Assuming that this plan is righteous, then I'll need some help.* Good thing he had a couple of corrupt lobbyists and a rogue CIA Officer on his side.

He left work at lunch and headed home. *First, I'll need to involve the lobbyists.* He called Arjun with instructions, and later that afternoon, they met in Dupont Circle for coffee. Afterward, Arjun returned to his office and handed Julius a disposable phone. A note was attached that read, "7:00 PM."

"J.J., Mark wanted me to give..." Julius touched his finger to his lips and pointed Arjun toward the door without a word, just as he had promised Mark he would do.

At 7:00 exactly, the phone rang from an undisclosed number. Julius and Davis were huddled by it in the otherwise empty office.

"Gentlemen, I assume that it is safe to talk?"

Davis was anxious. "Whoever this is, we are simply answering a phone that was..."

Julius cut him off, "Yes, it's clear. Is it safe on your end?"

"Yes. These are both untraceable disposable phones."

"Okay, that's out of the way. Why are you contacting us?"

"I need your help. I've been replaced on the Summit Team and need to regain my spot."

Davis snorted, "What are we supposed to do?"

"I need you to use one of your firm's overseas entities to wire some money."

Julius cringed. "We have lived up to our side of the bargain, this isn't a demand for more money is it?"

"No, it's not for me. It's to convince someone to stay home from the upcoming trip so that I can take his spot. He has certain debts and this sum would persuade him."

The lobbyists dubiously glanced at each other. Julius asked, "How much?"

"It's a little over $10,000, $10,250 to be exact. A tiny amount for you, but unobtainable for me. I will text you the bank account information for you to wire it."

The two breathed easier. Davis said, "Hell, I can hand that to you from my home safe."

"Don't be a fool. No personal contact, no ties. Just follow my instructions." Mark hung up the phone. *Tomorrow I'll need a visit from the CIA.*

The next morning, Raleigh waited outside for Mark to retrieve him from the visitor's gate. He was an employee of the Central Intelligence Agency who had been officially summoned to the White House by a Presidential Advisor, but he was still darting his eyes nervously. It didn't help that he appeared completely out of place with his long hair, scruffy beard, and ill-fitting suit.

As Mark escorted him in, Mark spoke over his shoulder, "Nice duds, did your mom dress you?"

"I don't wear suits. You're lucky I had this in the back of my closet." Raleigh leaned forward and whispered, "You're not still on the Summit Team, is this the smartest thing to be doing?"

"Relax, there are no recording devices here. And I may not be a part of the travel contingent, but I'm still advising, so I'll be a part of all preparations including the official prep meeting tomorrow. For today, we'll be fairly inconspicuous." Mark led him toward the E.E.O.B. "Besides, there's someone I'd like you to meet."

Mark knocked on the door to the Secret Service H.Q. and the two were led inside. He told Raleigh, "Follow my lead and keep this guy's attention focused on you."

Charles came out of his office. "Mark? I have to complete the final prep for the Summit so I don't have time to chat."

"I know, sorry about the disturbance, but I wanted to introduce you to a good buddy of mine from the CIA, Raleigh Simmons." The two shook hands. Mark continued, "Actually, Raleigh was a Special Forces Operator for several tours in the Middle East."

Charles smiled, "Oh, good on you. I was 2MarDiv in Fallujah and Ramadi for a few tours."

Raleigh's face lit up, "That was some heavy work."

"Yeah, it kept me busy."

Mark pointed to the Armory. "Show Raleigh what you've got in here."

"Oh, he's seen munitions before."

Raleigh obviously caught on to Mark's idea, "What do you carry, the M9?"

"No, Sig Sauer 229."

Charles led them into the room. He began to discuss weaponry with Raleigh as Mark slipped over toward the magazines lining the rack. He ran his hands over the magazines of ammo, hovering at the blanks. "Raleigh, you've got to see this." Mark was pointing across the room at the skull and crossbones.

Charles said, "Uh, Mark, that's not exactly public knowledge."

Raleigh smiled, "The 'Hell's Bells Box.'"

Charles chuckled, "Yeah, it's not in the regs, but I'd rather have it and not need it, than need it and not have it." He put it on the table and opened it up.

Without looking, Raleigh said, "Let me guess, frag grenades, smoke grenades..."

Charles nodded, "Spoken like a man who's had one of these."

"Roger that."

Mark got closer holding his hands behind his back. He gestured with his head, "Show Raleigh that rifle over there."

The two men turned and looked as Mark slammed the box shut. The startled men turned back.

"Whoa, be careful with that Mark."

"Sorry, thought someone was coming into the room."

Charles looked around. He said, "Yeah, we'd better put this away," as he locked the box and placed it back on the ground.

Mark said, "Well, we've got more work to do on the Summit prep, but do you think you could do me a favor while Raleigh is still here?"

"Uh, sure what do you need?"

"Can you get us into the Executive Residence?"

Raleigh gave him a cross look. "Uh, Mark, I don't want a tour that bad."

Mark shot him back daggers. "Yes, you do. You told me it was on your bucket list."

Raleigh backed down. "Oh, well if Charles has time."

Charles shook his head, "I don't know that's really frowned-upon."

"Come on, POTUS is out of town, no one is going to care."

"Why don't you sign him up for one of Jamie's tours?"

"He's only in the building today and it'll only take a minute. There's something in the pantry that I'd like him to see." He winked at Charles.

Charles smiled with recognition and chuckled. "Okay, just real quick though."

The three walked over to the White House, passed through the checkpoint for the Executive Residence and entered the kitchen. Mark walked directly over to the pantry and said, "Get a load of this." He opened the door and sitting on the ground was a pallet of Spam containers.

Raleigh's eyes bulged. "That's a lot of processed meat. Are we sure that this guy never served in a war zone?"

Charles laughed at the reference. Mark looked around the room. "Charles, how do they get a pallet of meat in here?"

Charles pointed over at the back wall. "See the roll-up door over there? That's where deliveries are made."

"All deliveries? So, the pizza guy just checks in at the front gate and knocks on that door?"

"No, only scheduled deliveries and security personnel are allowed to approach from back there."

Mark stared at the door. "Oh, got it," he said distantly. He turned on a dime, "Okay, time for us to get back to work."

Raleigh hustled along with Mark up the stairs until they were alone. "Thanks for the tour, but shouldn't you be working on how to get back on that Summit Team?"

"That's what I'm doing, I just need to work out the details. For now, I need you to head back to Langley."

"I thought that you needed my help here?"

"Can you get your hands on a CIA Security Protective Service badge and van?"

Raleigh stopped. "Uh, that would be an enormous effort."

"Relax, I'm not asking you to give up your life or anything." Mark said this as he opened his eyes wide to emphasize his meaning.

Raleigh shook his head. "Right, sorry. I can get it done."

"Good, head back there now and do that. And I read in your file that you were trained on how to covertly enter enemy compounds, so you can pick a lock? Say, on a townhouse?"

Raleigh looked surprised by the reference to his past, but nodded confirmation of his skills.

Mark said, "Then I need you to get a hold of a lock-picking set."

After lunch, Mark sat at his desk and looked at his calendar. He had only three days left until the Summit Team departed. He took a deep breath and called the Director of the East Asia Office.

"Hello Mr. Rutherford, how can I help you?"

"Jeannette, please call me Mark."

"Okay, Mark, we're a little busy preparing for tomorrow's Summit Briefing. How can I help you?"

"Sure sure, sorry to bother you. I was hoping that Raleigh could be added to your group of attendees tomorrow."

"Oh, he's not really part of our official briefing."

"Understood, but I would like him to attend in case he can provide further insight to me."

She paused. "I appreciate your confidence in Raleigh, but we have other more senior..."

"I'm an Advisor to the President and I would like him there. Is that a satisfactory reason?"

She exhaled. "Of course, I'll alert him immediately."

Mark hung up the phone and waited 30 minutes. He called Raleigh.

"Mark, I just got a call from the Director." He said this pleasantly, but his voice was laden with concern.

"Were you added to the group for tomorrow?"

Raleigh said gritting his teeth, "Yes but not everyone here is so pleased with this."

Mark was cautious, he couldn't be certain if the phone line was secure. "Great, your insight will be invaluable. Say, why don't we meet in five hours at the old hang out. We can have a beer and chat."

At 7:30 PM, Mark pulled up to the Fort Marcy parking lot in his mustard-yellow Nova. It was empty save for Raleigh standing at the front of his car looking toward the woods. He covertly signaled for Mark to park a few spaces down, who was alarmed by the cloak and dagger. He got out and before he could speak, Raleigh lit up a cigarette.

"Pretend like you're on your phone," he said down to his lighter. Mark was confused but fished in his pocket for his phone. Raleigh blew out a puff of smoke. "I told you about this location, but it's more of a stop off to meet and transfer to another place. We're only a mile from Langley, so it is periodically electronically monitored and there are constant Park Police and S.P.O. drive-bys. Just keep it quick, no unnecessary details, till the end of my cigarette." He took another puff, literally burning up their time.

Mark pulled his dormant phone up to his ear. "Tomorrow you are cleared-in with your group at 10:00 AM, but you will come separately. Secure the credentials and vehicle that we had discussed and head to the delivery entrance on the Northwest side by the Eisenhower Executive Office Building. Once inside the compound, head to the security staging area outside of the kitchen that Charles had mentioned. By that time, he'll be in a final security briefing, but I'll meet you at the roll-up door."

Raleigh stared with a side-glance at Mark. "Are you nuts?"

Mark eyed Raleigh's dwindling cigarette. "I don't have time to explain everything. Just trust me."

"You want me to trust an untrained co-conspirator to execute a plan to surreptitiously enter the most heavily-guarded building in the United States?"

Mark watched the cigarette burn to a nub as his mind raced. *He's right, this is crazy. So how do I convince a CIA Officer and former Special Forces Operator that it's necessary to do something as bold as...* His head jerked up from the phone as he smiled. "A courageous soldier once said, 'Virtue is bold and goodness is never fearful.'"

Raleigh finished the last drag and stamped it out. "Okay, see you at 10:00."

Mark arrived home shortly before 9:00 PM and tossed his belongings on his couch. With all of the chaos of losing his spot on the Summit Team, he had pushed the communication session with Kim Yo-jong out of his mind. *I only have a little over an hour to figure out what to say to her, if it is in fact her.*

He stared at the Oz as the minutes ticked by. When the device's clock hit 22:00 hours, the text lit up. Mark held his breath as he awaited contact.

"Hello, I am here," appeared on the screen.

His fear subsided a little at the common nature of the greeting. He thought and typed, "Hello, are you well?"

After a moment's time, the response came, "Yes, thank you."

He stared at the text and began to panic again, *How do I tell if this is really her?* He took a deep breath. "We were alarmed by your last communication."

The cursor flashed for a bit. "The situation is perilous. I do not wish for this loss of life."

He thought about what he could say to confirm her identity. "Your English is impressive, where did you learn?"

There was a long pause. "I was educated in Switzerland." There was a further pause. "Given what I have told you, this is what you wish to discuss?"

Mark shook his head, *That was a stupid question, anyone familiar with Kim Yo-jong's history would know that she was educated in Europe. How can I tell...* Time ticked by as his eyes wandered up to the end of the last session- "Peace be with you." He had read this salutation before; it was a reference to the peace of Christ.

He typed, "No, you are right. These are trying times. Peace be with you."

The seconds ticked by as Mark held his breath. Finally came the response. "And also with you."

He exhaled; she had completed the customary Christian greeting. *In a country devoid of Christian adherents, that's about as good a confirmation as I'm going to get.* He looked at the clock and realized that he had less than four minutes left. "Thank you for warning us."

After a pause the reply came, "Something must be done to avoid great tragedy."

Something must be done, yeah I agree. Mark's eyes narrowed. "What if you were in charge?"

The response was quick. "I seek no office. Just to serve."

Mark thought, *It would be helpful if the altruistic were ambitious as well.* He stared at the response, repeating the word "serve" in his mind. An idea popped in his head and he grabbed his phone to scroll through the old Daily Verses. He nervously kept one eye on the time and after a lengthy search, he typed, "*For even the Son of Man did not come to be served, but to serve, and to give His life as a ransom for many.*"

There was a long pause and then she responded, "This is so. And He did not come to rule, but to set us free."

Freedom. Mark went back to his phone. "*It is for freedom that Christ has set us free. Stand firm, then, and do not let yourselves be burdened again by a yoke of slavery.*"

There was another pause. "Freedom to serve Him, not freedom from government."

Mark thought for a bit as the time ticked by. "Are your people free to serve Him? Are you?"

The cursor blinked as Mark darted his eyes back and forth to the clock. The reply came, "We are not free, therefore, I am not free."

Mark tapped his fingers on the table in nervous contemplation then wrote, "If you were in charge, your people would be free." There was another long pause. Mark held his breath.

"Yes, I would choose freedom. But I am not in charge."

Mark breathed again and checked the clock. He had less than a minute, no more time to look up verses. "Your people need an earthly savior."

Another pause. "I stood with my people. I was punished."

Mark watched the clock tick down to thirty seconds. He typed, "Do you agree that your brother must be removed?"

The cursor blinked. "I have a daughter to protect. I cannot know this."

Twenty seconds. "Will you lead your people?"

The prompt flashed.

Ten seconds. He quickly added, "We need your help." The seconds ticked down as Mark held his breath. *I need to know!*

"I serve where God places me."

The text went dark to signify the end of the session.

Mark exhaled and sank back into his chair. He thought about what he had learned. *She will serve... if properly motivated.*

- 25 -

The next morning, Mark sat at his desk and stared at his phone. He was breaking multiple laws, had lied to numerous people, and conspired with despicable men, but nothing felt as bad as what he was about to do to Charles. He had no choice.

At 9:45 AM, he called down to the Secret Service office. Charles was rushed given the proximity in time to his final security briefing. "Mark, gotta call you later. I'm about to give a briefing here."

"Charles, I left my I.D. in the Residence! General Hastings had to accompany me in this morning, but I can't keep hiding in his office. I need it to enter the official Summit prep meeting at 11:00."

"Oh, dammit Mark! I knew that was a bad idea. Can't you just get another badge? Say that you lost it at home?"

"Get a new one in an hour?? And what exactly do I say when someone finds it in the President's kitchen?"

"Oh jeez how would I explain that?" Charles obviously had begun to realize how this could directly implicate him as well. "Get down to the Residence entrance NOW and we'll look for it."

Mark timed his walk to arrive at the Residence checkpoint at 9:55. With the President in the building, no unscheduled visitors were allowed past. The two were cleared-through only after Charles used every ounce of his seniority.

"Find it Mark. I have five minutes." Mark mimicked frantic searching as he crisscrossed the kitchen. At 9:58, Charles said, "That's it, I'm leading the briefing that starts in two minutes."

"I could lose my job, Charles. I'm already hanging by a thread with my relapse. Just tell the Officer at the checkpoint that I'm part of the hospitality group for the Summit and I just need an extra minute in the kitchen." He gestured with his hands, "Just present it like it's normal for such an event."

Charles shook his head in frustration. "I can't believe this. I will instruct her to come looking for you in exactly five minutes to give it some legitimacy."

As Charles exited at a minute before 10:00, Mark ran to the roll-up door and made a slight knock. Raleigh knocked in return.

After five minutes had elapsed, the Secret Service Officer checked her watch and decided to head in. As she opened the door to the Residence, she found Mark standing there.

"All set, thanks for your understanding," he said as he hurried past her and up the stairs to the West Wing. The Officer shook her head and resumed her post.

The Summit Briefing began precisely at 11:00 and Mark took a seat off to the side. The various Agencies and groups with input on North Korea took turns presenting, however, they were brief given how little was yet to be settled at the event, and how little was planned to be accomplished.

At the end of the presentations, the President asked if there were any other points left to discuss. A lone hand was raised. "Mr. Rutherford, you have something to add?"

"Thank you, Mr. President. I just have one suggestion. I note that Mr. Kim's sister, Kim Yo-jong, will be in attendance. I would recommend that we try to highlight her presence somehow."

The murmuring began after he spoke, something Mark had grown accustomed-to. The President was curious. "Why would I do that?"

"Well sir, she has a history of altruistic work on behalf of the people of North Korea and she seems to have endeared herself to them because of it. One way to stick it to Kim would be to praise her work and hold her up in your esteem."

Davenport was unaware of the background of this woman and so he surveyed the room for reaction. The Secretary of State rose to the task. "Sir, Mr. Rutherford is correct in his assessment. She has shown great concern for her people and has been punished by Kim for such behavior. It would be a way for you to make a statement without further formal aggression."

Davenport nodded and smiled. The Secretary was consulted by an aide and rose to add a point. "This will be interpreted as quite an agitation for the regime, however, so perhaps I should be out of the room while you make any such statement of commendation. Try to make it seem more of an off the cuff speech. Press should not be allowed in to witness either."

Mark chuckled to himself and thought, *What a profile in cowardice.*

Davenport was pleased. "Great, so what will such 'off the cuff' remarks say?"

Mark leaped at the question. "Mr. President, I'd be happy to draft your statement... in conjunction with the State Department of course."

"Okay, Mark will draft, State will support. Have them to my office by noon tomorrow for final approval."

"Yes sir, I'll get on that right away."

At the conclusion of the meeting, Mark hurried back to his workstation to begin drafting the statement. He pulled the room schematics out of his briefcase and examined the positioning of the principals involved. He noted Kim Yo-jong's expected location toward the far end of the main table. He slipped the schematics back into the briefcase and placed the Oz in an inter-department mail pouch back to Raleigh. General Hastings entered the room and stopped at his desk.

"I'm impressed that you kept your head in the game, Mark. I feel like I may have acted rashly in giving Jamie your spot. I'm sorry that you won't be witnessing these remarks in person."

Mark looked up and smiled, "You can make it up to me."

At 5:00 PM, Mark made his way over to Ja'mae's desk and found him packing up his things. He said, "So, you've got to be excited about your first Summit."

"I certainly am. No hard feelings for taking your spot on this trip." He smiled like the cat who ate the canary.

Mark smiled back, "No, none at all. Enjoy the experience."

"Oh, I will. I'm headed home to have a night of beauty-need to look dazzling for my public in case I end up in front of the cameras."

He swiveled and started packing up his bag. Mark reached for his desk drawer. "Hey, do you have any gum in here?"

Ja'mae was distracted so he barely turned and simply waved him on. "Oh, I guess. Just look."

Mark fumbled a bit and closed the drawer. Ja'mae lifted his Gucci to his shoulder. "Okay, I'm off."

"Have a good night."

Ja'mae took a step and Mark stopped him. "Hey, you dropped your checkbook."

Ja'mae looked confused, but he took it from Mark's hand and continued toward the exit.

As he pulled the disposable cell phone from his pocket, Mark hollered after Ja'mae, "Oh and Ja'mae, don't forget to pack a toothbrush."

At 8:00 PM, Mark rushed into his apartment and turned on the national news. The story he was expecting was on every channel as he turned up the volume.

"Breaking news tonight, an aide to President Davenport has been arrested on suspicion of theft. He is accused of stealing, get this, a pallet of Spam meat containers from the President's pantry. The yet unnamed man, seen here during his arrest, somehow absconded with the meat product in broad daylight. The Spam was later recovered inside of his residence."

The scene on the news made Mark smile even as he felt a twinge of guilt. There was Ja'mae, in some type of kimono, with a beauty mask on his face, being led away from his

285

townhouse by Federal authorities. The caption underneath read, "Staffer Caught Spamming."

Ja'mae was shouting, "I don't eat Spam! Please don't report that I would eat such a thing!"

The broadcast continued, "Authorities received an anonymous tip this afternoon alerting them to the theft and the aide's involvement therein. Apparently, he was known to provide personal tours of the White House Residence and therefore had access to the pantry."

Mark shut off the TV and returned to his work on the President's statement. Later, he sent a final text message to the disposable phone that Arjun had delivered to the lobbyists. When the two men received the message, they copied the instructions left by Mark and deposited the cell at the bottom of the Potomac.

The environment was chaotic in the West Wing the next morning. Stunned staffers were darting about the offices trying to distance themselves from "The Great Spam Heist" as it was now known. Mark calmly walked up to his desk and resumed his post.

"Mark, in my office!" General Hastings was knee-deep in dealing with the aftermath of the events, however, he quickly added a, "Please."

Mark took a seat as Hastings rubbed his face. "I am absolutely astounded at Jamie's actions yesterday."

"Yeah, who'd have thought." Mark struggled to keep a straight face.

"I don't know what the *hell* could have possessed him..." he exhaled. "Well, he's obviously no longer working here. The good news is that you're back on the Summit Team. I know that the President will be pleased."

Mark nodded his head solemnly. "Okay, I'm ready."

"Good. State is awaiting your remarks on Kim's sister, so you will want to get that over to them with plenty of time for them to comment."

Mark returned to his desk and immediately emailed over a copy of his draft statement to the State Department. A staffer made a few slight changes and emailed it back. She followed up with a call. "Mr. Rutherford, the speech is fine, but..."

"What's the problem?"

"Well, not necessarily a problem, but we don't really see the goal with these comments."

Mark sat back in his chair. "I do, thanks." He hung up the phone on the confused staffer. At 11:45, Mark delivered the final approved version to the President's office.

That night, Mark sipped coffee and thought about how to say goodbye to his friends and relatives. He pulled out a pad and began to write. He ended with a quote from William Carey, a 19th Century missionary about whom he had read. "Expect great things from God. Attempt great things for Him." He rubbed his face and looked at himself in his bedroom mirror, *God, I hope that's what I'm doing.*

Thus completed Mark Rutherford's benediction.

- 26 -

The plane ride to Okinawa, Japan, was uneventful. Mark had been unable to sleep the night before, but made up for it on the long flight from Andrews Air Force Base. The entourage of planes refueled and were bound for Seoul, South Korea, within an hour's time. There, the staff, some security, and press would travel via motorcade to the Demilitarized Zone while the President flew in the Marine Two helicopter. While still onboard Air Force One, Mark made his way to the Secret Service quarters in the middle of the plane where he found Charles working on his equipment.

"Hey Mark, what're you doing in here? Don't you have important diplomat things to work on?" Charles's words were friendly enough, but the tone was something Mark had never experienced from him. There was a sharpness and a purpose in his every move. The man was preparing himself for action.

"Hey, just wanted to check in before we land. Things will no doubt get... hectic, so I wanted to talk now."

"Well, speed it up, we land in Seoul in seven minutes and then I'm on the job until we pull chocks for the flight home."

Mark appreciated the man's dedication and focus. He smiled, but he too needed to focus. "I just wanted to thank you again for your mentoring, and for your friendship."

Charles broke his concentration for a second and looked at him. "Of course Mark, I'm proud of you."

The room was silent. Mark had said his final goodbye, now he focused on his task. "So, now you're on the clock?"

Charles picked up his Sig Sauer. "Roger that."

Mark reached out. "Let me see that peacemaker. Once more before we land."

Charles grinned at this edgier side of Mark. He dropped the magazine out of his sidearm, cleared the round from the chamber, and handed it over grip-first with the slide open. "Here, don't go near the trigger."

Mark turned and walked toward the other side of the compartment. "Who are you paired with during the Summit?"

Charles replied, "Martinez." He opened a bag on the floor and started rifling through it.

Mark, seeing that Charles's attention was occupied, knelt down and opened the box with the skull and crossbones on it. He hovered for a few seconds and looked back over his shoulder. "Is he a good man?"

"Yeah, he takes my lead and has my back."

Mark quietly closed the box and walked back toward him. Charles stood and faced Mark who was now next to him. Mark smiled, "Let me load the magazine for you."

Charles nodded, "Okay hard-ass, show me what you've got," as he handed the magazine to Mark.

In one quick motion, Mark lowered the gun, shoved in a magazine, and presented it grip-first to him. Charles grinned, "Well, I taught you *something* at that range. If this Presidential Advisor position doesn't work out, I'll have to turn you into an Operator, Rambo." He closed the slide on the sidearm and slid it into his waist holster.

Mark said, "Rambo? I've got to have a better Secret Service codename than that."

"Well, I had been told last-minute that you weren't going to be on this trip, but now that you are, you would rate one. I can name you and record it officially. POTUS is "Phoenix," but you can pretty much pick any other name. What would you like us to call you?"

Mark looked down and thought for a second and then looked back up at him. "Pharaoh."

Once inside the anteroom reserved for the Americans, General Hastings assembled the Summit Team. "The presser and photos will take place at ten hundred hours local time in the front room. State and Press Secretary will take lead. There will be a one-hour break for food and prep, then the meeting itself will commence at 1130 hours in the main room. It is scheduled for less than one hour and culminates with the signing of the previously-negotiated documents. N.S.C. will take lead. After this, the President will deliver his specially-prepared remarks," he nodded toward Mark, "while State has removed itself to the anteroom," a nod toward State. "As soon as the statement is delivered, State will return to the room to escort the President out front to the Press Corps. Then we will break until evening for a dinner hosted by the South Koreans."

"General," Mark interrupted, "I was hoping to stand in the room while the President delivers the remarks that I prepared. Perhaps toward the far end of the main table?" Hastings thought for a few seconds about the last-minute request. Mark leaned in close and whispered, "You know, since you owe me one."

The General looked at him and nodded, then scanned the room and said, "If there are no concerns, then that is fine with me. I'll clear it with Secret Service for you to enter the meeting room as State exits." He turned toward the Secretary of State. "Then State will reenter at the conclusion, does that work?"

The Secretary was frowning, but nodded her assent.

Back in Washington, Ja'mae was being questioned by the Secret Service in a Federal lockup located in Anacostia. The full-blown sobbing had subsided hours earlier and now he was dabbing his eyes periodically while proclaiming his innocence. The Director of the Secret Service called the facility from his cell phone while walking through the entrance to the West Wing and spoke with the lead investigator, who was eager to update his boss.

"Sir, I don't buy the idea that this guy masterminded a theft of this intricacy. Originally, he was identified by an anonymous call, and given his access to the Executive Residence, he was thought to be a prime suspect. However, outside of the actual stolen items being found in his home, there are no elements of physical proof to tie him to the act of the theft, there is no hint of a co-conspirator to help him move a pallet of cans, and his demeanor doesn't suggest… *concern* over the gravity of the allegations."

"What do you mean by that?"

"Sir, he keeps insisting that he would never eat canned meat. He seems more anxious to have that issue cleared up with the public than he is about the charges."

"What? Well, maybe the meat was for a third party? Someone who paid him to pull this off?"

"The FBI is currently pursuing a Grand Jury subpoena for his bank records, sir, but that just doesn't seem likely. It's not like Spam is a valuable commodity. We're thinking maybe he was targeted."

"You're suggesting that he was set up? By whom?"

"We've interviewed the Secret Service Officers on duty during the affected times and one admitted that she allowed access to an individual who was not cleared for the Residence, but only on the direct urging of Agent Joeng."

"We'll deal with her later. Who was allowed access?"

"A staffer named Mark Rutherford."

At 1130 hours, the two leaders and their principals had gathered around the center table for "discussions." In actuality, very little was "discussed" as the two men despised each other and all issues had been previously finalized by their respective staffs. As the time for the statement on Kim Yo-jong approached, Mark maneuvered close to the alarm-enabled doorway.

The Secretary of State sauntered out of the room, smiling haughtily over the "accomplishments" of her Summit. Mark stood outside the room and held her back from the rest of her staff. "Madame Secretary, thank you for setting the stage."

As she confusedly shook his right hand, Mark dropped the papers in his left. She instinctively bent down to help Mark retrieve them. Before they were assembled, Mark stood up brushing her lapel.

He moved toward the room. "I don't need those, I know my lines."

The Director of the Secret Service burst into the White House Situation Room, "I need a direct line to the Summit Room!"

A startled Agent jumped to his feet and grabbed the secure phone. The Agent on duty in the Peace House answered. "This is Agent Morris... yes sir, Rutherford is here..."

"Please escort Mr. Rutherford out of the anteroom and sequester him away from the remaining team and then await further instructions."

Agent Morris looked around the anteroom. "Sir, he's already inside."

Mark stepped into the room and looked at Charles who was just inside the doorway. "Hey, you on the clock, Devil dog?"

Charles barely looked at him. "Always."

Mark buttoned his coat, "Good, stick near me."

With that, Mark moved toward the main table. Charles looked startled by Mark's comment and began to trail him.

He grabbed Martinez and approached the Agent in charge of the protection detail who was stationed by the President. He informed the Agent that he and Martinez would be standing by Mark as the President delivered his remarks.

Mark was amazed at how close he was to the North Koreans. Kim was seated in the middle of the table, opposite from Davenport, preparing to leave the room. His sister was seated behind and to the side of him. Only one Korean State Security Department guard stood between Mark and them.

The President saw Mark standing toward the end of the main table and pulled the note cards from his jacket. As staffers exited, he rose to deliver his prepared remarks. "Mr. Kim, if you would hold one moment."

A translator standing next to Kim came to life as he realized that the President intended to give a speech.

"I would like to say that the two of us may have our own differences but there are common ideas that our two countries can share. One of those is the pursuit of a better life for our respective peoples. In recognition of this principle, I wish to commend your sister, Kim Yo-jong, who has accompanied you today."

As the North Korean translator finished this sentence, Kim gave a stunned look to his sister who was as surprised as he. She began to instinctively bow slightly and move back toward the end of the table where Mark was standing.

"Her work in establishing orphanages for those left without families by yours and your father's regimes has been an inspiration to me and to the people of America. Your people can find great leadership in her and I think that we could both learn from her selfless work to love our neighbors as ourselves."

Davenport obviously didn't understand the final line he had read and looked at the card in his hand as if its words had left a bad taste in his mouth. Kim was seething and turned angrily toward his sister, who was visibly scared. She moved even further out of her brother's way.

The President was nevertheless satisfied with the jab he had delivered and turned to head toward the anteroom. As he did, the Secretary of State attempted to reenter the room. Alarms sounded to signify the presence of an unauthorized intruder. She looked down at her lapel and realized that her coded badge was missing. She threw up her hands and turned to exit.

Despite the fact that it was obviously just a mistake by the Secretary, the security teams from each country moved quickly to escort the two leaders out of the room and into their respective anterooms. As the remaining staffers exited, Mark stayed a few feet from Kim Yo-jong who did not appear in any hurry to rejoin her brother behind closed doors. With the focus of the security on the principals, Mark unbuttoned his jacket and maneuvered himself next to her.

"It is for freedom that Christ has set us free. Stand firm, then, and do not let yourselves be burdened again by a yoke of slavery."

The concerned woman looked at him in disbelief. "You!" She looked around, attempting to decipher Mark's intentions. She turned back to face him and shook her head in desperation. "I told you that I cannot. My daughter..."

She started to move away from him and he gently reached out to hold her arm. "Your work for your people was to bravely fulfill Jesus's command. Your work is not finished. You were the one who reached out to us to warn of Kim's objective and you know that if we do not act, millions will die. I'm sorry that you have this burden, but God placed you here, not me."

She looked down at his hand and then locked eyes with him. His gaze was thoughtful and calm as he wore a slight smile on his face. The Korean security personnel had maneuvered Kim out of the room and turned in surprise to find the two engaged in conversation.

Mark saw the reaction in his periphery. "I followed your brave example to find my own freedom in Christ, you did that for me. And now, I am returning this opportunity to you on behalf of your people. But you must be the one to take up the cross and follow Him." As he finished his words, he pointed upward.

Two North Korean guards frantically called over as they quickly moved toward the pair. Charles, hearing the commotion, grabbed Martinez and turned back. The doors to the anterooms locked and would not be reopened until the security protocols had been cleared.

Charles called, "Mark, you need to move away."

Mark's eyes narrowed. He looked directly at the North Koreans, reached into his jacket, and quickly pulled out his cell phone, mimicking pointing a gun toward Kim Yo-jong. The two guards stopped and trained their weapons on Mark. The two American Agents reached Mark, and without an understanding of the situation, flipped their jackets back to expose their sidearms as they placed themselves between Mark and the North Koreans. Threats were made in Korean, pleas for calm were returned in English with arms extended out.

Mark looked back at Kim Yo-jong as she locked eyes on him. "This is your moment. *If God is with you, then who can stand against?*"

Mark released her and moved toward the Americans. The release prompted the North Koreans to dip their weapons and move to grab her, within arm's length of Mark. With one fluid motion, Mark dropped his phone, grabbed Martinez's sidearm, and raised the barrel at the Korean guards' heads, firing two rounds in quick succession. The men dropped to the ground lifeless.

In the American anteroom, the group froze. A few voices were heard asking if those were gunshots followed by shushing sounds. The Agent in charge jumped into action.

"Cover Phoenix now! Confirm lock down of these doors!"

The Agents scrambled to surround the President. The C.A.T. Team rushed toward the door to the main room. They stopped and focused on the Agent in charge.

"Hold here with the President until we can confirm safe egress. Who all is left inside??"

Charles stood staring at the two dead Koreans. He stammered in disbelief over what he had witnessed. "Mark.

Oh my God, what have you done?" He looked over at Mark who was whispering to Kim Yo-jong.

The Agents' earpieces exploded with noise. "Joeng, Martinez SITREP!"

The commotion drew Mark's attention. Charles spoke into his mic, "Sir, two Koreans are down. Rutherford is the shooter, he is still armed."

The frantic response was so loud that Mark could hear it clearly. "Take him out!"

The shots had startled the Koreans in their anteroom as well, who then instinctively covered their leader. The head of security yelled into his mic but received no response from his guards inside. He instructed the security team to remain locked-down as he scanned the room. He gasped when he realized that one person was missing. "Where is Kim Yo-jong??"

Charles raised his weapon toward Mark's chest as he instructed an unarmed Martinez to retreat. "Mark, I need you to back away from the lady and place your weapon on the floor."

Mark smiled at Kim Yo-jong and patted her hand as it clenched his. She returned a slight smile and nod. "Charles, I'm sorry that I put you in this position. But it was necessary, this is how it's done."

"No, this is definitely not how it's done, Mark. Place the weapon down or I will be forced to shoot you."

Before Mark could respond, the door to the North Korean room burst open and several guards entered screaming. Kim Yo-jong was positioned in front of Mark as the Koreans yelled to see if she was okay. She nodded in their direction. One guard aimed his weapon directly at Charles's head while the others slowly maneuvered to obtain a clear line of fire with Mark. The Korean guard in charge instructed Kim Yo-jong to move out of the way, but she stood immobile, in fact, she stood taller in front of the American. Confused, the guard furiously instructed her to move so that she would be out of harm's way if he fired. She did not. A momentary silence set in.

Mark forced himself to look away from the danger and directly at his sponsor. "Charles, it's okay."

Charles was grasping for words to respond when Mark raised his weapon toward the Koreans. Charles cried out and fired his weapon. Mark's free hand slapped his chest as blood dribbled out over it. Kim Yo-jong held his arm as his body collapsed to the floor.

Charles groaned as his weapon lowered to his side. Almost imperceptibly he said, "Mark."

His earpiece wailed, "Joeng, report! What is your status??"

He slowly raised the mic concealed in his sleeve as his eyes welled. "Threat is over. Pharaoh is down."

Kim Yo-jong knelt and hovered over him, holding his head in her hands. She removed her jacket and laid it on his bloody chest. She whispered to him and kissed him gently on his forehead. She looked directly into his eyes as they closed.

Pharaoh had led his people to the gates of the afterlife.

- 27 -

When the confusion cleared, the Koreans converged on Kim Yo-jong and grabbed her. One guard maintained his bead on Charles who now had his head lowered to one hand. Martinez was consoling him while casting a wary eye on the foreign agent.

Charles raised his head and watched the Koreans furiously move chairs to look for something on the ground. Kim Yo-jong was led out of the room clutching her jacket in her hands. The Koreans spoke to one another, shrugging in frustration, and finally maneuvered to take Mark's body with them.

Charles moved to intervene and the Korean guard pushed his weapon further in his direction. Martinez held him back as the Koreans disappeared into the opposing anteroom. He spoke into his mic, "All clear."

The American door opened and the C.A.T. team swarmed in pointing sub-machine guns. The Agent in charge ran up to the two men. "What the hell happened? Where is Rutherford?"

Martinez spoke, "He grabbed my weapon and shot those two Koreans. Then he refused to disarm and," he looked over at Charles, "Agent Joeng was forced to neutralize him."

"Oh my God, the guy snapped?"

"I don't know, sir. But the Koreans took his body."

"Why would they do that?"

"I don't know, maybe they..."

"They couldn't find his weapon." Charles broke his silence. He looked up at the Agent in charge. "I know some Korean and understood most of what they said. They couldn't find the gun used to kill the guards, something about proof of American treachery, so they just took Mark with them."

The President pushed his way past his security and approached the Agent in charge. "What happened?? Mark did this??"

"It appears so, sir. He shot two Koreans and then was put down by Agent Joeng."

"Good God."

"Sir, I really need you back in the anteroom for your security."

As the President was led out, he was stopped by General Hastings who was absorbing the scene. "Sir, what about Rutherford's body?"

Davenport scoffed, "I'm not bargaining with the Koreans after this debacle, he did this on his own. As far as I'm concerned, he's gone."

The Press Secretary, who had been standing just inside of the anteroom, nodded his head at what he had overheard and raced toward his staff. As Davenport was pushed out of the meeting room, Hastings turned back to it and stared in a daze.

A commotion was heard from the North Korean anteroom as the C.A.T. Team trained their weapons on the closed door. From inside the room came the sound of several gunshots in rapid succession. There was yelling and then more shots. Then silence.

The Americans focused in anticipation. Voices could be heard from the room, but nothing else. The Agent in charge took control. "Everybody out now. Secure Phoenix and get him to Marine Two. Move!"

In the office of Julius Johnston, the two lobbyists were glued to the television when an urgent report interrupted the regular Summit coverage. "There is breaking news from Korea, reports of shots being fired inside of the meeting room of the Summit between the U.S. and North Korea. There are no reports of casualties or information surrounding the gunfire, but it is confirmed by reporters on the ground that shots have been fired."

Davis practically leaped out of his seat, "He did it! I can't believe it! This is going to lead to a MASSIVE arms race, maybe even a full-scale war!"

Julius smiled broadly. "I didn't think he had it in him." He poured two glasses of 30-year-old scotch and handed one to his partner. "To many years of active hostilities."

"Cheers to that."

As the President quickly boarded his helicopter and departed for Seoul, the remaining American Agents gathered their equipment and prepared to follow in their vehicles. General Hastings stood in the anteroom by himself, staring at the meeting room door.

Charles approached him. "Sir, are you okay?"

The old soldier snapped out of it and looked at Charles. "Yes. Just never get used to losing one of your own."

The thought visibly pained Charles as well, but he pressed on. "Sir, the yelling after those shots were fired in their anteroom."

"The Koreans? What about it."

"Well, I'm positive about what I heard, I just don't know what it means."

"What did they say?"

"They were screaming, 'he's dead, he's dead.'"

Outside the Peace House, the Press Secretary approached the Press Corps to make a hastily-prepared statement designed to confirm that the President was still alive. "I don't have a long statement right now. A few minutes ago, shots were fired in the main meeting room of the Peace House. At the time of the incident, the President was out of the room and is unharmed. I repeat, the President is unharmed. Unfortunately, an Advisor to the President was struck by gunfire." He dipped his head slightly in grief. "His name is Mark Rutherford. Given the events of the day, the President..."

Before he could continue further, several reporters began shouting questions. "Is he dead? Is the Advisor dead?"

Omar exhaled. "It is my understanding that Mr. Rutherford is deceased."

"Is that an official declaration of death?"

"Yes, as far as the United States Government is concerned, Mark Rutherford is gone."

Within the hour, FBI and Secret Service Agents had descended on Mark's home. It was mostly empty save for a disposable phone resting on top of a handwritten note. These materials were rushed out of the apartment for analysis. The Agents who remained behind combed through his belongings.

One Agent was examining Mark's medicine cabinet when he came across an empty prescription bottle. "Hey, I've got a prescription here. Think he was on anti-psychotics?"

"He definitely should've been. What's the prescription for?"

"Something called 'Biothrax,' ever heard of it?"

"Biothrax? Are you sure?"

"That's what it says. Why, what is it for?"

"Inoculation… for anthrax."

Charles sunk into his seat in one of the up-armored S.U.V.s used for transport. Several Agents were busy securing their equipment around him as the line of vehicles hastily withdrew from the compound and headed toward Seoul.

Martinez finished his prep and turned his attention to his partner. "Hey bud, how're you holding up?"

The weight of day's events had visibly worn on him, but Charles sat up straight to refocus on his work. "Uh, I'm here. Just need to snap out of it."

"Relax Charles, we've got you. You sit tight and I'll handle your weapons check."

Charles nodded in appreciation and handed over his firearm and extra magazines. Martinez ejected the magazine from the Sig Sauer and stared at it.

Charles noticed his focus. "What is it?"

"Charles, you had this magazine in the whole time, correct?"

"Yeah, I only let off the single round. I had no need to reload. Why?"

Martinez held the magazine up for him to see. The shaft was bright blue.

The two lobbyists were well into their second round of drinks when the buzzer rang from Julius's secretary. "Mr. Johnston, there are some gentlemen here to see you."

Julius rolled his eyes as he looked at Davis. He dropped his feet from their perch on his desk and stretched in leisurely fashion to the intercom. "I told you that I was indisposed for the rest of the day. Tell them to beat it." He chuckled as he resumed his lounging and pulled his glass up to his lips.

"Sir, these gentlemen are from the FBI. They say that they need to speak with you immediately."

Julius's glass dropped as scotch sprayed onto the floor. He bolted upright in his chair and stared at Davis. "Uh… please send them in."

The two men rose on unsteady feet and turned toward the door. Three Agents entered the room and one approached the men directly. "Mr. Johnston? Mr. Holmes? My name is Agent Ramos with the FBI."

The lobbyists looked at each other with their eyes wide. Johnston stammered, "Uh, yes, how can we help you?"

"Gentlemen, are you aware of a theft that occurred earlier this week in the White House Executive Residence?"

Davis answered, "We've been a bit preoccupied with other business, but yeah I heard some staffer stole some canned meat. Why?"

"Yes. An entire pallet of Spam to be precise."

Julius began to relax. "So? You can look around if you like, but we don't eat the stuff." The two lobbyists looked at each other and chuckled.

Agent Ramos smirked. "No, we've recovered the goods. It was in the home of a Mr. Jamie Thurman."

The blood drained from the faces of the two men. It did not go unnoticed by Ramos. "Oh, you've heard the name? Thought you might have. You see under the PATRIOT Act, any wire transfer over $10,000 from a foreign entity can be flagged by a financial institution and referred over to the Treasury Department in a Suspicious Activity Report. Given the recent arrest of Mr. Thurman, the FBI had been made aware of a $10,250 transaction from a few days ago sent to his bank account by an offshore corporation. And do you know who owns this corporation? Your firm."

Davis was shaky. "Well, you would have to ask our accounting department about that. Maybe there's some valid reason for it."

"Oh sure, that would have been our next step and certainly wouldn't have warranted this visit from us, except do you know what we found today? Mr. Thurman's name and checking account on a disposable phone in the residence of a Mark Rutherford."

Julius gasped. Davis nearly fainted. Agent Ramos produced the disposable phone for the two men to see. "Yeah, *that* Mark Rutherford. The one who was killed today at the Korean Summit. He left a note regarding his intended actions at the Summit which also implicates the two of you."

Julius steadied himself against his desk. "The guy is obviously a lunatic, he probably just had an axe to grind with us. Are you suggesting that you have proof that he contacted us using that phone?"

Davis chimed in, "Yeah, we don't know Mr. Rutherford. Check our phone records."

"There were only two numbers contacted by this phone. One contact was a call to the FBI, which was anonymous at the time, to report the theft from the White House. The other communications were made to a companion burner phone. These included a text message with the wiring instructions for Mr. Thurman's account."

The two men breathed again. That phone was long gone. Julius said, "Well, we don't have any knowledge of these phones so I'm sorry but we can't be of help to you. Like I said, he was obviously unbalanced."

The Agent nodded his head. "Okay, he must've just been a nutball then." He turned to leave and then stopped and looked back. "Except, maybe you could explain one last thing to me. If you had nothing to do with these cell phones, then how is it that they were purchased with a credit card issued in your firm's name?"

Panic spread across the faces of the two men. They turned toward each other in recognition of what Ramos was going to say.

"Both phones were purchased by an Arjun Chandra."

On Air Force One, the President was alone in his cabin. He sat at his desk with his head in his hand. "What was Mark thinking? Did he get this idea from me?"

The door burst open as the Secretary of State and several aides rushed in. Davenport stood enraged. "What're you doing? I told you that I don't want to be disturbed."

"Sir, we've just received word from the Peace House. It's been confirmed, Kim Jong-un is dead."

"What? How?"

"Apparently his sister smuggled a weapon back with her into the anteroom after Mr. Rutherford's incident. She killed her brother and then demanded allegiance from the State Security Department guards. The majority of guards apparently supported her and the remainder were either subdued or killed. The key military and government leaders have all pledged their support as well. She is in charge now."

"What? My God." His face contorted as he contemplated the magnitude of the information he had just received. "What will happen now?"

"She is scheduled to make a formal address shortly, but she has already made contact with the President of South Korea and has stated that she plans to move immediately to reunite the two countries under democratic rule."

Davenport shook his head. "I... I can't believe it."

"It's true, sir. The North Korean regime is gone." He stared blankly at the Secretary for a moment and then began to straighten his tie. As he pulled on his jacket, she looked at him confused. "Mr. President, what are you planning to do?"

A smile spread across his face. "I'm going to go announce the success of my Summit to the American people."

- 28 -

The reaction in America to the events at the Summit was exuberant. The President spoke in glowing terms of the brave actions of his close Advisor and "good friend," Mark Rutherford. Small groups of people spontaneously took to the streets to hail Mark as a hero.

After about a week, however, the Opposition Party began to ask questions about what Mark had done. How did he manage to gain access to a weapon? Did he have help? What he did was illegal under American laws, shouldn't there be a Congressional inquiry? What exactly did the President know and when did he know it? Critics and news outlets began referring to the incident as "Summitgate"; apparently, anything connected to the White House that had even the potential of wrongdoing now rose to the level of an impeachable offense.

It didn't take long for Davenport to begin distancing himself from the now "rogue" actor and there were few remaining defenders of Mark's actions in Washington. The only supporters left, according to the polling data, were the American people.

Raleigh was immediately identified by the CIA as a likely co-conspirator and he was sequestered in an interrogation room deep in the recesses of the Langley campus. The questioning lasted for the better part of a day before senior officials realized that nothing he had to say was going to be good for the Agency. It was at the point where he began to suggest that perhaps greater

Congressional oversight of the Agency would be the proper safeguard against recurrence of such an action that the Director of Clandestine Operations interceded. He suggested that maybe he could use an Operator like Raleigh for field work. Raleigh agreed.

Without continued aid from the political class in Washington, Mark's father was forced to abandon his efforts to seek the return of his son's body. Communication with the remnants of the government in North Korea was near impossible as speedy reunification of the two nations took understandable precedence. He was finally resigned to holding a graveside memorial to bury an empty casket.

On a bright Saturday morning, exactly two weeks after the death of Kim Jong-un, a handful of family and friends gathered at a private ceremony in the West End of Richmond. Most people at that point were now afraid to be associated with a mad man, but Julia spoke on Mark's behalf followed by General Hastings, and finally his father. George was too broken up to speak.

As the event concluded, Mark's father pulled George and Bella aside. "I saved this for after the ceremony, but I've got some incredible news. I was contacted by our estate attorney and she informed me that George's mother had apparently purchased a life insurance policy on Mark several decades ago. When Annabelle was born, Mark changed the beneficiary to her. You will be receiving a check for five million dollars."

Bella jumped excitedly. George gasped for air. All three hugged as the family left the cemetery together, the last remaining attendees.

As the three made their way out, a lone figure stood concealed, watching from a distance. A tear traced down his face as he watched the little girl skipping alongside the wheelchair. He lifted his hand to wipe away the tear, a hand which wore a large, emerald ring.

REVIEW & RECOMMENDED

Enjoy the book? Please leave a review:
Pharaoh: An Addictive Political Thriller

Also Recommended:
Reagan and the Russians: Perspectives from my six years on President Reagan's NSC staff
By Colonel/Dr. Tyrus W. Cobb

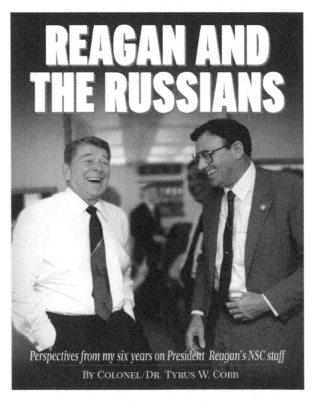

Biography of Ty Cobb

Ty Cobb in Fallujah, Iraq (left).

Legend has it that Ty Cobb gained his love of political intrigue fiction while attending Langley High School, which borders the CIA in the Washington, D.C., suburbs. At that time, his father, Col. Tyrus W. Cobb, PhD, had been called up from his post as a Professor of Soviet Studies at the United States Military Academy, West Point, to serve under President Ronald Reagan as Special Assistant for National Security Affairs. Following Ty's graduation from law school, he was admitted to the Bar in Nevada and California and volunteered to work for the Department of Defense Coalition Provisional Authority in Baghdad, Iraq. Upon completion of this assignment, Ty served as an Aide in the Office of the Deputy Secretary of Defense in the E Ring of the Pentagon. He was later elected to two terms in the Nevada State Legislature and currently resides in Las Vegas, Nevada, with his daughter, Elizabeth where he works as an author and attorney.

Made in the USA
Las Vegas, NV
19 March 2021